THE WARWICKS

OF

SLUMBER

MOUNTAIN

Other Fiction
by Cheryl B. Dale

Romantic Suspense

Intimate Portraits
The Man in the Boat
Set Up

Paranormal/Gothic Romance

Treacherous Beauties

Light Mystery

Taxed to the Max
Overtaxed and Underappreciated

Vintage Mystery

Losing David

This book was previously published in 2012 by MuseItUp Publishing.

Copyright Information
Copyright 2012-2014 by Cheryl Dale
Published by J&H Press
Previously Published by MuseItUp Publishing
Cover Art by J&H Press
Content editor: B.L. Wilson
Line editor: Greta Gunselman

ISBN: 978-0-9908695-2-8

www.cherylbdale.com
cherylbdale.blogspot.com
cherylbdale@hotmail.com

THE WARWICKS

OF

SLUMBER

MOUNTAIN

by

Cheryl B. Dale

J&H Press

CHAPTER ONE

LIKE EVERYONE ELSE in our north Georgia town, I tried not to attract the attention of the Warwicks.

I failed twice. When I was seven and didn't know any better, I made friends with one of them.

My father died.

A harsh lesson, but that's how I learned the Warwicks were as different as the townsfolk claimed.

Even their name.

They didn't pronounce Warwick *war-wik* according to the spelling. They said *wohr-itch* in a British manner, with an imperceptible twist of the lips. And from their intimidating, fascinating mystique, they might well have been British aristocrats.

With their black hair and pale complexions and enigmatic eyes in long oval faces, they drifted through town on the way to and from their mountain fortress overlooking Lake Lassitan. Except when dedicating a new clinic or library built with Warwick money, or hosting a charitable tour of their fabled home or antique yacht, they kept to themselves.

Oh, the Warwicks spread their wealth throughout the community and were unfailingly polite at chance meetings. But they did not mingle. Not with us ordinary folk.

They acted like lords of the manor. The mountain and its mansion made up their estate, our town their village.

The second time I met a Warwick, I wasn't yet eighteen.

I knew better than to get involved, but some people don't learn from their mistakes.

Not that I had a choice. No hint of Warwicks troubled me as I paddled my canoe over a restless lake under an early September moon. Not even when the familiar tug came.

Come. Help.

"Damn, damn, damn. Not now. I'm nearly home and I'm too tired," I muttered, and then shouted into the night, "Go away, I don't have time to look for you!"

The Voice didn't listen.

Come. I need help. Please. Help me.

Gram's house lay five minutes away. My feet hurt after working eight hours at Margo's Mart-O and another four hours waiting tables at the cafe. I didn't want to turn into the black void that marked the lake's middle to rescue some animal in trouble.

You have a gift, child, I heard Gram chiding as though she sat beside me. *Accept it. When The Voice calls, you better answer.*

Tender-hearted Gram would disapprove if I refused help to any creature, however small or insignificant.

"Crap. It's probably another muskrat like the one trapped under the dock last week."

No use. I couldn't rationalize away Gram's disappointment. I turned away from the comfortable lee of the shore.

Whatever odd quirks of nature created my faculty, whether the talent was handed down from my father's Cherokee forebears or my mother's fey Scotch-Irish ancestors, I had long since learned Gram was right. The Voice was a force to be reckoned with.

It might be a gift, as she labeled it, but I would never prize it. That night, exhausted and wanting my bed, I doubly resented the call.

Though past midnight, a few sailboats remained out, their sheets reflecting moonlight like drifting ghosts. Once a cruiser hummed its distant chant.

The night smelled like thick lake water and, occasionally, fish.

I sank the oar with a methodical ease acquired from paddling to and from my jobs. The canoe skimmed over the water's chop.

Too bad coming back wouldn't be nearly so fast. The wind would be against me then.

Brightness, far down the lake, interrupted my rhythm.

A huge yacht that would have looked more at home on the ocean glittered its way toward the dam. Colored lanterns and dancing people lined the deck. Music blared, punctuated by occasional echoing laughter.

Cleopatra's barge must have looked something like that to the slaves lining the Nile. It would have been ablaze with light and dressed-up people having fun, too.

"Well, this ain't Egypt, folks. And I'm sure not anybody's slave."

The Warwicks were celebrating tonight.

Must be nice to be a part of that charmed circle who enjoyed themselves without a thought about tomorrow. Happy and carefree, the biggest decisions whether to wear the yellow dress or the red, the diamond ring or the ruby. Worried about nothing but weight or boyfriends or which college to go to.

I had to spit over the side to get rid of the bile roiling up.

The yacht rounded an island and snuffed the sparkling gaiety. Damning my momentary weakness—what good does envy do?—I dug my paddle in.

Somewhere out there, a stray dog or half-drowned rat or some other poor animal needed rescuing. Maybe it'd be nearby so I wouldn't have to detour too far.

At last, after what seemed like hours, in the middle of the lake and far away from islands or shoreline, the canoe crested one of the waves raised by the wind. Ten yards away, the moon outlined an oval.

A human face.

What supported it? A block of plastic foam ripped from a boathouse by summer storms? Driftwood from a tree trunk felled by rough winds and worn smooth by the currents?

Imagination, a legacy from Pop that had earned slaps from my mother, ran riot till the canoe dropped into a watery swale and temporarily obscured the face.

My arm cramped, but I was closing in and paddled with renewed energy.

The face belonged to a figure who clung to a cushion. Not a boat preserver, but one of those plump plastic-covered cushions for outdoor furniture.

He could have fallen off a boat. Or been tossed into the lake during some horseplay. The freedom of the lake attracted people who drank too much and did stupid things.

The wind diminished. I stayed my paddle so the canoe could drift alongside him. "Do you need a ride?"

He raised his head slightly. "Why on earth would anyone think I might need a ride?"

His drawl was north Georgia modified by foreign influences. The assurance bestowed by wealth permeated his words even as he lay helpless and half-submerged on a makeshift float in the middle of the lake in the dead of night.

Warwick assurance. Before he had finished his first sentence, I recognized him and clenched my teeth to keep from smarting back.

Oblivious, he swept one arm toward the sky. "Can't you see that glorious crescent moon up there? Isn't it obvious I'm out for a moonlight swim?"

Gareth Warwick, whose grandmother presided over the thirty room structure on the mountain jutting up from the lake and who, with his kin, enjoyed the opulent yacht cruising toward the dam. He was poised and sure of himself despite being abandoned in the water.

With good reason, since he was one of the charmed clan.

Eccentric, erratic, philanthropic backers of the community, the Warwicks were rumored to be fabulously wealthy and secretly corrupt. They were admired or feared, according to who did the telling. A lot of people said it was wise to whisper when speaking of the Warwicks.

I'd not known that ten years ago, but lessons learned in heartbreak aren't forgotten. If he didn't want help, I wouldn't press him.

Bending over the paddle, I turned the canoe.

"Hey."

I headed back toward Gram's.

"Come back. For pity's sake, don't you know when somebody's teasing you? Hey!"

At a splash, I stopped and glanced back.

He had left the cushion to swim after me.

"Of course I need a ride." The breathless words betrayed no anger but merely surprise that his teasing had offended. "D'you think I normally wear this kind of stuff to swim in the lake? Can't you tell I'm kidding?"

No, and I don't like sarcasm.

Even if that might be amusement trembling beneath his arrogance.

I like being laughed at as little as I like sarcasm, but I prudently kept my mouth closed. The last thing I needed was to get on the wrong side of the Warwicks.

It might be coincidence that my father, healthy one day, had died of an unsuspected heart condition the next. Right after the Warwick matriarch had told him she didn't want me playing with her grandson, this very same Gareth.

Coincidence maybe, but I didn't believe it.

Rumor said that if you crossed a Warwick, your children would sicken, your plants would wither, your dog would die, your car engine would blow up, and nobody would be surprised if your body ended up in the deep waters below the bridge spanning the lake into the next county.

Not that the Warwicks would have to go that far to be revenged on me this time.

A whisper to the right authorities would be sufficient to put me back in my particular hell. Soon I'd be eighteen, able to chart my own life, but now . . .

No sense in gambling. I wouldn't defy any of the Warwicks. Not even a half-drowned one like Gareth.

The wind faded. By the time he swam to where I waited, sulky waters were tranquil.

He reached for the side of the canoe.

"Hold on." I stuck my paddle in his face. "Hang on to the side and let me tow you to shore. You'll tip me over if you try to get in."

"No, I won't. I know all about canoes."

The breezy condescension irritated as much as his catching the edge of the canoe alarmed.

"Don't do that. You'll turn—"

The lake this September night was cool. I came up sputtering, water streaming from eyes but paddle safe in hand.

"You ass!" I'd love to use the paddle on his head. "I told you you'd tip me over!"

"If you'd stayed still, we would've been fine. When you moved, you threw us off balance." He didn't hide the laughter. Gareth Warwick wasn't sorry to see me dunked. "Come and help me turn it right."

His self-confidence made me think twice about hitting him.

He'd dumped me out on purpose because I'd threatened to leave him in the water.

Clutching the oar made getting to him awkward, but then, side by side and heaving in unison, we righted the canoe. I threw the paddle inside. "Let me go around before you try to get in. We have to climb in together, at the same time."

"Sure. I know."

"Like you knew how not to tip me over?" I bit my tongue. *Stupid. Don't provoke him.*

"If you hadn't moved, the canoe would have stayed steady and we would have been fine. I was balanced—"

Tuning out his excuses, I swam around to the other side. Counting to three aloud, I hoisted myself over the side and hoped he was doing the same. He was and managed his part creditably enough. He more or less fell into the bottom.

I had to scramble over him to get settled so my chest ended up at his face. He giggled into my boobs except it wasn't really a giggle. It was more like a low-pitched abrupt laugh. If he'd been anyone else, it would've sounded nervous, but Warwicks had no need to be nervous. They probably didn't possess nerves.

"You don't have on a bra." His breath made a warm spot on my wet windbreaker. A hand crept up. He might have been trying to push me off, but he wasn't trying real hard.

"Keep your hands to yourself, bubba." Any touchy-feely stuff and I'd throw him back into the water, Warwick or not.

"It's kind of hard to keep out of your way when—Oof!"

I took my knee out of his stomach and finished crawling over him, satisfied he wouldn't say anything else. At least for a few minutes.

While he caught his breath, he stayed motionless. Quiet. I retrieved the paddle and took my seat in the rear. What was that reek? Rum, maybe. Rum mixed with some kind of exotic fruit.

The aroma brought back images of carefree people on the glitzy yacht. The jealousy that welled up made me sick.

Take deep breaths.

I tamped down the nausea and let go the anger.

Gram always told me to be thankful for what I had and not to begrudge others what was theirs. Her advice was sound but sometimes hard to follow.

So I wielded the paddle and tried not to want too much stuff I'd never have. A shame my unruly tongue wouldn't stop flapping. "People who drink and fall into the lake usually drown."

The wind had unaccountably and completely died, but he didn't try to sit up. The canoe could have been a downhill sled on black glass, so smoothly did it glide. The chop I'd fought getting to him might never have been.

"Drown?" He gave his funny abrupt laugh and stretched his arms. "Not me."

"Hah. You're lucky I came along to pull you out."

I managed not to shiver. Must be from the soaking clothes. The night air wasn't that cold.

"But you did." His arrogance was back. If it had ever gone away.

I clenched my jaw. He was too chipper, too cavalier about his rescue.

One small consolation, at least he didn't recognize me from our childhood encounter. I couldn't take him bringing those days up. Not after losing Pop. "It's a wonder you weren't run over by a boat. If a propeller had got you, it would have been ugly."

From his position in the canoe bottom, he cradled his head with his arms. "My mother says I'm a water baby and that the water takes care of its own. Looks like it does."

Chills crawled up my back.

Gareth Warwick didn't sound like he was boasting. Gareth Warwick sounded like he believed his own words.

No, he was having fun at my expense again.

Or maybe not. All my life I'd been warned about the Warwicks.

I couldn't stop the shiver this time, and it wasn't from wet clothes or the cool night.

"That's one place folk like us don't need to climb," my father had always said whenever we fished in the cove behind Gram's house. He would nod toward the looming mountain. "The Warwicks don't much like company. They can't keep us off our own land, but there ain't no need to go on theirs. Mind, don't you ever go any farther than Gram's hedgerow up there, Lindy."

Whenever my mother bothered to notice me, she would echo

Pop's warning. "Stay away from Slumber Mountain. Them kind of people don't like uninvited visitors."

Even Gram, who wasn't afraid of anything or anybody, held reservations about the Warwicks. "They'uns be different, child. Hit's not good for folk like us to mix with their sort."

Well, I hadn't chosen to mix with them tonight. That cursed Voice had chosen for me.

My arms ached each time I dipped the paddle and so did my lungs.

No wonder. I was doing all the work.

We'd soon fix that.

"Are you awake?"

He didn't move. Had he passed out?

"Hey, I asked—"

"I'm looking at the stars," came the dreamy reply. "Aren't they gorgeous? Like you could reach out and touch them. Have you ever imagined what it'd be like to fly through the stars on a night like this? When the sky is clear as crystal and only an occasional wisp of cloud covers the moon? Like that one over there. It looks like netting on a woman's breast."

"No." I wondered how much he'd had to drink, whether he could paddle.

"No, what?"

The dreamer had forgotten his question. "No, I've never imagined what it would be like to fly up through the stars. I have too many other things to worry about." Like buying gas for Gram's pickup and shoes for myself.

Friday was payday.

If the weather held so I could use the canoe to get to work every day, a half tank of gas should last till the next pay check. Then I'd have enough money to buy shoes. Maybe some new jeans. Or at least some pants from the thrift store.

Stuff like that didn't bother Gareth Warwick.

He lay supine in the moonlight, hair spilling over the coat sleeves under his head. One foot rested on each side of the canoe. "I bet flying through those clouds would be like flying through lace. Or cotton candy. What d'you think?"

"No idea."

A dark strand fell across one of his eyes, begging to be brushed back.

I must be coming down with a cold. "Don't go to sleep before we get to shore." If he passed out, I'd never wrestle him out of the canoe.

"I'm not sleepy." He added as if reading my mind, "Or drunk. The adults had cocktails, but I only had one cup of punch and it didn't have much champagne in it. Grandmama only let them use one bottle so we could have some."

"Just one bottle, eh?" What was I going to do with him? True, Gram lived at the foot of the mountain and the Warwicks lived on top, and we could drive to their house from hers in five minutes flat.

But by water the distance trebled. I would have to go past Gram's cove, round the point of the mountain, and halfway up another finger of the lake to reach the Warwicks' dock. After all that, I'd have to turn around and come home.

Thirty or forty minutes of hard paddling, minimum.

The best thing was take him to Gram's and let him call someone to come get him.

Yeah, that should work. If I could keep him awake.

Talk to him. "Is that how you got out in the middle of the lake? Trying to fly to the stars on one cup of punch?"

I thought he wasn't going to answer but he did, and his voice sounded the same as before. Soft-spoken but clear, with a hint of twang that years in foreign boarding schools—the Warwicks always sent their children to Europe to be educated—hadn't eradicated.

A pleasant voice if it hadn't belonged to a Warwick.

"I fell off the boat," he said.

I couldn't resist. "A bad night for flying?"

He was too buzzed to recognize scorn. "No. I didn't try flying tonight. We were having a, um, a family debate that—" He paused. "Bet you can see the boat. It should be close to the dam."

Changing the subject. Must have realized he shouldn't discuss Warwick business with a mere human. "I saw it going in that direction before I picked you up. It's long gone by now."

"Good. I don't want to get back on it anyway. I wasn't having much fun." He sounded as groggy as I felt. "Everyone was arguing. That's why I came up on deck, to get away from them."

He gingerly sat up in the bottom with his back facing me. Dark curls fell to his coat collar. He rolled his neck around, and then each shoulder. "Is this Blue Creek Cove?"

"Yes."

If Gareth Warwick could pick out Blue Creek Cove at night and in his condition, he was more familiar with the area than most. Knowing where you are on the lake is always tricky. It sprawls over thousands of acres with hundreds of inlets that look alike, branching off from the main fingers. Even in the daytime, experienced boaters can lose their way.

Strange how someone so comfortable around the lake had fallen in.

Forget it. What happened to him wasn't my business. The logistics problem was. "Can you call someone to pick you up when we get ashore?"

"Probably." He yawned. "Do you have a cell? Mine's in the lake."

"On my budget?" I snorted. "Not hardly. We'll be at my grandmother's house in a moment. You can use her phone to let your folks know you're all right."

He yawned again and stretched his arms. "There are a hundred people on board the boat. Eating, drinking and making merry. Or arguing. I doubt any of them will miss me."

As he eased onto the canoe's middle seat, something suspiciously like empathy sprouted.

Was he really so overlooked, so disregarded, that he could fall into the lake and drown with none of his family the wiser? Was there no one who cared about him either?

Poor little rich boy. Maybe we were more alike than I thought.

He leaned over and trailed his fingers in the water.

Pity fled.

Here I was, working my tail off and he was making like a girl boating with her boyfriend. He could at least spell me with the paddle. I poked him with its tip. "You wanna do this awhile?"

"Oh, I don't think I'm able," he chirped. "I was in the water a good forty minutes before you came along. After drinking all that alcohol you think I've had, I doubt I could hold a pencil, much less a paddle. Sorry."

Sure he was. Stewing, I got us to the stretch of water fronting Gram's property and ran the canoe aground. Hard.

Gareth lost his balance and fell backward into me. His arm came down over mine and his body warmed my chest through his damp clothing. I felt the curve of his back and the strength of his hand against my arm, the whisper of a shoulder grazing my breast.

I gasped.

He jerked away before I could push him.

I slapped the back of his head anyway. "I told you to keep your hands to yourself!"

"Sorry."

The contact may have been unintentional, but that didn't help the revulsion at a male touching me. Any male, accidentally or not. "Can you get out?"

"Sure." He climbed out, but staggered when he started up the bank.

I hopped out, gritted my teeth, and offered a hand.

He waved it away. "I'm okay."

"You nearly fell."

"Yeah, but I'm okay now. Thanks anyway. I don't need you."

"Fine." I wasn't about to offer again. I didn't like touching him any more than he liked me touching him.

With the terrain so rugged and him halfway high, it took a while to get up to Gram's house.

He never asked for help. Once, in the midst of him stumbling and me lagging behind in case he fell, he let out that dumb low laugh that made me want to smack him.

On the porch, I stripped off my wet jacket and left it on the porch swing, but as I opened the door, my mouth dried. What if he thought my bringing him into Gram's house was an open invitation? What if he came on to me? He was bigger and stronger than me. What if—?

Jeez, get a grip.

Any girl Gareth Warwick might go for would be nothing like me. A lowly cashier and part-time waitress would be perfectly safe because Gareth Warwick didn't want anyone like that even touching him.

Inside, the dim lamp Gram had left on exposed the ratty furnishings. From the rear of the house came her snores. Lucky she was a sound sleeper.

"Try to be quiet. My grandmother's asleep. The phone's over there. You need me to dial or can you?"

He looked at the phone as if it was a strange instrument.

No. As if he was debating whether or not he wanted to use it. Was he as drunk as I thought?

Then he gave his dry chuckle.

My tense muscles relaxed. Of course he was drunk. He was sloshed, incapable of picking up the receiver. I was right the first time. He'd probably never seen a rotary telephone like Gram's, vintage 1960 or so. He didn't know what it was.

I did. "Tell me the number."

"There's no use calling. Everyone's on the boat. Or nearly everyone." He didn't seem concerned as he surveyed the room.

Not that he had much to see.

The tiny living room was furnished with an ancient sofa and chair, a boxy television, two scarred end tables, and an ugly floor lamp. A worn recliner held an unfinished baby sweater Gram was crocheting for a friend's grandchild. A shabby afghan spilled on the sofa alongside a knotty pillow. A notebook I used to track income and expenses lay open on the coffee table.

It was a messy, lived-in room though I doubted Gareth Warwick would describe it as such. More like impoverished or Early Hovel.

Not that I cared. "If you can't call anyone at your home, I'm going to dial 911."

"Do you live here?" Through the kitchen door he spotted the Formica table and chairs.

"No. I just drop by to borrow the phone." I stuck my finger in the nine hole, but before I had time to dial, he bridged the distance across the room and closed his hand around mine.

His quick bound surprised me as did his grip. Shocked by its strength, I froze.

His long fingers gleamed white against my tanned wrist.

When I looked up into his face, warmth moved from his hand up my arm to my breasts and face, downward to my hips and legs.

I found that, after all, I didn't mind his touch.

He smiled crookedly. "You don't really want to call 911, do you?"

"No," I whispered.

"Then you take me home."

Thinking about the encounter afterward, I mostly recalled the long and symmetrical lines of his face. Compelling and coldly perfect like some of the old Grecian statues.

He wasn't much older than me, but his character was already set. Black eyes, their almond shape outlined by thick lashes, stared out with open humor beneath upswept eyebrows. Caught in their depths, one hardly noticed the patrician lips that curved with the same self-mockery that had echoed in his laugh.

In later years I could see him clearly in my mind, too clearly at times for comfort, but I didn't notice much of his appearance while we stood staring at each other. I was conscious only of my knees shaking while a lazy heat spread throughout me.

Instead of examining what that heat meant as a more astute person might have done, I wrenched away. "I can't take you home."

His breath exhaled.

Long. Shuddering.

His hands clenched and one of them moved.

Skittish, I stepped back.

He didn't reach for me but massaged his left shoulder. The light in his eyes died, leaving them opaque and unrevealing.

I rubbed my wrist, not because it hurt but because it tingled from the imprint of his hand. He might be a lot more sober than he acted. "Listen, your people are going to miss you and be worried. You'd better let them know you're all right."

"I will." He turned persuasive. "I will if you'll take me home. I don't live far from here, and we can call the boat from my house."

Gram's ancient pickup had barely enough gas to get to the grocery store tomorrow for senior discount day. Besides, the only access to the top of Slumber Mountain lay in a tortuous narrow road that I would hate to negotiate this time of night.

No one with sense would go onto the mountain after dark.

My head tried to shake no, but my conscience held it steady.

If Gram had been awake, she'd have clucked over his wet clothes and found him an old pair of sweats and made him coffee and told him we'd be glad to run him home.

Warwick or not.

My Gram was a good person, but she was asleep, and I was dead tired.

I gnawed my lip.

He fumbled in his pocket. "I'll make it worth your while."

What I'd taken for a dark suit was a tuxedo, its doubtless perfect lines spoiled from the dunking. The shirt ruffles drooped and the starched collar lay limp against his tan throat. The black tie dangled, undone.

How wonderful it must be to take tuxedos and parties on yachts for granted when people like Gram subsisted on social security and food stamps.

Gareth, clueless of my resentment, triumphantly produced a sodden wad. "See?" When he fumbled to separate the bills in the money clip and failed, his smile faded. "Oh well. Never mind. I've got dry money at home. Plenty of it. Say a hundred?"

"A hundred?" I had to swallow. "Dollars?"

"Uh huh."

A hundred dollars meant a full tank of gas and shoes to replace the ones nearly worn out after six months of waiting tables. Maybe a little left to stick in the kitty for jeans.

No, I couldn't let him pay for something Gram would expect me to do anyway.

I could almost hear her. *We can't take his money, child. Wouldn't be right not to help a body out iffun we can. He may be a Warwick, but he's still a human being.*

He mistook my silence. "Okay, two hundred then. Run me home and I'll pay you two hundred. Cash on the barrel. What d'you say?" He raised hopeful brows.

I despised Gram's quaint moral code and myself for adhering to it but might as well give in. "I don't want your money. Let me put on some dry clothes on and I'll take you."

"Great." He went into the kitchen, plopped down on one of the dilapidated vinyl chairs, and folded his arms across his chest. "Go to it."

At least he knew better than to sit on Gram's sofa in his wet clothes.

"In case you're wondering," he addressed my back as I went toward my room to change, "I'm Gareth Warwick. I live on the mountain behind you."

"I know who you are." I looked over my shoulder to meet his gaze squarely. "And I know where you live."

Safe inside my room, I leaned against the door and closed my eyes.

Memories washed over me. Sunny summer afternoons. My father coming home after his shift at the mill, picking up his fishing kit, and calling for me. Carrying our poles through the trees to the river at the base of Slumber Mountain.

What Pop said every time: "Once our people owned all this land, Lindy. All this land and more. And the mountain, too. Got it after the Revolutionary War when they run out the Cherokee. Then taxes climbed and there was some bad crop seasons."

I knew the story by heart. How the Warwicks bought the mountaintop, and then more of the land. How the government had taken a bunch of the farm for the lake when the dam was built half a century ago.

Of her family's original tract, Gram held only ten acres at the foot of the mountain.

I was too young to understand Pop's regrets. No matter who owned the land, I could still climb trees and swim in the lake and collect lacy moss.

When I stumbled across Gareth crying in the woods after his grandfather's death, I was picking up pretty rocks. He was nine, two years older than me, but he didn't know how to fish.

So I showed him how to bait a hook with fat wriggling earthworms dug up from Gram's garden and how to yank up the line. For a few days we shaped a tenuous friendship over bobbing corks and on tree limbs made for swinging out and dropping into the lake when we got too hot.

Then one day the Warwicks discovered he had a playmate. Gareth's grandmother made her driver stop at Gram's house and got out of her big car. She spoke to my father briefly.

After she left, Pop repeated his warnings about the mountain that brooded over us and the people who owned it. "You can't play with Gareth no more. His people don't like it. We don't have much truck with Warwicks anyways. They been hellbent on buying us out from the time the Cherokee left." He spat. "They got most of our land now, but it won't do 'em no good."

He aimed a faraway gaze up at the peak, looking at something I couldn't see no matter how hard I tried. But I never forgot his words.

"The mountain won't talk to 'em, Lindy, not like it does to me and Gram. Not like it will to you one day. We'll always be tied to the rock, no matter who owns it. It'll always be ours."

That night, Pop had died, and my mother began her nomadic life, taking me far from Gram.

All because of the Warwicks.

In my tiny bedroom, under a naked overhead bulb barely illuminating the shabby red maple bedstead and chest of drawers, I swiped my eyes.

Fool. Pop's dead and the only way Slumber Mountain will ever be yours is for you to get enough money to buy it from the Warwicks and that's not likely to happen. Even if you wanted it back. Even if they wanted to sell. Damn them.

I had learned long ago not to believe in miracles

CHAPTER TWO

DRY JEANS AND tee shirt did wonders for my black mood. Combing my hair, I thought about putting on lipstick.

Thought was all. Why bother? A Rand was just one of the peons, and a Warwick wouldn't bother to notice if one of the peons had on makeup or not. A Warwick wouldn't have bothered to notice a peon, period, if she hadn't pulled him out of the lake.

He should have remembered me.

Aw, come on. Why would he? A few days of playing together, a little girl loaning him a fishing pole because his grandfather had died and he was sad and she felt sorry for him.

Why should he remember something from ten years ago? More to the point, why did I?

Because I still hurt. Gareth Warwick may have missed his grandfather back then, but I bet I missed my father more.

Resentment laced my grief.

Gram would be horrified to know I was capable of such. It wasn't Gareth's fault he'd been born with plenty while I hadn't. It wasn't his fault that his family held the mountain while mine had lost it. It wasn't his fault my father was dead and my mother an alcoholic who couldn't protect herself, much less her child.

When I emerged, he sat as I'd left him. Composed, quiet, preoccupied. Black lashes covered eyes that focused on nothing.

How could any male look so beautiful and yet so masculine? "Ready to go?"

A quick movement of his head made me wonder again if he'd drunk as much as I thought. "Yeah, I'm ready."

Driving him home, I decided he had. No one whose alcohol content was anywhere near the legal limit could be half so garrulous.

He began by asking me to talk to him. "I don't want to go to sleep on you."

"I'm not the talkative kind."

"All right, then I'll talk to you. What shall I talk about?"

"Tell me how to keep a drunk from getting rowdy."

His strange chuckle acknowledged my dig. "You needn't worry. I'm not drunk but when I am, I'm never rowdy. I'll tell you about the party tonight, shall I?"

"No need to bother."

"I knew you'd want to hear all about it. Grandmama had the dock lit up with little white lights. The yacht, too, from bow to stern. And there were these neat Japanese lanterns strung up over the outside tables. All colors. Red, blue, yellow. Then, when we got on the yacht . . ."

As I drove, he detailed everything, from the number of tables set up—twenty-one—to the Sasaki table vases that held gardenias, from the recipe for the champagne punch to the variety of delicacies—lobster and sushi—on the buffets.

His ramblings got on my nerves, but I gritted my teeth and let him talk.

He told about cruising the lake under the night sky and eating on the deck beneath the lanterns. He described the lights on shore winking as they went by. Even his unexpected swim, he said, was invigorating. The water had been soft and cooling as he floated and looked at the stars and picked out the ones he knew.

"What happened? Did you fall off the boat?"

The torrent of words checked. "No-o-o. Not exactly. I'd been, um, talking to a cousin. We don't always get along and things got . . . Anyway, I went back to the stern to cool off. One minute I was looking down at the wake in the water and then, boom, I was in it. I guess I grabbed onto a chair when I fell overboard. Lucky for me. When I came to, I had its cushion so I hung onto it till you came."

"You were unconscious? It's a wonder you didn't drown." There had to have been some horseplay involved, maybe between him and this cousin.

"Nah, not me. I told you, I'm a water baby." He rushed on as if anxious to forget his plunge.

He discussed the town's growth and the new senior center his grandmother had recently financed. He told me about his schools in Switzerland and England, and how much he'd missed the Georgia sun. He spoke of jaunts through Europe and Africa, and other places I'd never been nor could ever hope to go. He described stores catering to the rich that I'd never enter, and the celebrities who used them that I'd never meet.

He chattered nonstop all the way to Slumber Mountain. I learned about the childhood pleasures he'd enjoyed and the adult pleasures he was poised to enjoy.

Cross with envy, I drove with tight lips.

It never occurred to me that he talked to keep from thinking about the people on the yacht because I had no idea of what had taken place or what was taking place as we drove.

Nor did he.

Years later, maturity convinced me he must have suspected something was wrong from the time he was pushed into the water. This night, though, I was simply one stranger taking another home, and that was more than fine with me.

We pulled up to a gate, and Gareth stopped in the middle of a story about a Wimbledon match to tell me the code to put in. The headlights caught some dark figures to the side, but the dogs, big hulking animals, watched us and let us pass without a single bark.

Like they knew a Warwick was passing.

When the pickup started the steep climb to his home, he fell silent. He'd talked so much, he was hoarse.

I missed his prattle.

The only sound was that of the engine. No. That hammering in my head was my heart.

The headlights glowed weaker than usual. Any moonbeam was blocked by trees rising on either side, their large outspread limbs leaning to embrace overhead and form a corridor. The truck crawled up it on a narrow, twisting road.

I wished Gareth would start talking again. Anything would be better than the monotonous hum of the motor and the blood pounding in my ears.

I ought not to be coming up here.

All the old stories rushed back.

Teenagers out to vandalize the mountain's rocky face when their car plummeted over the side. Pets wandering toward the summit and never coming down. Weird lights dancing in the dead of night on the mountain's peak. Hikers stopped by huge dogs as they went past the unmarked boundaries of Warwick property tacitly forbidden to outsiders. A lingering aura from primitive revelries at the top during an earlier period when forests still covered the land.

My father's death . . .

But I'm taking a Warwick home.

Surely I would be safe. I was invited.

By the time we passed several rows of cars parked in lots beside the road, I'd settled down. Then doubt returned tenfold when I stopped in front of Paladins Rest itself.

Imposing in size and appearance, the Warwicks' residence was sited on the highest point of Slumber Mountain. The original home, built in the eighteen hundreds, had burned in the early part of the last century under mysterious circumstances still speculated about in town. Its replacement was a substantial five-sided two-story structure made famous by architectural magazines and inclusions in numerous television shows on home designs.

From them I knew that, depending on which outside room one stood in, custom tinted windows framed magnificent vistas of the forests or the town or the lake several hundred feet below. Each inner room overlooked a large courtyard and dramatic gardens.

But no matter how much I had learned, reading about it or viewing photographs and videos of Paladins Rest was not the same as seeing it. I gaped at the massive shape looming above us.

I did not want to be here.

The house should have appeared ungainly because of its five sides, but it didn't. Balanced and attuned and perfectly situated on the main point, its presence dominated the mountain like an alien spaceship in disguise.

Feeble light from within did not seem welcoming.

Gareth directed me toward garage doors set in solid rock beneath the house. "In there." He rolled down his window and called, "Open sesame."

When the doors rolled open, I must have jumped because he loosed the low sound in his throat that passed as a laugh. "Black magic," he intoned. Seeing me recoil, he quickly reverted to his normal tone. "No, I'm joking. Voice activated."

No reason to be afraid, idiot.

I still wanted to turn around and speed away as fast as Gram's truck would take me. "I'll let you out here."

His impatient sigh hovered. "The elevator's inside." His unspoken *stupid* hung in the air. "You'll want to come in and collect your money, maybe see the inside of the house."

"I told you, I don't want your money."

He slanted a look at me, lashes not concealing a hint of malice. "Afraid, are we?"

Gareth Warwick was amusing himself.

"Me? Afraid? Ha! Say something else funny."

The moment the words blurted out, I realized the mistake. Better to have said that I had no interest in seeing the house and that I had to get home. I opened my mouth to explain why I couldn't stay.

"Good." He grinned like the Cheshire Cat. "Some people around here seem to have a silly phobia about the mountain. Glad to hear you aren't one of them."

Too late now. Consigning my bad vibes to purgatory, I drove the pickup into a well-lighted garage hewn out of solid rock. Several cars were already parked there, and he had me pull up beside a large Mercedes. When I cut off the engine, an eerie quiet descended.

Trying to vanquish claustrophobia, I briskly opened the door. "Can you get out okay?"

He could and did. He was also able to lope without staggering to the elevator.

So he couldn't be as drunk as he pretended even if he did still smell of some potent brew. Since I didn't have to get too close, it didn't matter. I would see him inside and leave.

On the elevator, the lights faded unexpectedly. From his corner, Gareth picked up on my panic. "Not as tough as you make out, are you?"

"I'm tough enough to deal with you."

His mouth twitched. "The lights dim automatically so you can look out at night. Behind you. See? Most people like the view."

I turned.

The back of the elevator was glass, revealing the driveway's last turn among the trees. On one side, the town twinkled in the distance like fairy lights while on the other, moonlight reflected off the black lake far below.

Pretty view but not reassuring. My heart pounded as we inched upward. By the time we emerged into a massive hotel-like lobby, I was ready to turn tail.

The scent of roses blasted us, not unpleasant but strong. From a porcelain vase on a low table in the middle of the spacious room, two dozen or more oversize roses fanned out to spread their heavy perfume. I'd seen red roses before, but never ones like these. They looked as unreal as they smelled, with huge petals perfect ovals and bright blood-red.

They could have been conjured up from some magical greenhouse, but they suited the surroundings.

Goose bumps rose.

"Come on," Gareth urged. "Right over here."

My unwilling feet lagged after him toward a fireplace at one end, tall enough to hold an upright man and wide enough to hold four or five men standing shoulder to shoulder. A pair of wing chairs faced it. A small fire blazed though it was September, and Georgia Septembers are seldom cold.

"Why in the world do you need a fire this time of——?"

"Yeeeeeeechhhh!"

A form, wild and shaggy and screeching, erupted from its hiding place beneath a bombé chest.

It shot toward us.

I jumped back. "Ohhh!"

A flowing apparition rose from one of the chairs behind the squealing creature. A human scream pierced the air over the cat's cries.

I bolted. Smack into Gareth's shoulder.

He, giving his strangled laugh, caught me. His arms closed around me cautiously until he held me fast.

"Let me go!" The darkness and the mountain that had unnerved me on the way up were nothing compared to the attacking beast and the banshee behind it.

"It's all right." Gareth's grip tightened. "Auntie El, it's me," he called over my head. He gave me a reassuring shake and murmured, "Come on, Lindy. It's only Grandmama's cat scaring my aunt. He loves picking on Auntie El and Auntie El can't learn that screaming just makes him worse."

I barely understood him. His hold did not lessen as I struggled. He was warm and solid, and I stopped fighting him.

The punch on his breath mingled with remnants of spice aftershave and clear lake water. Forgetting humiliation, I slumped against his chest as his words sank in. His hand might have caressed my hair, but the sensation was so feathery-light that perhaps I imagined it.

My own sob yanked me back to reality.

I never cried. And Gareth Warwick mustn't think I needed him for any reason whatsoever.

I straightened and pushed him away.

For a fraction of a second, his arm remained outstretched as if to embrace me again.

Another step back quelled the temptation to let him.

The cat, a huge white creature with powder-puff fur, wound about Gareth's foot, its previous wild screams muted to a loud purr. Its candid gaze seemed to say, "Why no, don't blame me. That had to be some other cat howling at you just now. I'm much too nice a cat to do anything like that. See how well-behaved I am?"

"Gareth, stop that beast's mewling and make him go away," the apparition commanded.

Gareth spoke to her with the same calm he'd used to quiet me. "All right, Auntie El. He's leaving. There was no need to scream like that. You've scared Lindy."

Lindy. I hadn't told him who I was. I wasn't about to remind him of that long ago summer. "I'm not scared and I didn't tell you my name." I put more distance between us.

"Yes, you did. When we walked up from the lake." He used a foot to shove the cat aside. "Go away, Jacinth. You've caused enough trouble. We'll talk later."

The cat protested, but Gareth ignored it. He motioned with his head for me to go forward. "Surely you remember."

The thumping of my heart confused me.

What had we said? Had I told him my name?

No, I'd waited to see if he mentioned that summer ten years ago and he hadn't. Perhaps I'd slipped up. Or perhaps he'd gone through my billfold.

Of course. That was exactly what he'd done. Rifled through my billfold while I was changing clothes.

Fury overrode fear. I'd left my windbreaker with my wallet and the night's tips in its pocket, drying on the porch swing. Wide open to his prying. His snooping around my stuff was much more likely than my forgetting I'd told him my name.

He'd gone through my things, looked at them, fingered them. He had no right.

Anger faded as he herded me past the sulking cat and toward the ominous woman who stood in wait.

His aunt, in a long brown housecoat with flowing lines and bell sleeves, could have been a monster bat. The planes of her face, still registering exasperation, proclaimed her Warwick lineage. She waved a tissue. No, it was a handkerchief. "Gareth, what are you doing here? You're supposed to be on the yacht."

A quick glance caught the full force of his smile. Sweet and vulnerable and guileless and sexy. I was a little sorry that the smile was aimed at his aunt and not at me.

"I fell off, Auntie El. I fell off and no one noticed."

"My goodness." She blinked at his bedraggled evening clothes. "You fell in the lake?" The whites of her eyes were streaky and her nose red, explaining the handkerchief she now pocketed. "And they didn't notice? How could they not notice?"

He shrugged. "They didn't. If Lindy hadn't come along in the nick of time, I'd have been run over by a motorboat and cut to pieces and killed dead."

His aunt took his exaggerations seriously. "Goodness gracious me, how awful. What were you doing to fall off the yacht in the first place? Gareth, you've been drinking. Oh, stars, who let you drink? Not your mother, I know." She frowned. "I hope your cousin wasn't drinking, too."

"We just had some of the champagne punch. Grandmama watched them mix it. She said we could have some."

His aunt's mouth tightened. "I wish Annora wouldn't do things like that. And now see what happened. Won't she and your mother be upset when they miss you. I'd better go let them know you're all right."

"I only had one cup of punch. Mom'll want to fuss at me anyway so no need for you to bother to call. I'll do it as soon as I change."

She pursed her lips. Then, "All right. I'm sure your mother will feel better hearing from you herself. I'll enjoy my tea and fire while you find yourself some dry clothes."

The cat, quiet since Gareth had spoken to it, sprang up on a chair and looked at us with a speculative gleam in its eyes.

I could have sworn that same gleam was mirrored in Gareth's eyes before he lowered them, but I was doubtless mistaken.

Time for me to go. "Ahem."

He looked up, all innocence. "I haven't forgotten you, Lindy. This is Talitha Rand's granddaughter, Auntie El. You probably remember her. Or at least remember Mrs. Rand talking about her. Belinda Kay Rand. I don't know how she found me in the middle of the lake tonight, but I'm not joking, she probably saved my life. Lindy, this is my Aunt Eleanor. Auntie, why don't you give Lindy a cup of tea and show her some of the house while I change? Come on, Jacinth, you rascal. Keep me company. Auntie El wants you gone."

The cat jumped up into his arms.

I was too shocked at his belated admission that I had rescued him and my belated realization that he had recognized me, to protest when he swept out with the cat and left me with his aunt.

This was not good.

His aunt didn't help my anxiety by staring at me. She might be outwardly cordial, but she was still daunting. Jet black hair held a tinge of gray at the temples. Her skin was unwrinkled except for tiny lines around the eyes and mouth. Fiftyish or so. Thin, and extremely tall.

I myself was five nine, and the top of my head might reach the tip of her aquiline nose. Aristocratic lips like Gareth's had parted slightly when he introduced me but were a thin line now.

Her gaze locked on me like I'd surprised her.

Of course she was surprised. I was the poor little neighbor girl who had no business being in the magnificent home of the Warwicks.

The chilly air brought up goose bumps again. "There's no need to show me around. I just wanted to make sure he got in safely. After his dunking, he didn't seem too steady on his feet."

She tore her eyes away. "No, no. Come over by the fire, dear, and warm up." The queen being gracious to her subject. "My, aren't you a pretty little thing with those big blue eyes. And what lovely hair." She picked up a strand and sifted it through long fingers.

Gareth had long fingers, too, but hers reminded me of claws.

"Natural blonde, is it? I seem to recall you being a towhead when you were little."

I refused to cower. "Um, yes. Yes, ma'am." Gram's lectures on manners bubbled up at the most inopportune times.

"How nice. Nowadays, blondes generally come from a bottle."

"Yeah. Well, I just brought Gareth home." I didn't care for this intimate examination. I didn't want anyone touching my hair or any other part of me despite my welcoming Gareth Warwick's arms not five minutes before. "I need to get back."

"I insist you have tea. See? It's all ready. I was just about to have some."

She busied herself in a corner at a tea tray that looked like those seen in old movies. Coming back, she held out a steaming cup. "My own special blend. Wonderful for soothing jangled nerves. I've enough steeping for Gareth, too, once he changes. Try it. It'll make a new person out of you."

Did I dare? Why not? A shot of hot tea might calm my nerves.

I took the cup, a delicate porcelain affair with roses on the side and an intricate gold pattern around the rim but fumbled. Hot liquid sloshed out onto my jeans.

Oh no, I should have known better. "I'm sorry." I rubbed at my legs as if to erase the stain. "I didn't mean to spill it."

"My fault entirely. Don't you worry, we'll have you dry in a jiffy." She fluttered over with a tea towel.

When I took it, she eyed the double triangles on the inside of my wrist that most people think are tattoos. Unlike most people, she said nothing.

After I was dry and holding a refilled cup, she took my arm. "Now you come over here and sit down."

"I really need to—"

"I insist. Tell me all about yourself." She put me in the wing chair next to hers.

I couldn't stay here. "Should we let the people on the boat know Gareth's all right?"

"Gareth will call them. He'll be out soon to thank you. Drink your tea, dear."

A nervous swallow proved the flavor innocuous, but the hot liquid did relax me.

Surprising how good its warmth felt. Especially with the fire's heat soaking into my bones. The Warwicks must keep the air conditioning on high all summer to keep the house cool enough for a fire. Their electric bill must be awful.

Not that it mattered. Rich people could afford such eccentricities.

"So. You're Talitha Rand's granddaughter." Eleanor picked up her own cup. "I haven't seen you in a long time. Or Talitha for that matter. I hope she's well."

The kind tone made me think that perhaps I had misjudged her.

The cat had frightened her and she was obviously not expecting a stranger to waltz in. She had reason to be tetchy.

"Gram's fine. And I've been away." Short answers should cut off further questions.

The tea's heat joined that given off from the fire. Spices, strange and wonderful, tickled at my taste buds. The second sip was more flavorful than the first.

"Away?" She drew her handkerchief from a pocket of the robe. "I see. Were you born here in Lassitan?"

"Yes." Now to gracefully leave. The last thing I needed was a Warwick digging into my life.

After a second cup of Eleanor's wonderful brew, I didn't mind her curiosity so much. She was sympathetic, and it had been a long time since I'd been around anyone besides Gram who cared anything about me.

"Do you have other family, dear?"

Despite my reluctance, I found myself telling her about losing my father when I was seven. "He was wonderful. He used to do things with me. Play ball, take me swimming, fishing in the river. Stuff like that."

There was no need to mention that he'd died after I had befriended Gareth, that I'd been convinced the Warwicks had a hand in his death. That was childish imagination.

Instead, we went on to my mother. No need to talk about Mother's drinking either. I skipped to where she'd barely been able to cope after Pop's death, how we'd moved all over the southeast while she tried to forget.

I left out the uncles, too, but not how I'd tried to look after Mother. I even admitted she'd gone to AA after accidentally setting her bed on fire with a cigarette. "It helped for a while. Then she remarried last year, but I came to live with Gram because—"

I stopped, aghast. I hadn't meant to reveal so much about myself, especially about my mother's husband. I'd never tell anyone about those terrible months. I wanted to forget them, to expunge the shame.

"How old are you, dear?" was the next question.

"Eighteen," I lied.

She smiled a perceptive smile, and looked into her teacup as if reading leaves.

Seventeen years and ten months and twenty-one days, the words came from somewhere.

I started.

Was that right? Ten months and twenty-one days? I took another gulp of tea.

Those were my own thoughts I'd heard, not the demanding Voice that occasionally intruded. No one in this house could know my age. I was a stranger to the Warwicks. The words must have come from inside my mind because they couldn't have come from anywhere else. I'd been counting the days until I was eighteen.

My subconscious, that's what it was.

Eleanor got up and pushed an ottoman toward me, wearing compassion like a mask. "I'm going to check on Gareth and make sure he called the yacht so his family won't be worried. You put your feet up here and rest, dear."

I'd worked from six in the morning till two in the afternoon at my cashier's job in the county across the lake, and then gone down the street to the lakefront restaurant where I waited tables from four to eight. The long day, capped by having to haul Gareth Warwick out of the water, meant I was exhausted.

I shouldn't obey her. I didn't have time to rest. But I propped up my feet and sank back into the plump upholstered chair and drank more tea.

My eyelids drooped. My hands clenched around the cup. Someone lifted them, cup and all. Gentle warmth enveloped my legs before hands and cup were laid back down on a rough texture.

Eleanor had thrown a blanket over my lap. I should open my eyes and thank her.

The scent of roses lay like another, ethereal mantle, no longer pungent but delicate and welcome. I floated in that evanescent state between waking and sleeping.

"How do you know?"

A man spoke next to me. I roused but not to the point of waking.

There was no man in the room. I was dreaming. Dreaming as I reclined snug and safe by the fire.

"It's obvious." That was Eleanor's voice.

She sounded close. And real. Was I dreaming?

Heavy eyelids strained, lifted.

Two strangers stood beside Eleanor Warwick.

One, a heavyset middle-aged man, wasn't one of the tall, lean Warwicks. He was stocky and coarse-featured, with a broad forehead, thick sensual lips, and a pug nose that looked as if someone had pushed it in. He did not exude confidence like Eleanor nor arrogance like Gareth. He fidgeted.

The other one, peering over the shorter man's shoulder, was quite elderly, with stooped shoulders and white hair. His soaring brows and long face proclaimed his relation to Eleanor. He might have been her brother or uncle or cousin, but no matter the relationship, he was a Warwick through and through.

While the first man wore regular slacks and a yellow golf shirt, the older one wore some kind of loose, billowing outfit like his sister/niece/cousin.

Strange kind of lounging garb, but these were Warwicks.

I was right. This had to be a dream.

The three stared down as the fire cast writhing shadows across their faces.

Placid and incurious, I looked up at them. They had nothing to do with me.

"If it's true, she's come too soon." The heavyset man ran his tongue over a full bottom lip, and then the top one. "How do you know?" he asked again.

"Listen to me, Jeffrey." Eleanor exaggerated her patience. "Look at her right wrist, and you'll believe me."

Jeffrey came over and raised my arm, turning it so that he and the other man could study the inside of my wrist and the five moles there. A line connecting them would outline a bow tie.

I couldn't stand men touching me, but I didn't complain. If this hadn't been a dream, I would have jumped up and thrown the cup at this Jeffrey.

Even if Warwicks would curse me.

But it had to be a dream. Not a single drop sloshed out of the cup as he moved my arm.

Eleanor pointed to the moles. "The mark is plain."

The older man inhaled.

She looked smug. "Well?"

"I see it." Jeffrey carefully returned my nerveless hand with its cup to the woven throw on my lap and looked down at my face.

I still couldn't move, couldn't speak, could only stare back at them.

The older man cleared his throat. "I suppose you're right, El."

"Of course I'm right, Alonzo. Now we have to make a decision. And quickly."

No fear, no horror, no panic swept me. Not indignation, wonder, or concern.

My body was here, but my psyche hovered elsewhere.

Mentally, I remarked on the absence of emotion, but that was all I did. All I could do.

Dreams are like that.

The older man rubbed his eyes. "We have a decade before the next awakening, El. There are no records of anything like this happening before. Not ever. We'll never hold her that long. She's come too soon."

I had no interest in what they were doing or why they were watching me with such calculation. As for their conversation, the words were simply sounds.

If I paid close attention, I bet I could see them form shapes in the air.

Before I could try, Eleanor Warwick put long fingers to her throat and pulled out a pendant or amulet of some sort. She closed her hand around its pink radiance as if coming to a decision. "Nonsense. There's no such thing as too soon, Alonzo. Only too late. Now that we know who the mediary is, we simply figure out how to keep her available."

"Bind her." Jeffrey's harassed air gave way to determination.

Alonzo and Eleanor looked at him, the older man in astonishment and Eleanor with approval.

Alonzo was the first to respond. "Bind her? Now?"

I listened, a passive observer to a discussion over my head. Literally and figuratively.

"Of course," Eleanor agreed. "Jeffrey's right. She can be bound at any time. Indeed, that's the only answer. She must be bound."

The old man frowned. "Can binding hold her for that long?"

Eleanor humphed. "For ten years? Oh, come, Alonzo. You know very well any male Warwick can bind her for ten years or longer. Will you do it?"

Horrified, Alonzo stepped back. "I can't. I'm not capable. I'm past the age where I could even—I'd be afraid to try lest I couldn't bring her back."

Jeffrey's large rabbit-like teeth worried his lip. "Can't you do it, Eleanor?"

She waved an arm. The bell sleeve swished. "No, dearest. Were it for a month or even a year, yes. But for any longer, a female must be bound by a male. Normally the patriarch would do it, or the most able one available. Cavanagh would be perfect, but he's taking care of—"

She darted a glance at the older man, who still hadn't recovered from the thought of having to do whatever it was they wanted him to do. "He's with the others, going over our future as caretakers. No, we can't wait, dear. She must be bound before she leaves this place tonight, and the only qualified males here are Alonzo and Gareth. And Alonzo refuses."

"Then Gareth will have to do it," Jeffrey said.

"Yes. Gareth's proficient enough." Alonzo sighed in relief at finding someone other than himself. "Gareth's more talented than me.

Lots more talented than me or anybody else. Even your Cavanagh, El. If anybody can do it, Gareth can."

"Do you think it wise?" Eleanor asked Jeffrey. "Gareth is so . . . careless." She glanced pointedly at Alonzo. "In view of everything else happening now, the discussions over the future methods and all, will it be safe? Ought we to use him at this particular moment?"

"Wise or not, he's here and the others aren't." Jeffrey set his jaw. "Besides, it's only a binding, isn't it? Gareth may not be needed when the, uh, when the time comes." There was a small silence. "Gareth might not choose to be here for the actual ceremony. I mean, we never know, do we?"

Eleanor hooded her eyes.

Puzzled, Alonzo looked from one to the other. "Of course he'll be here. Gareth's a part of the elder line. He has to be here."

The surreal atmosphere of flickering lights and heady rose perfume fascinated me. It was like looking through a glazed window at a wonderful fantasyland.

"You'll have to make the bargain," Jeffrey told Eleanor. "Alonzo and I'll talk to Gareth if you'll deal with her."

Eleanor hesitated, as if she would argue, but finally shrugged. "Yes. I'll deal with her." Her words sounded unaccountably flat.

"Don't you want me to help you?" Alonzo asked her.

"I need you, Alonzo," Jeffrey said. "Gareth will listen to you when he might not to me."

Alonzo opened his mouth as if he would protest, but closed it again. Then, "That's true. Still, I've always been able to explain these things better than Eleanor. Oh, very well."

The two men disappeared. Literally disappeared. I looked at Eleanor for a split second and when I looked back, they were gone.

What an amazing dream.

Housecoat flowing, Eleanor glided across the floor, knelt in front of me, and took my numb hands. "Belinda, dear." Her words caressed me as she chafed my hands. "You poor thing, how you've suffered. You deserve something to make up for the past, don't you? I can help you."

She tipped up my chin.

Her eyes were like Gareth's, almond-shaped and almost Arabic with their dark outlines. Beautiful eyes that brimmed with compassion. "What would you like most to have in the whole world, dear?"

I thought of my father, tried to tell her, but failed.

Eleanor patted my cheek. Her hand was cold. "No, dear, that's impossible. That's in the past. Your father is gone and you can't bring him back. No one can change the past, but the future's yet to be written. The future can be formed, molded in a way you can decide on. Think, dear. What do you want your future to be like?"

I remembered Gareth on the drive to this house, his talk of countries I'd never seen, possessions I could never afford, friends I'd never have. People happy to know him, anxious to please him, willing to love him.

I remembered how I'd felt, knowing I meant so little in the world that it hardly mattered I was alive.

"Success." The word came out harsh and dry.

Could that be me speaking? My lips had definitely moved, but that didn't sound like my voice.

"Success?" Eleanor's hands tightened on mine as if seizing on a mistake I'd made. "Success meaning . . . ?"

The dream caught me in its spell. "Wealth," I croaked. "Fame. Admiration."

So that I could hold my head up high, never worry about anyone's opinion ever again. So that no one like Gareth Warwick or his family could look down on me as being lowly and insignificant. So that I need never apologize for what I was, or what I had been, or what had happened to me.

Eleanor smiled, as if understanding why I hankered after such things. "That can be arranged." Her eyes narrowed. "What would you give for, say, ten years of success, Belinda?"

Ten years. I could amass a fortune in ten years if I was careful. I could take care of Gram. I could save enough so that I need never again be hungry or homeless. No one would ever have me in their power again.

I could show everyone, including Gareth Warwick, that I was a person to be reckoned with, not one to be scorned or pitied.

My detachment had eroded.

"What would you give, Belinda?" Eleanor asked again, almost crooning as she held my hands.

Someone sighed. Me. "Whatever it took." Yielding to desire drove out the hoarseness.

"Would you surrender your soul, Belinda?"

I couldn't think. She reminded me of the white cat, all purrs and velvety fur before unsheathing sharp claws.

No. This was a dream. I could agree to what Eleanor asked and not be obligated.

No one should give up her soul. Gram would shake her head in sorrow that I would consider such a thing. *Child, child, think what you're doing,* she'd say.

"Would you, Belinda?" Eleanor pressed her advantage. "For

enormous wealth? To have people look up to you? To be able to have anything your heart desired?"

Gram's image vanished. "Yes," I muttered.

Agreeing wasn't truly making a bargain for my soul. If the dream was real, such a bargain would be wrong. In my own fashion, I tried to keep the standards instilled in me by my father and strengthened by my grandmother. Trading one's soul was immoral and unthinkable.

But this is only a dream.

What did it hurt to dream? I'd never surrender my soul in real life. Never.

Eleanor bent closer. "Think about it, Belinda. Pretty clothes, valuable jewels, magnificent homes. Men wanting you, women admiring you. The very best cuisine, the finest hotels, travel to different lands, money enough to gratify every whim. No one daring to snub you."

Ah, she knew my deficiencies, Eleanor Warwick did, and she played on them like a master with her seductive images.

She stroked my hair. "It would be another life for you. A new life. You could forget the old one. Cleaning up after your mother drank herself into a stupor and threw up all over the kitchen. Keeping to yourself instead of going to parties like the other girls. The times you were pawed and slapped by the men she brought home."

I hesitated.

She whispered, "Why, you could completely wipe out those horrible months when she married him, Belinda, when he raped you and she allowed it. When she blamed you for tempting him. Think of it. You could forget all those terrible things and put them in the past because you'll be a different person. A whole new person. When you're successful, it would be like none of the bad things ever happened."

Her words were a siren's song. All the pain sealed up inside seemed far away already. The future stretched out, bright and secure. I'd be someone else, not Lindy Rand. I'd be pristine and guiltless and unhindered by my past. I'd never again feel tainted and contemptible.

Yes, yes. My mind reached out eagerly to confirm the promise.

"Only if you choose it, Belinda," Eleanor murmured as if I'd spoken aloud.

She stroked my arms, but her touch no longer bothered me. Only Gram had caressed me with affection since Pop's death.

Eleanor still crooned, her face nearly touching mine. "It takes such a little thing to become a new person, Belinda. Do what I ask, and I'll keep my side of the bargain. You'll have everything your heart desires. I promise."

I wanted to give in because since I'd lost Pop, no one besides Gram had loved me. Because I was tired of working sixty hours a week to survive. Because I hated feeling dirty.

"What do you want?" I croaked.

"I only need to borrow your soul for a little while, dear."

Even then, on the verge of submission, I wavered.

Though the pictures she drew were enticing, and her promises for the future seemed genuine, a sense of self-preservation warned me they were too good to be true.

Still, I wanted to believe the dreams, the promises. Oh, how I wanted to believe. "For how long?"

"That you loan out your soul? Only a few minutes. You can have it back afterward."

A few minutes. What would it hurt to loan my soul for such a little while? I'd get it back. Eleanor had said so.

I whispered, "I'll do it."

Before my mouth closed, Eleanor was rising in triumph. I saw her through misted eyes, a towering figure in cascading robes.

"You're doing the right thing. Trust me."

"Yes," I murmured. Deep in my being I didn't trust her or even myself, but my hunger for acceptance meant I was lost.

From somewhere in the backrooms of the great house, a cat screamed out. I didn't flinch.

"Did you persuade her?"

The man who was not a Warwick had returned to linger in the shadowy light behind Eleanor. I'd been vaguely aware of his entrance but at his words, I saw him clearly. His unsmiling vigilance reminded me of a great bull.

"Yes, Jeffrey," came Eleanor's muffled answer. "She's agreed."

I had sold my soul.

No, I had *loaned* my soul.

CHAPTER THREE

AFTER ELEANOR COAXED my agreement, I was transported away. No person or thing carried me, but still I went.

One moment I sat in the wing chair with her and the stocky man hovering over me, and the next moment their images dissolved while I floated in a gray soundless atmosphere.

Dreams are like that sometimes. Neither was I surprised to find a dim room materializing around me, far removed from the rose-scented living area where I'd drunk tea. I had no inquisitiveness whatsoever about where I was or how I came to be there but waited, with what was for me, extraordinary patience.

Five walls I counted, all draped from ceiling to floor with some kind of shimmering cloth that lay in silky creases. Every few feet a griffin, sculpted in gold and adorned with sparkling stones, gathered folds of material with its claws. The light was uneven because it emanated from branches of lit candles, supported by the griffins' outspread wings and backed up to round mirrors which captured and threw back the weak flames.

The room remained quiet and still, save for the wavering light.

I lay on a soft mattress suspended in the middle, not shocked or even alarmed by the absence of my clothing. A sheer cloth covered me from neck to ankles, but did not conceal the aureoles of my breasts or the darkness of my pubic mound. I might as well have been naked for all the good the cloth did.

In dreams people sometimes shed their clothing, so neither fear nor anticipation nor wonder struck me. I waited like an eager spectator for the next portion of the fantasy.

Somewhere in the background unseen currents of air made wind chimes tinkle. The same currents carried a scent of spices and lavender. Gone were the odoriferous roses.

I rejoiced in the fragrance. Beneath the sheer material, my nipples swelled and budded as if in slow motion. The silken fabric caressed their tips, heightening the sensation of promised delights.

At some point, envy and fear and suspicion had fled. I was cleansed and benevolent. Expectant in the way I'd been when my father had been alive to take me with him on his outings. Optimism replaced all the regret, all the hurt.

Pinpoints of light stabbed the coverlet. The ceiling over the bed gave way to a huge expanding circular opening that brought the night sky down to enclose me.

How natural the illusion.

Now I could understand what Gareth meant when he spoke of flying through the skies. The twinkling stars and gauzy clouds veiled the moon. Easy to imagine myself up there in the midst of the planets, soaring like an unfettered spirit.

Whyever had I thought him drunk?

Time, a little or a lot, elapsed. I waited, aware of everything around me except for the passage of time. My arms lay relaxed by my sides, the left one slightly turned to show the five familiar moles.

Two on either side and one in the middle. Perfect in their patterns and matched sizes. Some graphic artist might have marked off the quarter inches and inked in template dots. A line through them could make two connecting triangles.

As I floated, suspended in time and space, Gareth Warwick appeared from nowhere and stood against the shimmering folds of drapery. He wore a loose white garment, the material opaque but as delicately fashioned as that covering me. His hands and bared chest were as ivory as his face. I knew without seeing that all his skin was as pale.

With each step he took, the muscles in his arms and shoulders and thighs rippled beneath the silken raiment.

Gareth wouldn't be tanned, but his stomach would be flat and his body hard.

Something inside me sparked, flickered.

He came forward until he stood at my feet. His hair, dark and brushed straight back from his face, shone as with an unholy halo. His eyes were black as midnight and as obscure. He was beautiful, so beautiful that my heart turned in upon itself, and a strange joyful fire began to burn in the pit of my stomach.

No one had to tell me that I'd been waiting for him.

"They said you agreed. Is that true?" Any trace of alcoholic languor had vanished. No longer playful, he was grave, lips set in a purposeful line.

"Yes." The whisper did not sound like mine. Had I really agreed? Panic threatened, but receded.

I'm dreaming. What did it matter what I had agreed to so long as this was just a dream?

So long as Gareth stood before me.

"You know what happens to your soul? That a part of it stays here until you return for it?"

"Yes." Again that unfamiliar whisper. My soul would be loaned out, but only for a while, as Eleanor had said. Then I'd have it back, and everything would be as it was before.

Except she hadn't promised I'd be the same. And I wouldn't be. Not after living this moment.

I knew that, too.

"Do you understand what it is you undergo?" He almost but not quite brushed my calf with the tip of his finger.

Delicious waves of heat emanated from the depths of me, simply from the suggestion of a caress. "Yes, I understand."

I lifted the corners of my lips, enticing him, inviting him closer.

That had to be the essence of the bargain between Eleanor and me. A few hours for Gareth to touch me, touch my soul, use me as he willed. I was to be prostituted, body and spirit, but I no longer cared. A vision of Gram and my father, their faces creased in pain, appeared and then fled before rising urges.

I wanted Gareth. I wanted him wholeheartedly, with a desire I had never imagined could exist. The memory of the engaging boy he had once been, the nebulous bond we had formed, had remained concealed inside me like a seed lying dormant. Now it sprang forth in full bloom.

Somehow I had let that boy become a part of me until, without him laying a hand on me, with only one look from his inscrutable eyes, my body was roused and eager for whatever he chose to do with it. I had never been so vibrant, so quivering. So alive.

The longing made me physically ache.

He hesitated, his face more stolid than before, if that were possible. "I don't suppose it will matter in the end," he muttered, and the waiting was over. "Give me your hands."

He might not share my memories of our connection, but it didn't matter.

Such an effort it took to raise my hands. But he wanted them, and I knew, the same way I knew his feelings for me were not as strong as mine for him, that I would have to offer them, that he would not pick them up himself.

Somehow I gathered the strength to raise my hands. He took possession, examining both with gentle care before putting them together and catching hold of my middle fingers.

He trembled a bit as he held them.

Or perhaps it was my hands that trembled.

I never felt the pricks, but I saw scarlet drops spring up, drops of blood that were persuaded into thin streams by dint of massage from his lean fingers. He straightened both my arms in a prelude to spreading them wide.

I arched my back as if I had done this before, felt his body fall on mine. The mattress had become hard as a stone. As he lay on me, he stretched out with me, forcing both my arms down. My palms, awkward under his, flattened against something hard and unyielding.

Where was my soft mattress?

Gone.

We lay on a slab of gray rock barely wide enough to accommodate one person before sloping off. The mountain itself.

My bare skin pressed directly against its top, but I felt no discomfort because the rock conformed itself to my body. On the right, he pressed my bleeding finger against the surface of the smooth stone, inside a little cupped place where other hands had been positioned before.

The blood trickled out and disappeared into the rock.

The same thing repeated on the left.

As my blood flowed red before fading into the rock, I felt myself changing. Until I was . . .

Different.

Ancient and timeless and enduring. Tranquil and slumberous and massive. Solid and invulnerable and majestic. All-powerful and forgiving and predestined.

I became patience, content, fortitude. I became rage, even violence.

I was the mountain itself.

How long we lay there I couldn't judge. An eternity, a second? All were the same.

Drifting and at peace, I didn't want to disturb the harmony by moving. I wanted to lie there forever, tied to the mountain.

When at length Gareth began to remove my hands from the stone, I whimpered. I refused to be forced back into the real world and away from the peace of the mountain's center.

He held steady.

I struggled.

He continued to pull me away.

I twisted, trying to throw him off and keep my hands bonded to the rock. Perspiration beaded my forehead and damped the filmy coverings between us. I gathered together all my strength and all my emotions to use in escape.

His will was stronger than mine.

As we fought, soundlessly except for his harsh breathing and my anguished sobs, he inexorably forced my hands up, up and away from the rock, so that I came back to myself and eventually lay quietly beneath him, overwhelmed by what had happened.

Somehow he had taken me to the depths of the mountain's soul and brought me back.

He had changed me.

Still holding my slack hands, he lay on me as if exhausted.

When he finally roused himself, he pushed up on his elbows and looked down into my eyes. What he saw seemed to be what he expected but did not please him. "So it's true. You are the mediary." He gave his twisted smile, but the half-laugh did not come. "You're bound now. You'll come back here of your own accord when it's time. Back to the mountain."

Elation faltered.

I had become a part of the mountain and had glimpsed the peace that unanimity with nature could bring. Despite the sting of my fingers and the regret at being torn from the mountain's comfort, I was buoyant.

He had no right to depress me with his melancholy.

So I awaited his next move, impatient for whatever else he would do. Whatever happened next was at his inclination. I was still in thrall.

He grimaced, and then put my fingers into his mouth and held them, stanching my wounds with his tongue. His elbows, resting on the rock beside my neck, enclosed my face. A strand of dark hair, disheveled from our exhausting encounter, touched my cheek. Soft, silky.

My nipples budded.

His quivering body remained stretched out on me. His chest, because he was raised up on his elbows with his hands holding mine, barely grazed my breasts. The rest of him—his stomach, his thighs, his legs—followed mine intimately. His sex pressed into mine, chastely since his clothing and my cover separated us, but the heat had built to such intensity I thought we would combust.

Gone was the indifference that had afflicted me earlier. The brief flash of desire I'd felt before was nothing to my torment now.

I burned, I hungered, I ached for him.

For his touch on my thighs, for his tongue lashing my breasts, for his body joining mine.

"Gareth."

I lurched beneath him, tried to pull off the cloth separating us.

He recoiled at my need. His body stiffened as if he would hurl himself off me.

My arms, until now heavy and docile while he controlled my hands, lifted of their own accord to encircle his neck. "Gareth."

"I can't." His weary smile fled. His face over mine changed, lengthened. He hesitated. Desire vied with indecision. "Our code won't let me, Lindy. It would be wrong to take advantage of our closeness. Don't ask me this."

"Gareth." He was on the precipice of withdrawal. However much he felt the same passions that raged through me, he was fighting them. He was too near to leaving me unfulfilled and incomplete.

I wanted to scream for him to enter me and stop my agony. Had my words been intelligible, he would have heard me begging, cursing, pleading. "Gareth."

Perhaps he did hear.

"I can't. Even if you choose me, it isn't right. Not now." He was clearly torn. New beads of perspiration wet his forehead. The thin cloth over his chest was soaked. His breathing sounded loud above me. "I can't."

He was weakening.

"You can."

"Oh goddess." He turned his head from one side to the other as if fighting himself. Or seeking help. Then he looked back into my eyes. "Do you want this, Lindy? Are you sure?"

"Yes."

His uncertainty and resistance fled. I hardly heard his soft, "Then so be it. May the mountain forgive me for not being strong enough."

His will had won the contest earlier. He had brought me back from my fusion with the mountain despite my struggles. But here as man against woman, I was the victor.

Wind chimes tinkled again. A bouquet of spices mingled with lavender. He raised up on his knees and his clothing and my covering disappeared. When he reached down to part my legs, I saw the full length of his pale form before he blocked my body with his.

Then he covered my mouth with his mouth and I was lost.

The hard rock softened beneath me, changing back into an airy feather bed offering the softest support. The room that had been dim with gray and silver tints lightened and turned into a moving kaleidoscope of vivid colors. Reds and pinks and oranges and golds and yellows and greens and blues and purples and lavenders. Every color in the rainbow and some I had never seen, swirled around in a mist that enveloped and enclosed and kept us separate from the rest of the world.

I nearly drowned in the colors, was kept afloat only by his arms that held me against him.

Panicked, I cried out.

He tightened his grasp. "It's only colors, love. They're here to shield us, to protect you. They won't harm you. Don't be afraid. You don't ever have to be afraid with me. I promise you I'll safeguard you.

It doesn't matter that you're bound. I'll keep you safe, Lindy. Always. I promise."

He sounded far away, as if he wasn't with me at all, though I felt his body's warmth up and down me, and knew he was against me. And I believed him. Instinct told me he spoke the truth, that I could trust him as I could never trust any other.

No, I'd never have to be afraid with Gareth. He'd always protect me, keep me safe.

My heart expanded with the knowledge. The longing returned, stronger than ever. My body rose to meet his, welcomed the pressure when he entered. I went through a long, dark tunnel, where the colors lit my path and kept me from losing my way as I strove to keep up with him, racing beside him, inside him, inside me, racing toward the skies overhead.

We burst out into the stars and soared together.

Then we were bathed in white brilliance, and I cried out in jubilation as I had cried out earlier in fear. A thousand diamonds danced round us in the sky.

I would never let him go.

CHAPTER FOUR

I AWOKE WITH a start, the fire burned down to embers, the empty cup of tea still clutched in both hands. My heart pounded and my muscles were enervated.

Both my middle fingers hurt. On examining them, I saw tiny pierced places on each fingertip. Further inspection showed the pricks were caused by my tight grip at broken edges on the teacup where the handle had once joined the base.

To my horror, the handle itself lay on my lap.

It had snapped off during my sleep.

While relieved to see the origins of my dreams had a physical cause, I still felt sick. Eleanor Warwick would be furious that I'd broken her porcelain cup. The idea of becoming the focus of a Warwick's anger brought back my earlier fears.

The last time the Warwicks became angry with me, my father had died.

Coincidence, I told myself from my adult point of view as I tried to calm my beating heart. Purely coincidence.

Sound of movements came from somewhere in the huge reception area beyond the elevator.

Eleanor talking to someone else. "We ought to let her sleep. She's exhausted."

She wouldn't be so sympathetic if she knew what I'd done to her china cup.

"Auntie El, she needs to go home." Gareth sounded impatient. Almost petulant. A lot different from the Gareth of my dream. In it he'd been overpowering, almost heroic. In the flesh, he was simply a nineteen-year-old boy. A spoiled scion of a rich family. "I need to go, too. I must."

"My dear boy," a man's bass said, "you can't do anything even if you go down there."

"Don't ever call me that again." Gareth emitted an iciness I didn't recognize. "I'm not your dear boy nor will I ever be your dear boy, Jeffrey."

Jeffrey? So there was a reason for that name being in my dream. I tried to turn so I could see what this Jeffrey looked like and found neck and shoulders stiff from sleeping in an unnatural position. I stifled a groan.

The men didn't notice.

"I understand and forgive you for your attitude, Gareth. You're too upset to be thinking clearly." That same condescending tone had been directed against me and my mother too often; Jeffrey was telling Gareth he was too ignorant to know what was best.

Gareth recognized it, too. "I'm thinking quite clearly. I know what you've been doing behind Grandmama's back the past two years, how you've been manipulating everyone. Did you actually think she wouldn't find out you were the one who instigated the whole idea?" Gareth's voice betrayed him vying desperately for self-control.

"She understood that I'm trying to look out for the family's best interests."

"Best interests! I blame you and only you for what happened tonight. You hatched the whole greedy scheme. If you hadn't got Uncle Selwin to spring it on Grandmama without warning tonight, there would never have been an argument." Gareth's intensity was frightening. "And if they hadn't all been arguing, someone would have noticed what was happening."

"Go away, Jeffrey," Eleanor commanded. "We'll discuss this later. Can't you see the poor boy's too upset to be rational?"

A door slammed.

I got up on unsteady legs, but the other two didn't notice.

Eleanor put a hand on Gareth's shoulder. "Gareth, we may never know what happened tonight, but I'm deeply disappointed in you. Jeffrey has only the interests of the family at heart. He may not see the future in the same light as you and my sister, but that doesn't make him disloyal to the family. He simply has a different vision of where our future, our fortunes lie. Your grandmother understands—understood that. Annora was ever willing to listen to new ideas."

I put the teacup on a table. Coward that I was, I took care to place the handle toward the wall so that the jagged edge was partly hidden.

Better that Eleanor discovered the broken piece after I was safely away.

That isn't right, I heard Gram say. She would be scandalized that I didn't own up to the breakage, but I didn't care. Once I left this place, I'd never come back here again.

"I don't want to discuss it, Aunt Eleanor." Gareth was back to being the sulky boy. "I have to go. But if you think that you can push Jeffrey's plan through because of this, you're wrong. If Mom and Dad were—I'll never let them or Grandmama down by allowing . . ."

He put both hands over his face.

Was he about to cry?

He needed comforting. I started to go toward him but stopped. His aunt was here.

She kept her distance and watched him dispassionately.

Jeffrey, whoever he was, must have been the one to slam the door. There was no one to wipe away Gareth's tears.

Poor boy.

I immediately laughed at myself. In my dream, Gareth had been masterful, desirable, vulnerable. Here he looked like a teenager who'd been grounded for getting a speeding ticket. What a shame that in real life, men are never as exciting as women try to make them.

In any event, Gareth was a Warwick. He didn't need my sympathy.

I said abruptly, "I need to go."

Gareth and Eleanor whirled. They'd forgotten my presence.

"I have to get home. Gram might wake up and wonder where I am."

"You're awake," Gareth's aunt said, coming over with both hands outstretched. Her forbidding manner gave way to kindly warmth.

After my dream, I was leery of accepting that warmth at face value. Sometimes your subconscious highlights things you miss while you're awake. And Eleanor hadn't been very sympathetic toward her nephew just now.

I endured her grasp of my hands but not for long.

She overlooked my quick withdrawal. "You must have been exhausted, poor child. I thought it best to let you sleep for awhile. I hope you've managed to rest."

Gareth, changed into loose khaki shorts and garish Hawaiian shirt completely unlike the silken attire of my dream, was at her heels. "Here. This ought to cover what I owe you." Without looking at me, he threw a couple of folded bills on a table. His face was white as paper while his mouth was a thin line. He looked sick but no more so than would be expected from anyone going through a sobering-up process.

So that's how it's going to be.

The way he threw the money down, as if I were a hired underling, got my dander up. He didn't have to be so curt. He might have figured out I was his childhood playmate, but he obviously didn't put much store in shared experiences.

And he wouldn't even look at me. Guess that put me in my place. The poor neighbor. Dazzle her with the house and send her away with more money than she's seen in a while. Give her something to tell the town about. Make her day.

Well, I had news for him.

"I don't want your money. I told you I'd bring you home and I did."

He shrugged. "And I told you I'd pay you. It's yours. You earned it."

Like a lowly peon.

I wasn't good enough for Mr. Gareth Warwick of Paladins Rest to befriend or even look at. After I'd spent hours of precious sleep time rescuing him and bringing him home.

To think in my dream I'd trusted him with my life.

The damned nightmare had unnerved me, but I had enough self-control left to stand up straight and politely thank Eleanor Warwick for the tea. I left the money on the table.

She followed me to the elevator.

I said, "Thank you again. I'm sorry I fell asleep."

She pressed the button, brushed a hand against my shoulder. "The rest will do you good. And the tea. You'll see. Sleep will come easier tonight." The door slid open.

Maybe I'd get away before she realized her cup was broken.

The elevator faced a long corridor. The last thing I saw before the doors closed was Gareth walking down it. His back was rigid. The white cat slunk at his heels while the hands at his sides were balled into fists. He didn't look back.

Damn him. I was glad I had told him I wouldn't take his filthy money. I might be poor but I had pride. Never mind that I could have used even one of those folded bills.

Not now, though. I'd die before I took it.

His aunt went down in the elevator with me to my car, clinging to my arm and chattering. She hovered as if I were an honored guest about to leave after a party.

Or maybe a hired worker she escorted out to ensure no silver ashtrays went missing.

Thank heavens she hadn't noticed her broken cup.

"Don't mind Gareth," she said as I climbed into the old pickup. "He doesn't drink often and when he does, the Warwick surliness shows. We're just grateful you were there to rescue him. It's been quite a night. Really too terrible."

She hesitated. "And don't worry about the awful problems you've had with your . . . family. People usually end up paying for their sins. Right now, you're safe with Talitha. You can start to forget and that's the main thing."

I stared at her, shocked. She surely didn't know about my stepfather, did she? That couldn't be what she meant.

As I searched for words, her face, until now genial and sympathetic, lengthened into harsher lines. "As for the future, that's up to you, isn't it? You have choices. Are you planning on staying with Talitha long?"

The change of subject caught me unawares. "I-I don't know. For the time being anyway."

"I wonder if that's a good idea," she mused. "Sometimes it's better to be independent, to make your own way."

I gawked at her. "Gram likes having me with her."

"I'm sure she does." The hardness came back behind the surface. Eleanor patted my hand. "But you must do what's best for you. Give my regards to her, dear."

Was that a threat?

Gareth's grandmother had talked to my father the day before he died.

Pop had called me after she left. "Mrs. Warwick says you been playing with her grandson, Lindy, and the two of you been jumping off that big rock into the lake. You know better'n that. You could get hurt, even killed. You don't play with him anymore, you hear me?" Lines of worry creased his forehead. "I told you before, girl, we don't mix with the Warwicks."

"But he's nice, Pop. I like him."

"He probably is, but he's a Warwick. We don't need him down here, Lindy. Let it be."

Pop had died that same night.

After what had happened to Pop, I wasn't about to give Eleanor's regards to Gram. My hand shook so that I could hardly use the truck key.

I was the one who'd broken her stupid cup. She wouldn't take my clumsiness out on Gram. Would she?

Then I laughed. As if she could. Eleanor Warwick was human the same as everyone else. There was no way she could vent her spleen on Gram.

I don't remember driving back home. I remember starting the truck and leaving the cavernous garage, but I don't remember navigating the winding road down the mountain or seeing the dogs at the iron gate. Not even the dirt road that served as Gram's driveway.

The first thing I remembered after leaving the Warwicks' garage, was closing and locking the front door of Gram's house.

It was lucky I hadn't met another car coming up the mountain. I would probably have caused a wreck.

When I started to undress for bed, I found the bills Gareth had flung down on a table, folded up in a little wad inside my jeans.

Gareth or his aunt had slipped them into the pocket without my noticing.

Damn them. Who did they think they were?

I smoothed them out. There were two bills, each a hundred dollars. I felt dirty, especially when remembering how, when he'd brought out the money, he'd avoided my eyes as though I were something slimy, something so far beneath him he couldn't bear to look at me.

Double-damn him. I was a person, too. What happened to me hadn't been my fault. I'd tried to stay out of my stepfather's way. I hadn't asked him to rape me.

I might be damaged goods outside but inside, I was as good as the Warwicks or anyone else.

My reasoning didn't mend the crack in my heart.

What did I care what Gareth Warwick thought of me? Two hundred dollars was enough money to last Gram and me for weeks. I bit my lip and shrugged my shoulders and went to bed.

Strangely enough, despite my hurt pride, I slept better than I had in months. Eleanor's prediction proved true after all.

* * * *

THE NEXT MORNING, all the talk at the convenience store where I cashiered was about the fire on the Warwicks' yacht the night before.

One of the regulars, a local not much older than me who attended North Georgia College and University, was full of details as he paid for his gas. His brother was a deputy who had helped work the accident. "Something about a short in one of the lanterns. Looks like the fire spread too fast for anybody to notice. A lot of people died of smoke inhalation. The ones that survived had to take to the water to get away." His avid look belied the hushed tone.

"How horrible." I took his twenties and laid them on the register while I made change.

"Isn't it though? A real tragedy. You don't think about awful things like that happening to people like them, do you? I mean with their money and all, you would of thought they'd have smoke detectors all over the boat, wouldn't you? The help all got out but the Old Lady herself died, along with about thirty or forty Warwicks."

The cash drawer hit my stomach. The matriarch. Gareth's grandmother. She was among the dead. What about his parents? And didn't he have a sister?

I counted out change automatically. Gareth must have learned about the fire while I sat dreaming before the fire the past night. That was why he had looked so shattered when I started to leave, why he sounded like he was holding back tears.

He'd probably been crying before I saw him. No wonder he hadn't raised his eyes. No wonder he had been so short.

Falling overboard might have saved him from a worse fate than a late night dunking.

Later that same day, another regular at the convenience store talked me into going down to Atlanta's Lenox Square with her.

"Macy's is sponsoring this cool contest," she said. "The winner gets a five thousand dollar savings bond and some modeling jobs. Second place gets a thousand and third place five hundred while the next seven runners-up get a hundred each. My sister won five hundred dollars two years ago and she's been coaching me, but I don't want to drive down there alone. Why don't you come with me?"

I shook my head. "I've got to work Saturday."

"You said you're on the eleven p.m. shift. You'll get back in time. Aw, come on, Lindy. Ride down with me and I'll pay your entry fee. What've you got to lose?"

Nothing. It would be nice to spend a few hours daydreaming among chic clothes instead of washing my worn-out ones. Maybe they'd have a pair of comfortable shoes on sale I could afford. I could break one of Gareth's hundreds . . .

"Okay, but you're wasting your money on me."

* * * *

I WON THE contest.

The girl I rode down with was more excited than me and wasn't at all annoyed that she'd paid my way. She tried to refuse, but I insisted on repaying her the entry fee. Gram would expect me to.

After that, I was too excited about the five thousand dollar prize I'd won to think much about Gareth Warwick. Except when I saw his parents' and sister's names listed in the paper among the Warwicks who'd died on the yacht.

His devastation this time would be much worse than the summer when he'd lost his grandfather.

I pushed away pity.

He'd pressed money on me as if I were a servant. Or, remembering with heated cheeks my wanton behavior in that outlandish dream, as if I were a prostitute.

He'd only just learned about the fire, I argued. The poor guy probably wanted to go off somewhere to be by himself, had probably been crying already.

Despite his dismissal with two hundred dollar bills, I still had a soft spot for Gareth Warwick.

I'd used one of his bills right away to buy shoes and gas, but when I went to get the other, I touched it and ran my hand over it as I remembered that weird night.

Finally, I put it away.

It would be a good rainy day fund, I told myself, knowing even then that I'd keep it if at all possible. It was something to remember Gareth by.

Later, I heard he'd gone off to school, far away from Lassitan. Since I'd never see him again, I tried my best to put him out of my mind and for the most part succeeded.

By that time, Macy's had offered me a few store modeling jobs. One thing led to another until, a few months after my eighteenth birthday, I was working regularly. By the next spring, I'd made enough money to have a new roof put on Gram's house and buy myself a used car.

The next summer, too much happened for me to worry about where Gareth Warwick had disappeared to, and how he was doing, and why he hadn't returned to Slumber Mountain one single time since he'd left.

Local gossip, though, brought down from the mountain by the locals who helped keep up the house, said he blamed his great-aunt's husband for the yacht fire and his parents' deaths. "Big falling out in the family," they whispered. "Warwicks choosing sides. Lots of bitterness."

Gram shook her head when we heard Gareth had sworn not to set foot back in Paladins Rest until Jeffrey Tansey was gone. "It's bad to hold such bile inside. He'd best let it go."

I wasn't sure about that. Anger toward Mother and her husband would fester there forever. I could never forgive them because I couldn't let go of that hate.

There was no time to mull over Gram's advice, though. I was too busy.

My mother called one night, crying. "Arvin left me. He run off with this little tramp he met in a bar and left me flat."

"I'm sorry." I sounded unfeeling even to myself.

"Aw, Lindy, I know you never liked him. Guess you was right. I should of listened."

I could only mouth platitudes. "You're better off without him. He was bad. You'll do fine by yourself."

"But now I don't have no husband and no place to go. Lindy, do you think your Gram would care if I —?"

"No! You can't come here. There isn't room and I don't want you here. I don't want to see you." I wanted to throw up.

Mother drew a quavering breath. "I know you're mad at me, but I didn't have no choice but to stay with him, Lindy. You don't understand how a woman needs a man to count on. Your dad died and I didn't have nobody. You can't blame me—"

"You're right. I don't understand. Gram's got by for forty years without a man. I'm getting by without one. You chose him over me. Even after what he did to me, you still chose him. You'll have to find somebody else to keep you in bottles because I won't."

"I'm dried out, I swear I am! Besides, I'm your mother."

"No. Gram's the only mother I have. Don't bother us again. If you do, I'll take a warrant out against you for harassment."

Gram, knitting in her chair and listening to my end of the conversation, shook her head in sorrow but stayed silent. Even her compassion wasn't deep enough to issue an invitation for our home to be invaded.

"You slut! You Judas bitch! I'm sorry I ever had you! I hope you burn in hell!" My mother slammed the phone down.

When I replaced the receiver, my knuckles were white.

Pop had looked after me when I was young. After he died, I'd fended for myself during the years she'd dragged me around with her. Then when I ran away to Gram, the only time my mother showed any interest in me was when she needed something.

I regretted the phone conversation because of the ties we'd once had, but I'd never be able to love her again. She'd chosen a rapist over her daughter. The scar ran too deep.

A vague memory of something Eleanor Warwick had said about my family paying for their sins mingled with the recollection of scented roses. Was this what she'd meant? Was Mother's situation part of her payment?

Then common sense took over. I was being fanciful. Men like my stepfather always left the woman they cowed. Mother should have expected it. Those kind of men usually got what was coming to them, too.

I hoped he would die a painful, horrible death.

* * * *

RIGHT AFTER I severed ties with my mother, an agent visiting Atlanta saw me at Macy's and decided to represent me. She brought me to New York where I lived with her and her husband and six other girls in a three story brownstone.

All bones and chic hairdo, Ruth Sophia Bernstein didn't look like the motherly type. In fact, she and her husband were childless, but we girls were her bread and butter and she treated us all with maternal concern. She lectured us about skin care, sympathized with us about men, nagged us about proper diet, advised us about hair, scheduled our bookings, managed our careers, and chaperoned us while her husband David looked after the financial aspect of the business.

They made a good team, and I soon realized I could trust them.

At least, trust them to a certain extent. I would never again wholeheartedly trust anyone except Gram, but I believed Ruth and David meant well and wouldn't intentionally hurt me.

Ruth brought me along quickly. Within a few months, I was making more in an hour than I'd made in a year. Her husband seemed pleased I was interested in saving my earnings and took me under his wing to advise about investing.

The life wasn't all bouquets and balloons though. Curfews and dietary rules were rigorous and we disregarded them at our peril. During my tenure, girls revolved through the mansion at a pretty fast clip. One left after failing several times to meet the curfew standards Ruth imposed. Another was caught doing drugs, and there were no warnings, no second chances for her. One left after becoming successful enough to move into her own apartment.

Through all the fruit-basket-turnover, I persevered. Though I hated the city—the sounds, the clamor, the throngs of people were all alien to me—I threw myself into my work and began to get a reputation for being punctual and easy to deal with. Ruth started to get more and more calls asking for me.

By the next spring, I had settled in and nearly forgotten I was little Lindy Rand from Podunk, Georgia. I was even starting to forget about the Warwicks.

Until one morning I came back early to the brownstone, and my infatuation with one of them commenced all over again.

CHAPTER FIVE

THAT MORNING STARTED with the last day of a catalog shoot scheduled on Long Island, but the photographer's unexpected illness brought work to an abrupt halt after an hour. I had nothing to do for the rest of the day except go back to the brownstone.

When I came through the front door and started down the hall to the stairs, I caught a shadow out of the corner of my eye. In the living room off to the side, a dark-haired man stood with his back to me. He was in front of the mantel, looking into the unlit fireplace, and something about his lanky form was so familiar, I caught my breath.

Taking off my jacket and setting down my satchel, I said, "Hello. Are you waiting for someone?"

His back tightened at my words, but he took his time facing me.

I guess I'd known who it was from the moment I saw the black hair. Even so, when he turned, my stomach tightened into a hard knot and it was all I could do to breathe.

Gareth Warwick tried but didn't quite succeed in hiding his discomfort at my appearance. "Hello."

"Hey there," I got out.

He had changed some, filled out, become more mature. The shoulders might be wider, but the waist and hips were still trim. Something else was different, too, but a few moments passed before I realized what.

He had once worn an air of pleased wonder, like that of a baby discovering the wonders of the world for the first time.

No longer. He looked tired, wary.

He was as much at a loss for words as me. "Um, how, how are you, Lindy?"

"What are you doing here?"

There was the slightest pause. "I came to see Ruth."

"You know Ruth?"

"Yes." His unease fled. He relaxed. A tiny smile brought back the confidence I remembered from old. "She was a friend of my mother's."

"Ruth?" I couldn't imagine the down-to-earth Ruth being a member of the Warwicks' social circle.

Ruth appeared with a tray containing cups and food. "My cook made a coffeecake I thought you might—" She saw me and stopped so sharply I thought the cups would spill. Confusion and guilt vied. "Belinda. What are you doing here? I didn't expect you back for ages. What happened?"

The gears began to click. I wasn't supposed to be here; ergo, I wasn't supposed to learn that Gareth had come to the house today. "They took Herb to the hospital. They think it's food poisoning so they had to cancel the shoot. They decided to make do with what he'd already done."

"How terrible. I hope he's all right." Her mouth said the right words, but she wasn't thinking of Herb; she was looking at Gareth for guidance.

Gareth who had come to see Ruth while I was safely out of the way. I had spoiled their plans because a photographer happened to eat the wrong thing.

I said to her, "I didn't realize you knew the Warwicks."

"Oh?" Ruth set the tray down carefully, adjusted a plate, moved a cup. "There was no reason you should have known. Some of my girls worked in a series of marketing campaigns for a perfume company several years ago. Gareth's mother Amelie and I became friends then."

"It was my mother's company," Gareth murmured. "She started it and played a big part in running it."

I looked from one to the other, still putting the pieces together. "Is that how you found me?" I asked her outright. "Through the Warwicks? Was that how you happened to be in Atlanta looking for another girl to add to your stable?"

My accusation drew a half-smile from Gareth. "I told you she was quick," he said to Ruth.

Ruth bit her lip. Her usually controlled hands fluttered nervously. "As a matter of fact, Gareth did call and ask me to look at you, Belinda. However, I wouldn't have taken you on unless I thought you had real potential. If you think I signed you solely as a favor to Gareth, you're wrong. I'm in business to make money, not extend charity."

They both watched me to see how I would react.

Common sense overcame the first flush of anger that Gareth could pity me so much that he would beg favors for me from his mother's friend. I would still be waiting tables while getting odd modeling jobs at Macy's if he hadn't pulled a few strings.

I forced a smile. "Then I'm beholden to you, Gareth. Thank you."

He sensed my coolness. "I thought you deserved a break, Lindy. I didn't let you know because if it hadn't worked out and Ruth decided she couldn't use you, then you would have been disappointed."

Damn my pride.

I had helped him once and he had wanted to repay the favor. In the midst of his own problems, he had remembered me and taken the trouble to help me.

"Well, it certainly has worked out well for me. I'm grateful you thought about me. Really."

Both he and Ruth looked relieved. "Then let's have some coffee," she said to Gareth.

Determined not to let them have their private chat, I sat down, uninvited. I suspected the tete-a-tete, intended to take place while I was safely absent, was to have been about me.

We drank coffee and they ate coffeecake made by Ruth's cantankerous cook strictly for guests; we girls weren't allowed such delicacies. Ruth chattered about my career, what she planned for my future, how pleased she was with my progress.

She finally got up to take the tray away and left us alone for a moment.

"Do you ever go back to Lassitan?" Gareth asked, looking at me over the edge of his cup. The barest scent wafted toward me, a spicy aftershave I still recalled.

"Not often enough. Don't have time. I miss Gram something awful though. When I do go down, it seems like I only get to spend one night with her before I have to get back here. And when I have to leave her and Lassitan, I hate it. Readjusting to New York is so hard that it's easier to stay here all the time."

"Yes," he agreed in a detached way, "sometimes it is easier to stay away from home."

He wasn't talking about me. He was talking about himself.

As Ruth came back, he changed subjects. "Other than it not being home, how do you like New York?"

I shrugged, unwilling to say how much I disliked it in front of my agent. She was a native New Yorker. "Haven't seen much of it. I've been pretty busy working."

"Too busy to see New York?" He pretended shock. "We'll go out tomorrow."

Half of me wanted to go and the other half didn't. I never dated. I distrusted men. Gareth was different, though. I felt comfortable with him. Safe.

When I wavered, he laughed his curious husky half-laugh. "Afraid of Ruth? She's already told me you were resting for a few days after this shoot. I'll bet she won't bite if you decide to have some fun."

He almost looked like the carefree boy I remembered. "Tell her, Ruth."

"I think it would be good for you," Ruth urged. She obviously would have agreed with anything Gareth said, but she was genuinely concerned that I showed no interest in the opposite sex. In fact, once she found out I wasn't a lesbian, she had made me an appointment with a psychiatrist. I found out later Dr. Lebersten's specialty was sexual dysfunctions, but I liked her and still saw her. For my own reasons.

Now Ruth bent toward me. "You've only taken off a few days the entire time you've been here. And you never do anything just for fun. Go!"

Still I hesitated. "There are some things I need to get done."

"Like wash your hair?" Ruth rolled her eyes.

Gareth smiled kindly at me. "Afraid?"

"I am not!"

So I found myself trapped by him again, but this time I didn't mind.

We did the whole sightseeing bit. The Statue of Liberty, MOMA, the Nine-Eleven memorial site, Ellis Island, Central Park, and a myriad of other attractions and landmarks. I didn't have any friends to go around with, and I'd never taken the time to explore the city on my own, but with Gareth I roamed around like a tourist. I still missed Gram and Lassitan, but the painful homesickness lessened with him there.

As each day passed, I grew more comfortable in his company, but I never once forgot he was a Warwick. Little things reminded me. The way traffic lights always changed so we could cross streets when we neared. The way a cab was always handy whenever he wanted one. The way crowds parted to let him through. Even at the jammed hot dog stand, he got our order without waiting.

I first thought these occurrences were coincidences. Then I began to take the little conveniences for granted. After all, Gareth was a member of the magical family who lived on the mountain. Why should he be any different in New York than he was in Lassitan?

So from the beginning he seemed like an old friend, like the little boy I remembered from childhood. After a few days of us hanging out, he fast became something more.

As I waited for him to pick me up on that fifth morning, the doorbell rang. Joy filled me.

It was a parcel delivery man in the doorway.

My heart fell.

After signing the delivery sheet and closing the door, I put the box on the hall console for its recipient to pick up and stood immobile, trying to analyze my sharp disappointment.

The past days spent with Gareth had shown me how his lashes narrowed when he teased me. I'd learned how his shoulders set when he made up his mind. I'd felt how gentle his fingers were when they took my hand.

Was this how love started? Was love what I felt, that made me so happy when I was with him and so downcast when we were apart? That made me so depressed when a delivery man showed up on the doorstep instead of him?

Love! How stupid. What did I know of love except what I'd felt for Pop and Gram.

And that wasn't the kind of love that meant kissing, touching. Sex.

I couldn't think of sex. The thought made me ill.

But when Gareth finally came, the sun seemed brighter, the trees greener, the grime of the city disguised by a golden glow.

I felt different with him. I felt happy. I didn't mind him touching my back or holding my hand as we walked.

That's when I admitted I cared more for him than I should.

That day, we had no plans. We ate lunch, necessarily skimpy on my part, and laughed and talked. Later, we walked down the streets hand-in-hand, looking in shop windows, commenting on wares and prices, sometimes going inside if an item caught our interest.

When I heard a frightened voice in my head, I tried to ignore it. We were outside a pet store. All too often, pleas from such places left me a quivering mass.

I couldn't rescue all the lost creatures in the world, but their cries still hurt.

This time I couldn't escape seeing the source. A puppy, a scared bulldog pup with a brown circle over one eye, its nose pressed to the glass.

I grabbed Gareth's arm to steady myself.

The sudden lunge startled him. "What's wrong? You're white as a sheet."

There was no way I was going to explain about The Voice. He would think I was crazy. "I can't stand to see animals locked up and crying."

"Like that puppy? I'll buy him for you if you want."

"Ruth won't let me have a dog. She'd die. She can't stand animals of any kind. Come on. Let's get far away so I can't see him." Or hear him. "I'll be all right if I can just get away from here. Please."

He put his arm around my waist and we started walking.

A little distance away, he stopped and faced me, gripping both shoulders. "You're still shaking."

"I hate to see animals caged up." My voice stayed steady, but tears exploded anyway. I tasted the salty wetness on my lips, felt the rivulets running down both cheeks.

I never cried. Humiliated, I wiped my face savagely with one hand. Then again with an elbow. I'd learned to hide my weaknesses, especially around men.

"Whoa!" Gareth was alarmed. "People will think I'm being mean. My hotel's around the corner. Let's run up to my room, shall we? You can wash your face and rest a minute."

With another man, I'd have scoffed. I'd heard every excuse to get me alone and in bed.

But this was Gareth. I didn't protest. Perhaps I should have, but I didn't.

Nor did I wonder that his hotel was off the beaten path. While nondescript, it wore an air of dignity that older buildings sometimes have, but there was no hint of opulence.

Later, after he left me with so little forewarning, I remembered its lack of grandeur and only then wondered why a Warwick would not have stayed at a more exclusive place. His family could have owned a brownstone like Ruth or leased a penthouse in a luxury hotel for their personal use. (It was even later, after I met Cavanagh, that I learned they kept an apartment overlooking Central Park for use whenever they came to the city.)

At the time, though, I didn't question Gareth's choice of lodging. I did notice his room was decorated like a Holiday Inn. Danish modern furniture filled both walls. A flowered comforter covered the king bed while solid maroon draperies blocked out the sunlight.

Functional and impersonal, but not even close to a five-star hotel.

I went in and Gareth closed the door. He pointed to the dressing area. "Bathroom's there. Do you want some coffee or something to drink? There isn't any licorice tea like you like, but we have sodas in the fridge."

"No thanks. Nothing for me. I just need to wash my face. Good thing I didn't put on makeup this morning." I tried to laugh. "I'd have raccoon eyes if I were wearing mascara."

"You always look great. With or without makeup."

Inexplicably shy, I escaped.

The bathroom was sufficient but not luxurious. I took a white washcloth from the plain metal rack that also held towels. The counter around the sink was not wood or marble, but ordinary durable plastic. A few mini-toiletries sat in a basket to one side. A shaving kit monogrammed with GW lay on the other.

When I touched the leather, a faint spicy scent wafted up. I wanted to open it and look inside, find out what he deemed important enough to carry around with him. But I heard Gram's admonishment: "Tain't yours, Lindy."

So I wet the washcloth and looked at my swollen features in the mirror.

How stupid to let a frightened puppy get to me. I hadn't lost control and cried like that in years. Cold water helped me compose myself, but it didn't do much for my red eyes.

When I came out, Gareth noticed. "I've got some eye drops you can use." He went into the bathroom and came back with a tiny vial. "Look up at me and I'll put them in." He stood so that his body nearly touched mine.

I tipped back my head, acutely aware of the intimacy. He carefully held my lid up and dropped the liquid in, and then wiped off the excess. After he finished the second eye, his fingers lingered on my cheek. His head bent down, dark eyes inches from mine. "Do you know what I like best about you, Lindy?"

"No." I could hardly whisper, caught up in the Warwick spell as I was.

"I like that you're as beautiful inside as you are outside."

My face burned. I had not expected that. "I'm not as beautiful inside as you think I am."

"Yes, you are."

I wanted to kiss him, to throw myself on him and have sex with him. At the same time I was afraid of the physical aspects of love.

By now I knew that I did love him. Despite the turmoil inside, I was absolutely sure of that one thing. What I didn't know was how he felt about me.

Only one way to find out.

I leaned into him. He didn't pull away. Our lips touched. My arms went round his neck, his around my waist.

The kiss began chastely enough, but soon began to change, sparking, simmering, building.

His tongue gently followed my lips' crease, and then parted my mouth. Its tip explored my tongue and each tooth as if delighted with what it found. He kneaded my back as we kissed, worked his way down to the curve of my butt.

We clung together for some time, tasting, caressing, enjoying each other.

I was the one who slipped my hand inside his shirt, touching his bare skin and making him jump. I was the one who pressed his hips into mine, who put his hardness where I needed it, who loosened his belt and tugged at his underpants.

He was the one who pulled back, breathless. "I didn't intend this, Lindy. I know you . . . We shouldn't go any further. You don't . . . It's happening pretty fast. Maybe too fast."

"I've been waiting five days."

He made a choking sound, caught my hair in his fist. "God knows I shouldn't, but I don't think I'm strong enough to resist you. Sure you want to do this?"

"Yes." I was as breathless as he. "Oh yes."

Shoes, shirts, jeans went flying. Boxers, panties, bra followed. In moments, we were naked. I scrambled into crisp sheets as he put on a condom. One more second and we were wrapped around each other.

His hand slipped between my legs, massaging, preparing me. In spite of desire, my body stiffened. I tried to hide the flinch, but he stopped. "You're not ready for this."

"Yes, I am. Really. I am. It's just that I've never done it very much. I'm not good at it."

I'd die before I admitted my only sexual knowledge came from my stepfather raping me.

No! I would not think of the man, let the black memories ruin what was happening with Gareth. I managed to smile. "Go on. Please."

He brushed my hair back from where it had fallen over one eye. His breath was warm on my jaw. The hair on his legs roughened mine. His heartbeat in his chest echoed in mine. "I don't want you to be sorry afterward."

"I won't be. Please, Gareth." I pulled his face to mine, willing him to understand. "I'm just afraid you might be sorry. Please don't be disappointed if I can't do it right. I can learn."

The little half-laugh softened his features, made him more lovable than ever. "Of course you can. We both can. That isn't what worries me. I don't want to botch this for you."

"You won't."

"You have too much confidence in me."

"You won't hurt me."

"No," he whispered. "Not intentionally. I'd never deliberately hurt you. Tell me. Right away. If it hurts or if you want me to stop."

"I won't need to. I want this."

He began to kiss me again, and when his fingers touched me, pushed aside the curls and found my center, I didn't recoil. After a bit, my body reacted to his caress and he started to enter. I bit my lip to keep from crying out. He realized I was in pain and stopped. "Are you sure you want to do this?"

"Yes. Please."

He waited, taking it slowly, easing himself in by degrees so that when we were finally joined, the discomfort was minor.

The entire time, he kept asking, "Are you all right? Are you sure you're all right?"

And I kept answering, "Yes. Oh, yes."

I didn't lie.

Desire had fled but in its place was a gentle contentment. When I put my arms around him, he began to push at me with slow strokes. He never hurt me, never rushed. While the wild lust I had felt earlier was gone, a yearning still flowered. Under his hands, I relaxed. When his tremors begin, elation came. After years of fear, I was able to love a man, to go to bed with a man.

Perhaps I was on my way to being normal.

His breathing slacked. His heartbeat slowed. "Lindy, you didn't . . . Next time it'll be better. I promise. But are you sure you're all right?"

"I'm more than all right." I threaded my fingers through his hair as he curled up against me, spent. "I'm perfect."

He gave his abrupt half-laugh. "Yes, you are. You are absolutely perfect."

I knew I wasn't, but with Gareth, perhaps I could one day escape my past and come close.

CHAPTER SIX

WE SPENT THE rest of the afternoon in bed, investigating each other's bodies, marveling at what had happened between us. Learning how to make it better.

I couldn't remember the last time I felt so happy.

When he told me, I was stroking the back of his head where it rested. His cheek lay against my stomach. The sheets were damp from our bodies, diffusing the scent of sex. I couldn't see his face and his words were muffled.

"I have to leave soon."

I loved his hair, fine and straight like black silk. I heard his words but didn't want to understand. "Yeah, my curfew doesn't give us much time for dinner."

"That, too. What I mean to say is that I can't stay in New York much longer."

My drowsy afterglow vanished. My fingers stilled. "You're leaving New York?"

"I don't want to. Not now."

I couldn't think, could barely speak. "Then don't go."

He raised his head. "I have to, Lindy. I've overstayed my time already."

The warmth of well-being that had surrounded me the past few days turned cold. "I see."

There was no way I'd let him know how his words affected me. I pushed him away, sat up, and swung my legs over the side of the bed. "When are you leaving?"

"Soon."

Not wanting him to see the panic that must surely show, I kept my profile to him. "How soon?"

"This weekend."

Today was Thursday. "I see. Where are you off to?"

"Europe."

I watched my hands clasp around my knees because I couldn't look at him yet. The tears were gathering. "Are you going to school there?"

"That, too." He rolled nearer, brushed his fingers against my thigh. "I didn't think it would be so hard. I'm sorry. We shouldn't have done this, I shouldn't have let it happen like this." He stroked my leg. His palm was warm. "I knew better but I couldn't think of anything except you. You make me forget everything but how much I want you. This afternoon makes it even harder to leave you."

Story of my life. The brass ring close, but still out of reach.

He'd never know how much this hurt. Never. Needy women always drove men away. I would not be a needy woman. "I'll miss you, too, Gareth. When will you be back?"

When he didn't answer at first, I wished he wouldn't answer at all. I was afraid of what he would say. I heard him get up, felt his body slide across the sheets so he sat next to me.

He eventually did answer. "I doubt I'll get to New York again. I have no reason to be here and my studies are going to be pretty rigorous over the next few years."

As bad as I'd feared. "You won't come back at all? Not ever?"

"I can't. Not for the next few years." He looked as miserable as I felt.

I swallowed, trying to think, trying to breathe. "I'm taking two weeks off this summer to visit Gram. Maybe I'll see you in Lassitan."

"No." His face hardened into lines I didn't recognize. Frightening lines of determination, anger. "You won't see me in Lassitan. I won't be going back there either. Not for a long time."

Because of the quarrel with the unseen Jeffrey. Like me, Gareth was not one to forgive. But he had other relatives who flitted in and out of the house there. His aunts and uncles, his cousins.

"Your family's there. How can you stay away?"

"The family who mattered most to me are dead," he said dispassionately. "My parents and sister. Oh, I'll go back. I have unfinished business. But not any time in the near future. There are too many other things I have to do first. Finish college for one. Maybe go for a master's."

I poked at the sore forming on my heart. "So I'll never see you again?"

"I didn't say that, but I'm going to be busy for a long while." He reached out to touch my arm. "And so are you. Ruth says you have a great future, Lindy. She believes in you. She thinks you can go far."

My heart could be made of lead. "Well, if I don't, it won't be for lack of trying." I took a deep gulp of air, smiled to mask my unhappiness. "Thank you for everything, Gareth. For getting me on with Ruth. And this week. I've really enjoyed this week."

"So have I." He offered me his left hand and I took it, held onto it, breathed in the spicy aroma mingled with the remnants of our intimacy. Was it just moments ago he'd poured out his hot semen? Shared himself with me? Made me love him?

We were both somber as we sat there, me with breaking heart, him . . .

I didn't know what Gareth was thinking until he said, out of the blue, "Lindy, don't go back to Lassitan."

"Don't go——? My grandmother's there, Gareth. I can't abandon her."

"No, I suppose not." He hesitated as if searching for words. "Whenever you do go back, stay away from the Warwicks."

What a strange request. Warnings from Pop or Gram, I could understand. But Gareth? He was a Warwick. "Why?"

The curious laugh was a pale imitation. "Some of my family aren't nice people, Lindy. I'd hate for you to be hurt by getting involved with them."

He meant Jeffrey. "I rarely see your family. Besides, I can look after myself."

He studied me, seemed satisfied with what he saw. "Maybe you can, but don't take chances. Steer clear of us, Lindy. Sometimes I think there's a jinx on us."

"Not you."

He shrugged. "I promised you I'd never deliberately hurt you. You can count on that."

"I believe you." I didn't. Not really. He couldn't mean it and leave me like this.

He still held my hand. "You know I hope you have only good luck in the future, Lindy."

"For you, too, Gareth."

"I'm sorry. I wish things were different. I wish I could stay here and see you every day. I wish we could be together, move in together, go to movies and concerts. Be like any other normal couple."

"I wish all that, too." I gave him my biggest smile. "But don't be sorry we had today. I'm not."

"Neither am I. Don't forget me."

My mouth dropped. "You ask me that? How could I ever forget you?"

He smiled sadly, kissed my hand.

I would not show my heartbreak. Instead, I got up, briskly gathered up my clothes, and headed for the bathroom. "We need to eat if I'm going to make curfew."

When I was alone with the door closed and locked, I cried.

He was leaving and he had never assured me I would see him again. This one afternoon might be all we ever shared. The tears poured out while I tried to stifle my sobs. When I finished, I used the few eye drops left in the vial to disguise my weakness.

At that time, I still had some pride.

When I came out, Gareth was dressed in his jeans and tee shirt, long hair neat as if he'd never been in bed. He did not look happy.

"Ready?" I asked brightly. Gareth Warwick would never know what an effect he had on me. I wouldn't open myself up to his pity again. There was still time to make sure he had a hard time forgetting these last days with me, and I'd make the most of it. "I don't know about you but I'm starving. I may splurge and have dressing on my lettuce."

* * * *

THE NEXT DAY my intentions to brand myself in his mind went kaput.

We had planned one last excursion, ice skating at Rockefeller Center, but he didn't show up.

At ten-thirty, a half hour after he was due at the brownstone, I alternated between worry that he'd already left for Europe and irritation that he hadn't bothered to call and let me know he was delayed.

David had an early appointment across town, and Ruth had gone out for the day. The other girls were either at work or elsewhere, too. No one was in the house but the formidable cook everyone hated. I certainly couldn't vent to her. So I paced.

I shouldn't have gone to bed with him. I had frightened him away. I was too clingy. The sex disappointed him. He'd discovered I'm not what he thinks. He guessed how dirty I am, what my stepfather did to me.

No. None of that could be true. We had left on excellent terms last night. He had kissed me tenderly, held me, reminded me to bring a jacket this morning.

At eleven I started calling his cell but got only a canned response.

By twelve, I was convinced something terrible had happened.

With the doorbell came exhilaration.

Gareth hadn't stood me up. I'd accept the flimsiest excuse so long as he was safe and hadn't abandoned me.

When I opened the door, David stood there, briefcase in hand.

"Thanks, Lindy. I couldn't find my key and I really want to shed these clothes." His office was nearby, but he'd donned a suit and his favorite Brioni tie for the business meeting. He noticed my expression. "What's wrong?"

"Gareth was supposed to be here at ten. He hasn't shown up."

He frowned. "Have you tried his cell?"

"A dozen times. It goes straight to voicemail."

"Hmmm." David thought a moment. "What about his hotel? Have you tried there?"

"I don't have the number."

"What's its name? What street is it on? Can you look online and get the number?"

I squinched my eyes in frustration. "I can't remember," I finally confessed.

The day before, I had been in such a state, going and coming, I hadn't marked either the name of Gareth's hotel or its street address.

David stood undecided.

"I know about where it is." I grabbed my sling bag and said over my shoulder, "Maybe he's there sick or something. I'm going to run over and check."

David called after me, "Let me know what's going on. I'll be at the office."

After wandering around several familiar streets from the day before, I finally found the one with the hotel. Once inside the lobby, I couldn't remember Gareth's room number or even the floor.

Airhead. Why didn't I pay attention?

I asked at the desk.

The clerk might have had a hangover or some other problem. I could have throttled him for his lethargic typing on his computer. "Sorry, no one's registered by that name."

"But he was here! I don't remember the room number but he was here yesterday."

"Sorry." He looked over my shoulder at another person walking up.

I blocked the counter. "I have to find him. He may be sick."

The haggard clerk was reluctant to say anything more even after I explained the situation.

In desperation, I described Gareth.

He shook his head. "We have so many people coming and going, I could never remember any one person." He tried to peer round me at the waiting customer.

I blocked his vision. Maybe Gareth had checked out this morning. "Can you at least tell me if he was registered here before today? For last week?"

His impatience grew. "I'm sorry, I really can't."

Opening my bag, I found my billfold and pulled out a twenty dollar bill.

The clerk looked at it and glanced toward a colleague who'd come up to help the other customer. "I really shouldn't."

I went back to my billfold, found a fifty and added it to the twenty. I put my hand over the bills. "Please."

With a little more enthusiasm, the clerk clicked more keys on his computer. After several minutes, he checked the spelling I repeated, and then shook his head. "I'm sorry, ma'am. We've had no guest here by that name. At least not within the past twelve months."

Stunned, I barely managed a murmur of thanks and staggered from the desk.

I stopped to look around. Yes, this was the lobby we'd entered yesterday. Those were the funny round ottomans and the plump maroon chairs with matching sofas. Those were the elevators we'd taken upstairs.

This was the hotel, but evidently Gareth had not registered under his own name. Why hadn't I noticed what button he'd pushed on the elevator, which floor we'd got off on?

Not knowing what to do, I started back to the brownstone. What had Gareth said yesterday about going away?

Leaving soon. He had told me he was leaving soon. Could he have already left?

No. He wouldn't have said we'd go ice skating if he'd meant to leave before our date. Besides, he wouldn't go away without telling me. Would he?

When I got to the brownstone, David had gone on to his office. I called him for advice.

He was busy. "Try the hospitals."

I started calling hospitals with no luck.

As evening came with still no word from Gareth, Ruth and David came in. Like me, they didn't know what to think.

"He is a Warwick," Ruth said thoughtfully. "They do strange things. Still I would have thought he'd call if he had to break your date. They've always been good about things like that."

"Of course he would have called. Gareth would have let me know he wasn't coming," I said. "I'm sure of it."

I believed that until three days later when a huge bunch of lavender in a porcelain vase was delivered. Typed on the card were the words, "I'm sorry I had to stand you up and we couldn't go ice skating. Thank you for making my last days in New York so pleasurable. Gareth."

Ruth approved the gesture. "Nice vase." She leaned closer. "Looks like Chinese famille rose porcelain. And I wonder where he got lavender this time of year. It certainly smells wonderful."

With heavy heart, I buried my face in the fragrant spikes.

So he's really gone. Without saying goodbye.

I'd never see him again.

My next assignment started immediately so work helped. Still, the subsequent days went by in a gray blur where I, when alone, was prone to mope about Gareth.

Then came another present. A basket this time. "A guardian to keep you safe," read a bold hand I had never seen. "Her name is Asima."

There was no signature, but I knew who had written the card and sent the bulldog with the brown circled eye.

Ruth shrieked at the sight of her. "A puppy! What in God's name does Gareth think you're going to do with a puppy? He can't stay here!"

"I'll hire a petsitter."

As Ruth expostulated, I picked Asima up.

I would keep her. I would. As I held her and stroked the soft muzzle, disappointment with Gareth for leaving and never saying goodbye gave way to comfort. This wasn't the end. "If you won't let her stay, I'll move out. Zoe's been talking about going in with someone to buy an apartment. I think we could live together without too many problems."

Ruth stopped whatever she was about to say. She didn't think I was ready to move out, even with a roommate. I knew I wasn't ready. But no need to tell her that.

I guilelessly hugged Asima.

Ruth caved first. "I shouldn't do this, Belinda. I'm breaking my own rules."

David, who had been reading his newspaper while the discussion raged, dropped the financial pages to look at her in astonishment. "Are you feeling okay, babe, or have you lost your frigging mind?"

Ruth grunted. "He'd better not be making any messes."

"It's a she," I said softly. "She'll fit right in with all us other girls, won't you, sweetie?"

With Asima, I felt Gareth had left me something of himself. She brought me out of my funk and helped me get back to living.

* * * *

BEFORE ANOTHER YEAR passed, Ruth booked me jobs that paid thousands of dollars for a half hour's work. I traveled to remote and exotic locations all over the world. Companies hired me to promote their products, magazines used me on their covers, designers asked for me at their seasonal showings, even though my height didn't meet their six foot requirements. Public relations departments and misguided fans showered me with flowers, food, jewelry, clothes, cosmetics, and all sorts of expensive junk I neither wanted nor needed.

Through it all, I was alone.

I suspected, once Gareth left New York, that I might never see him again. His goodbye, while not final, had been firm. I told myself that I would forget him, that I should go ahead with my life as he was doing with his. There was no reason that my path would cross his, or, for that matter, any of the Warwicks' paths.

My mind knew all this logically, but my heart didn't. I thought of him every time I got out fresh underwear and touched the hundred dollar bill that I kept tucked away in that drawer. The memories attached to it were painful, bringing back the humiliations of my earlier life that I'd vowed to forget. But I couldn't give the bill up.

Not only a talisman, the bill held a sentimental attachment to Gareth Warwick. He had touched it, given it to me. Thought of me even while his own life was falling apart.

And there was Asima. Her presence was a reminder how much he'd cared. She gave me hope that one day Gareth would return. No matter how long I had to wait, I would.

Despite the inner longings that occasionally assailed me, on the whole I managed to cope without him.

Not that I didn't think I saw him countless times as my career skyrocketed.

Once on the ski slopes in Colorado, a man on the lift, going up in modish togs, looked past his vertical skis and lifted his sunglasses to reveal dark, indifferent eyes. As I started with recognition, the lift droned inexorably on, taking him to the top and away from me. I searched every face I met that week, on the slopes and on the streets of the resort town where we stayed.

No one with Gareth's pale patrician features could be found.

Again, doing a sportswear commercial on an island in the Bahamas, I cavorted and posed on the beach for the camera crew, until the sight of one familiar face among all the natives—this island was an undeveloped, out-of-the-way place, lacking the usual amenities and the curious tourists strolling its white sands—arrested me.

Surely those soaring brows could belong to only one person.

"Move!" the director shouted, and I automatically went through my paces.

Afterward, the islanders denied seeing any man such as the one I described and I slunk away feeling stupid.

Still, my imagination continued to play tricks. Once as I lounged on the deck of a private yacht, I could have sworn his lean figure walked on the shore. Once during a studio commercial when a crowd of people outside the windows looked in, his face stood out in their midst. Again in Egypt, I posed in the forefront of the pyramids as a camel trotted by bearing a rider agonizingly familiar. And in a casino in Monte Carlo, I was certain he peeked from behind a croupier directly at me.

On these and other occasions, I caught myself visualizing his presence when he wasn't there. On far too many occasions for comfort.

Those were the moments when my heart would rise to my throat with unexplained longing, when the disavowed need in my gut made its presence known. Those mere glimpses of an aloof, aristocratic figure charged my senses and caused my blood to race.

Invariably they turned out to be false and after a while, my heart would plummet to its normal place in my chest while slowing to its normal rate, and I would continue with my normal routines.

Yes, I was reconciled to my life, and satisfied. Or as satisfied as I could be.

After all, I was a success, wasn't I? Despite the fact I was beginning to hate the constant exposure to people and the constant pressure to display a celebrity's face.

After five years with Ruth and David, I bought my own apartment and hired a live-in maid. That was a hectic period in my career. Everyone wanted me, but Ruth and I both knew I could easily be pushed into the background by the next young and coming model. We did our best to accommodate clients while I was still a hot commodity.

The work hadn't been bad in the beginning but as the years wore on, more and more people clamored for my attention and for my time. There came a day when I tired of it. I was simply a piece of meat being marketed. Marketed profitably for me as well as others, true, but marketed nonetheless.

My mother's death when I was twenty-four made hardly a ripple in my busy life. My only reaction was guilt that I couldn't grieve at her passing.

The shrink I saw regularly, Dr. Lebersten, told me that was natural. She also echoed Gram's advice about my anger.

"Pent-up bitterness," she admonished, "will turn its poison inward and you'll be the only one hurt." She suggested I forgive and forget my mother's indifference to what her husband had done to me.

I might eventually be able to forgive my mother, but I would never forget.

Success hadn't made much difference in my self-esteem. There were few people I trusted enough to confide in. With my hang-ups about men, I doubted I'd ever be able to find anybody besides Gareth I could love or who could love me.

That was when I began to question my life and my goals.

One consolation was that I didn't intend to stay in my profession forever. My ambitions lately centered on retirement to a small house in the country, perhaps in the Ozarks. I didn't have to go back to Lassitan where Gareth no longer came and went. With enough land for a garden and a stream for fishing, Gram, Asima, and I could dwell simply and without stress, far from the life I had come to despise.

Far from the Warwicks.

By the time I turned twenty-seven years old, despite regular payments sent to Gram, I had a tidy sum of money put away. Thanks to David's care and my own prudence, I was well within reach of a comfortable retirement for me and Gram. I sent away for some real estate books about the Ozarks.

Gram died the next January, though, leaving most of the money I'd sent her through the years in her bank account. She'd always been a frugal woman and had accumulated a tidy sum. Besides her savings, she also left me her house and land at the foot of Slumber Mountain, the only real home I'd ever known.

Losing Gram was far worse than losing my mother. Gram had been my mainstay for too long. Now I was completely alone. Besides my grief, I was afraid of what her death meant to my own life. Before, I had at least had a goal. Without Gram, retirement seemed pointless.

More and more I sought solace in the hundred dollar bill Gareth Warwick had once given me. It served as a bridge to my memories of him as well as a reminder that one day he might go back to Lassitan.

As would I, I decided.

There was no reason to flee to the Ozarks. I could return to a place I loved, a place where I'd been happy. I would fix up Gram's house, go back to school, do something with my life. Something important, something good. I might teach, go into social work, do whatever I could to help abused girls like me.

Perhaps one day I might even meet up with Gareth again.

So I would go back, but not yet. The fees I currently commanded were enormous. I'd work another year or two, put as much money as I could into the bank until demand for my services dried up. Then I'd go home and start over.

Home to Slumber Mountain.

That was how things stood when I met Cavanagh Warwick the August before my twenty-eighth birthday.

CHAPTER SEVEN

I WOULDN'T HAVE met Cavanagh Warwick except that he came to a party I attended. Ordinarily, I would never have gone myself, but Ruth insisted. She was determined I garner an introduction to the noted French movie director being honored.

"I don't want to go."

"You must. He's looking for a model to use in his new project. He's got tons of backing and if he chose you for the part, it could open a new page in your career. He can't choose you if he can't meet you."

"I don't want to be an actress."

"Don't be ridiculous," Ruth scoffed. "This is the natural next step for you. And everyone wants to be in one of his films. Rumor says he's got some big LA names begging to read for this script." She turned a deaf ear to my pleas of exhaustion and arguments I needed more sleep. "I don't want to hear about it. You have to go."

In the end, I put on my vintage black Balenciaga and went.

The weather was unusually mild for that time of year so the air conditioning had been turned off and the doors to the penthouse's patio opened to let the crowd spill outside. Though we were atop twenty floors, taller buildings surrounded us and there was no view. Having made my obeisance to the great man himself, I took the first opportunity to escape and find a wicker island chair in a little alcove that looked out from behind palm fronds onto a corner of the patio.

My hiding place offered refuge from everyone but a perseverant stock broker who latched onto me. His presence kept away others more raucous so I encouraged him to expound on his career while I sat back and emptied my mind. This relaxed state meant I was also free to inadvertently eavesdrop on other conversations.

"They're takin' that car apart!" From the patio, one of Ruth's residents with a southern accent as thick as mine had once been, called attention to a crime going on far below. "We need to call the police or somethin'!"

Candela was one of Ruth's girls I occasionally tried to mentor, one of the girls who reminded me of myself when I was her age. Laughter drowned her indignation.

I should probably get up and go outside and put my arm around her and explain how things worked in the big city.

I was lazy in my seat, though, and unwilling to push back into the crowd. Before I could talk myself into moving, a cynical male, blunter than I would have been, let out an obscenity. "Why bother? By the time the police get here, they'll be long gone."

Another advised, "Girl, in this town you mind your own business. He's right. No use wasting our time. Come back inside so you won't have to worry over it."

"But they're takin' everything! Even the tires. How can we look at it happen and not do somethin'?" Candela's concerns faded as she was led away.

Once I would have been as horrified as my little protégé, but no longer. Candela would soon accustom herself to the ways of New York, too. Or she would give up and go home.

"She claims she's a witch." The different accent of another woman cut through the vacuum left by Candela's exit.

New England, I decided from my alcove hideaway. Probably Boston.

The broker paused to catch his breath, peering over his wineglass to make sure I was listening.

"Do go on," I murmured, looking up at him from beneath fake lashes while my hand languidly pushed the twist of lime around the rim of a glass containing ginger ale. "I had no idea trading stocks was so intricate."

A man on the patio behind us snickered. "A witch? Oh, come now."

"Statistics show," my companion began, taking my invitation to continue as a sign of interest, "that once a stock—"

From the patio: "No really," the woman protested. "She says she's a witch. A white witch, of course."

Someone laughed.

The same woman said indignantly, "There are such things. Trust me." Her 'are' sounded like 'ah.'

Naturally someone from Massachusetts would believe in witches. I smothered a yawn, nodded intelligently toward the stock broker as if the numbers he spouted were the most fascinating data I'd ever heard. The beginnings of a headache made me wish I were home in bed.

From outside, someone different scoffed, "Witches! I bet you believe in fairies, too."

Another person tittered. A modern clock without hands that hung over the wet bar read ten o'clock. In another fifteen minutes I would check on Candela and leave, whether Ruth complained about my antisocial behavior or not. In preparation, I put my glass down on a nearby glass table with its base sculptured into a swan.

"What's the difference between a white witch and a black witch?" a man in the outside group asked.

"White witches use their power for good, for the worship of the Almighty," the woman from Boston answered reverently. "Black witches use their power for earthly gain and worship the devil."

"How do you tell them apart?" a different woman asked.

"Very carefully," a new person answered, and the tone of his voice—the timbre, the accent—made me sit upright.

The stock broker's mouth opened in surprise at my sudden move.

Despite ears pricked for the sound of the previous speaker, I heard only erupting laughter and automatically asked the broker, "So this means exactly what?"

He enthusiastically leaped to explain whatever it was he was saying while I concentrated on the people outside.

"Very carefully indeed," the woman from New England chided. "You shouldn't make fun of things you don't understand."

"What difference does it make?" the other woman asked.

Another male said, "Cavanagh can make fun if he likes. He knows all about witches."

Cavanagh. For a second I was reminded of Gram's house and the Warwicks. Of Gareth Warwick and his southern, European-tinted drawl.

How foolish to become so excited by an unknown man.

Sitting back, I focused half-heartedly on the broker busy explaining to me exactly why I ought to let him take a look at my portfolio. I'd taken his measure in five minutes. With him, all I had to do was ask a few questions and I needn't worry about holding up my end of the conversation. He enjoyed hearing himself talk.

It was bad of me to encourage him, but I shushed my conscience and pretended to be considering his advice.

This party ran together with all the others, along with the faces of all the people who attended them, each of them mouthing the same old things, each one trying to put on a good front while scheming how to get what he or she wanted from the people milling around.

I despised being here. I never enjoyed the schmoozing part of my profession, but I had always managed to pretend. Until recently, I accepted it as one of the distasteful facts of life.

Then Gram died. Without her, the hobnobbing with people necessary to my career seemed pointless. I was unsettled, bored with the parties, with the people, with everything I'd become in the past ten years.

Once I had thought being successful would make me happy, and so it had for a while. Until I realized happiness did not lie in whether I was successful or not, but in something deep inside me apparently lacking.

I was as restless as ever.

But if success hadn't changed me and made me content, maybe something else could. Retirement to a different life would do away with my apathy. I could get away from the hangers-on, the would-be celebrities, the users.

Then I could be myself. If I could decide who that self was.

I had been Belinda for so long, the only thing I remembered about plain Lindy Rand was her overwhelming envy of normal people.

And the shame that still lingered.

The witch discussion continued heatedly on the patio. Shifting positions, I stole a glance but had no success in putting a face to the unknown Cavanagh. The lantern-lit darkness hid everyone's features. Only silhouettes were visible.

"Seriously, Cavanagh, how do you tell them apart?" the second woman persisted. Cigarette-damaged vocal cords made her words husky. "What if you think you're dealing with a white witch and she turns out to be a black witch instead?"

While I pretended to drink in every word that came out of the broker's impassioned lips as he yammered about annual yield and blue chips and bear-market bargains, my ears strained to hear the reply across the patio.

The man who'd said Cavanagh knew all about witches, piped up. "Who do you have in mind, Liselle? Give us a clue. It's not that crazy woman in the herb shop you use, is it? Because if it is, she's no witch. And she's not selling witch's potions, either. If I had a mind to, I could tell you a thing or two about her the police wouldn't mind knowing."

Several people laughed, but Liselle was indignant. "I'm not talking about anyone in particular. No, I mean it, I don't know any witches. Not personally. I'm just curious. If you're dealing with a white witch and she turns out to be a black witch, what happens to the spell you ordered? And how do you tell which kind of witch she is?"

The second man, Cavanagh, stepped into the light as I risked another furtive glance toward the group.

Our gazes met and held.

He smiled at me, an indolent, intimate smile, as if he knew I'd been listening. When he spoke, he addressed me directly, surprising the little group around him who hadn't noticed me or the broker among the palms. "How do you think you can tell a good witch from a bad witch?"

So I met Cavanagh.

Broker forgotten, I realized at once that he was a Warwick.

I don't know how, what sixth sense or forgotten memory told me, but I recognized him nonetheless. The lean body, the patrician face, the flawless skin, the air of possessing knowledge the rest of the world lacked. The accent had first given him away, but the other characteristics were there.

Though I'd never seen him before in my life, I recognized him for who he was.

His question drew me out of my lethargy. Ignoring the broker's dismay, I answered without thinking. "You're asking the wrong person. I don't believe in witches of any kind, white or black, bad or good. I think they're figments of fertile imaginations."

"Really?" Slanted eyebrows shot up while the sensual mouth curved in laughter, reminding me too vividly of another face I'd tried unsuccessfully to forget.

Gareth's smile had held that same crooked twist. Gareth had been a nice little boy and the last time we'd met, seemed well on his way to becoming as nice a man. But that was years ago. I hadn't heard anything from him since he left New York.

He'd forgotten me. I wished I could forget him.

So I knew nothing about what kind of person this Cavanagh was, only that he was a Warwick.

"Really," I answered firmly, not looking away. One thing the past years had given me was an air of assurance. I'd learned that my opinions were as good as anyone's and sometimes better, and that people around me were often as insecure and ignorant as I was.

Cavanagh mocked me with a chuckle not too unlike Gareth's. "I'll bow to your superior knowledge."

Instinct warned me not to let him get too close. His appearance alleviated the boredom of the night, but I wasn't sure at what cost. To be confronted with a living, breathing reminder of my past after existing with Gareth dancing in the shadows of my mind for the last ten years, was something I hadn't expected. I refused to be drawn back into that bitter void of wanting something I couldn't have.

We exchanged measuring looks before Cavanagh allowed himself to be coaxed back into his conversation from his precipitate entrance into mine. The woman pulling at his arm was obviously infatuated with him, but then women would always be attracted to the Warwicks. Money brought its own kind of charisma. Money with looks and a mysterious ambience was a combination impossible to resist.

"Contrary to what most people believe," I heard him drawl while he looked into the woman's smitten face, "there are no black witches and no white witches. All witches are equal. They're like everyone else. Some are bad and some are good."

Which are you? I wanted to ask, remembering my childish fear of the Warwicks. A second later, I was laughing at myself. The Warwicks were not witches but people. Wealthy people, true, but people nonetheless.

"You were talking about annual yield?" I murmured to the uncertain stock broker, letting him resume his monologue.

Content with my scrutiny of Cavanagh, I didn't try to hold his attention. He was a Warwick, blessed with their abundant and notorious charm, but he wasn't Gareth.

Immediately afterward, I left the party assuming that I'd never see Cavanagh again.

Nor did I especially want to see him. That's why I didn't ask Ruth about him. He might be a Warwick, but he wasn't the Warwick whose image dogged me everyplace I went. He wasn't the one I wanted to forget, the one I couldn't help but remember.

I didn't think any more about Cavanagh, but Cavanagh, it seemed, thought about me.

* * * *

THE FOLLOWING DAY, I had a business brunch with Ruth and a new sponsor that lasted several hours. When I came home afterward, I found Cavanagh Warwick sitting in the elevator lobby of my apartment building. A huge bouquet of flowers partially hid his face until he rose to meet me. The well-cut suit emphasized wide shoulders and slim hips. His tie looked like a Prada and his shoes were handmade. A gold signet ring matched real cuff links.

"Belinda," he said.

I was so taken aback I barely mumbled a greeting.

Cavanagh should never have gotten so far into the building. However had he managed to ingratiate himself with our doorman, an ex-Marine impervious to bribes or threats? I depended on Ike, as did other residents of the complex, to keep unwanted intruders out.

The mannerly Cavanagh ignored my confusion. "I'm sorry I didn't get a chance to introduce myself last night." He thrust the flowers at me. "When she heard I was coming to New York, my mother asked me to deliver these on her behalf."

"Your mother?"

"Oh, I'm sorry. I'm Cavanagh Warwick. My mother's Eleanor Warwick. From Lassitan."

Eleanor's son. Why wasn't I surprised?

I took the flowers, touched them, lifted them to my face and breathed in the odor of roses mingled with that of carnations and other flowers. The roses were hothouse blooms, the kind delivered to me in droves every month from admirers or sponsors. These were long-stemmed American Beauties, deep crimson and prettily formed.

An image of the impossibly red, overly aromatic monsters I remembered from that unforgettable night half a lifetime ago popped into my head.

I willed it away.

He went on easily, "Mother saw your picture on City Country magazine this month. You know. The article they did on you and your apartment?"

"Yes."

"She pointed it out to me when she found out I'd be here this week." He added as an afterthought, "I recognized you right away at the party, but before I could get loose from my friends, you'd left. I hope it's all right. My coming here without calling, that is."

"It's very kind of you to take the trouble. And it's more than kind of your mother. I only met her one time and the circumstances weren't that happy."

"So I understand. You, however, seem to have made a lasting impression on her." He grinned, and like Gareth's that I recalled from so long ago, the grin made him look cute and endearing and quite harmless.

Having fallen victim more than once, naïve though I had been, to Gareth's charm, I couldn't fault my intuition for warning me away from Cavanagh. I edged toward the elevator.

He followed. "May I?" He pushed the button.

In a moment of weakness, I asked him to come up for a cup of coffee.

My bulldog Asima—elderly now but still convinced she was a puppy—waddled out to greet me. She stopped short at the sight of Cavanagh.

Cavanagh saw her, but ignored her as he moved into the living room. Asima stood on her short bowed legs and watched him disapprovingly. Not until he sat down did she come over to stand at my feet. And then she didn't sit or lie down, but kept her gaze fixed on Cavanagh.

She'd never acted this way before. Always friendly to my few guests, she was a lovable ham who basked in attention from anyone. She usually trotted forward to sniff and grin at visitors and encourage them to scratch her ears.

Not Cavanagh, however.

Stretching his legs out on the Oriental carpet, he looked as if he owned the cream sofa the interior designer had so carefully positioned before the tiled fireplace. In fact, he looked as if he owned the room.

Like Asima, I wasn't sure I liked the way he made himself at home. This was my space.

Marguita, my housekeeper, brought out coffee and disappeared. I took a chair opposite Cavanagh. Asima followed, brushing against my legs before she finally settled down against them.

I'd looked her name up once. It was Arabic and meant protector or defender. Or guardian, as Gareth's card had said. She was living up to her name today, protecting me from Cavanagh.

I stifled a smile. The years hadn't dimmed my free-wheeling imagination.

Cavanagh drank deeply, and then gave a contented sigh before lounging back against the sofa cushions. "Mother's followed your career very closely ever since you left Lassitan."

Oh God, the teacup! She hasn't forgotten. She's after me.

I swear that was the first thought that entered my mind. Chills ran up my back as if someone were hexing me. It took an effort to rearrange my features into the impersonal expression I'd learned to don for people better avoided.

I was being silly. That broken teacup was long in the past. Besides, the Warwicks could afford a dozen porcelain cups.

After we discussed his mother and Lassitan and the changes going on there, he finished his coffee. Hospitality was satisfied so I stood up. Time for him to leave.

Asima scrambled to stand up, too.

I said, "Please be sure and thank Eleanor for the flowers. I appreciate your taking the time to look me up and deliver them. It's been really nice to talk to you about Lassitan."

In this instance, my usual dismissal didn't work.

He was slow to rise. "I appreciate your hospitality. I've thoroughly enjoyed visiting with you and seeing your apartment. It's as great as the magazine article said." Once standing, he made no move toward the door. "You must have dinner with me tonight."

My brows rose. I've never liked being told what to do. "Must?"

He threw out both hands in mock terror. "You've met my mother. You know what she's like when she gets annoyed. She specifically instructed me to bring you flowers and take you to dinner. Do you really want me to go home and tell her I couldn't obey her because you didn't want to go? She would have my hide." His look of appeal would have done Asima proud. "You don't want something like that on your conscience, do you?"

I didn't want to go out with Cavanagh Warwick, but the coldness witnessed in his mother years ago made me reconsider. I'd hate to get him in trouble with her. "All right. But it has to be an early dinner because I have to be in by nine. I'm leaving for a shoot tomorrow morning and have to be at the airport by six a.m."

"Great." We settled on a time and Asima followed us to the door. She made a noise in her throat when he turned toward me. He drew back, suspicious of her motives.

So was I. "Asima!"

Asima looked back, all innocence and with her usual placidity. As if the tiny growl had never happened.

Cavanagh spoke to me but kept one eye on her. "I'll be looking forward to tonight, Belinda."

"Can't wait." I closed the door after him.

Asima stood patiently until I locked it before aiming her reproachful gaze my way.

"No, I don't much care for him either," I told her. "But we still can't go around snubbing people we don't like. You, young lady, had better mind your manners. I think we'll see if Marguita can't take you out for your walk about the time Cavanagh picks me up tonight."

So Cavanagh and I had dinner. Against my better judgment, I ended the evening by consenting to go to a movie with him two days later. After the movie, I found myself agreeing to accompany him to an opening of a new play the next week. After that came more dinners and other excursions.

Despite Asima's disapproval, several weeks passed and I was still half-heartedly seeing Cavanagh Warwick.

Not that he was bad company. He was well-traveled, an interesting conversationalist, and an attractive man. But I didn't go out with men. I'd tried a few times after Gareth's abrupt departure, but my deep-seated distrust always interfered with a relationship progressing further than a couple of dates. That and my memories of Gareth.

My psychiatrist said my aversion stemmed from my stepfather's abuse.

Duh.

Dr. Lebersten also counseled me to move on. After all, she reasoned, I no longer feared my stepfather. I needed to let go of my anger. "That's the only way you're going to be able to have any kind of relationship with a man, Belinda," she said in her no-nonsense way.

Unfortunately, I wasn't ready to give up my inner rage. I was angry with my mother for letting it happen, but she was dead. I was angry with my stepfather for being what he was, and I would always despise him for what he'd done. The worst part was that I couldn't trust other men not to do the same.

Except for Gareth. And even he had been untrustworthy in the end, making love to me before leaving abruptly and cutting me out of his life.

After him, I'd made up my mind that I would be dependent on no one for anything ever again, especially no man. When my career soared, there was little free time to notice my lack of companionship. I had my agent and a small group of people I knew well enough to accompany to openings and galas and cocktail parties and receptions, but no one, man or woman, could sincerely claim me as a close friend. Not even the young models I tried to mentor.

I preferred it that way.

That's why when Cavanagh came along, I couldn't understand why I seemed unwilling, or unable, to break away from him. He was the first man I'd seen on a regular basis for any length of time. My agent and her husband didn't know what to make of my sudden sociability. Once they found he was one of the Warwicks, they overwhelmingly approved.

"He's so sexy! And he comes from a wealthy family and he obviously adores you," Ruth enthused. "Everyone knows the Warwicks are special people. Did you grow up with him?"

"No. Oh no. I never knew Cavanagh when I was growing up."

She looked at me, puzzled. "You were friends with Gareth. That's why he called me about you."

"Yes. I did know Gareth." My usual shell closed around the truth. "Gareth's different. I did him a favor once."

"But Cavanagh came to New York to see you."

"Not really. He came to negotiate with investors for some kind of resort their company is trying to build. His mother knew I lived here and asked him to look me up." I caught Ruth's jerk of consternation at the mere mention of investors. "No, he hasn't asked me for money."

"Leave Belinda alone," David said, overhearing. "Cavanagh's okay. Not that Belinda couldn't do better, if she wanted to. But on the whole, everyone I've talked to agrees he's a decent guy. In fact, I've spoken to his banker in confidence and he tells me that everyone knows the Warwicks have more money than the Waltons or Bill Gates. And anything they touch makes more. They shouldn't need Belinda to invest in any projects they might be contemplating. And that's strictly between the three of us. Personally, I think he's an okay guy."

"Ri-i-ight." Ruth and I exchanged significant glances. David might be a successful accountant, but he had the acumen of a five-year-old when it came to reading people.

Oblivious of our opinions regarding his character assessments, he went on, "But I'm like you, babe, I don't know why he hasn't made his move on Belinda before now."

Both looked me over, obviously speculating about my relationship with Cavanagh.

Their scrutiny made me uncomfortable. "Do you have that new contract ready for me to go over, David? Someone mentioned an insurance clause I need to make sure gets put in it."

"What kind of insurance clause? Who mentioned it?" If David had had doggy ears, they would have stood straight up.

I shrugged. "Something about, um, oh, if you two split up, I'm protected from conflicts of interest between you."

Ruth stiffened. "If we split up!"

"What! Where did you hear that? Who said that to you?" David immediately began to assure me he and Ruth had no intentions of splitting.

The change of subject went unremarked by both of them.

As for their speculation about my relationship with Cavanagh, how could I explain it to anyone when I didn't know what to make of it myself?

I wasn't physically attracted to him. I was never physically attracted to anyone with the exception of Gareth. I rather thought my past experiences had made it impossible for me to feel that way about most men, and Gareth was far out of reach.

Maybe it was because Cavanagh was good company. Entertaining when I wanted to be entertained, quiet when I wanted to be quiet. Willing to stand back and let me go at my own pace toward resolving my feelings.

At this point in my life, weary of my career and dreaming about retiring to a quiet place in the country, I guess I was more susceptible to a man's pursuit. Or perhaps with Gram gone, I needed someone to cling to, to fill the void of not having anyone who cared for me. Someone I could care for in return.

Or maybe it was because Cavanagh reminded me of Gareth.

* * * *

THE INEVITABLE CAME on my twenty-eighth birthday, after Cavanagh and I had been seeing each other for several weeks. When he picked me up for dinner and the theater that evening, he brought in a small gift box and a bottle of champagne.

The sight of the beribboned box took my breath.

I wasn't ready for a proposal. I didn't want a ring.

We haven't even slept together. It has to be earrings. A bracelet.

Before the door even closed, he handed the box to me eagerly. "Happy birthday, Belinda. Go ahead. Open it."

I took off the ribbon and paper as slowly as possible.

If it was a ring, I would tell him I was sorry but I didn't care for him that way. I'd say I wasn't ready to settle down or marry anyone. I'd say . . .

When I uncovered a small jeweler's case, my mouth went dry.

"Go ahead. Open it," Cavanagh urged, beaming. "Don't you want to see your present?"

The upraised lid did not expose the ring that I feared, but instead showed a thin gold chain with a pink stone pendant.

I let my breath out. The facets glittered as I let it dangle in the light. "How beautiful, Cavanagh. I love it," I said with complete sincerity. Thank God I didn't have to withstand a proposal. "Thank you."

He beamed. "It'll go with your black dress. Let me put it on."

While I held up my hair, he fastened it. The neckline was high and the pendant lay against the crepe, but still it felt cold. And I felt weird.

I can't wear this.

"This dress doesn't show it off." I fumbled with the clasp. I had to get it off. "I have a beige outfit with a sweetheart neckline that it'll look great with."

He was too polite to object, but he lifted a brow. "I think it looks fine."

I wanted to rip the chain off. "No. I'll save it." I finally got the stupid clasp open. "It's too special to be overlooked." Once it was back in its box, I felt better immediately.

Conscience again. I didn't want to take anything valuable from Cavanagh.

"All right. If you're sure. But I have champagne. Let's open it."

"I don't think we have time."

"We'll make time."

No. Don't.

The Voice I managed to subdue most of the time chose that moment to return and scream at me.

My psychiatrist said The Voice was my imagination. Too bad she wasn't inside my head right now. I'd show her imagination.

Cavanagh took the champagne toward the back. "I'll get us a couple of glasses."

I stood in the foyer, mute, wondering what The Voice meant.

Usually, the creature I heard cry out was in pain or terrified. Tonight the words seemed to come from the air around me and for no reason.

Asima growled when Cavanagh passed through the living area toward the kitchenette.

Big shock. Asima and Cavanagh didn't get along. I believe Asima had hated Cavanagh from the moment she met him. And Cavanagh, though he tried to hide it, did not care for Asima.

This night, when he disregarded her growls and began to rummage in drawers for a corkscrew, Asima wrapped her teeth around his leg.

His howl of protest sent me flying to the rescue.

"That damned dog has ripped my pants!"

I'd never seen him so enraged.

He tried to kick at her, but it was impossible with her hanging onto one leg. "She won't let go! Look at her!"

I peeled Asima off, saw there was no real damage, and divided my attentions while soothing both. "Oh my, Cavanagh, I'm so sorry. Your leg isn't even scratched, see? She hung her teeth in your pants and tore them, but it's a small rip. Hardly noticeable. I'll buy you a new pair."

Then to Asima, "There, there, baby, Cavanagh isn't going to get in your food dish. Is that what you thought? What a bad dog you are." I called my housekeeper. "Marguita, please come get Asima." And to Cavanagh, "We don't really have time to open the champagne anyway. Let's save it for another night."

He was stubborn. "No, this is special stuff. For a special occasion. And tonight is special. You're going to love it."

No!

The Voice—anxious, determined, frightened—burst into my head. Asima struggled with renewed vigor in my arms.

Was it Asima's fear I heard? What was she afraid of? Cavanagh?

"Well, I won't love it now." I held onto Asima to be on the safe side. "I have a camera session at noon tomorrow and we'll be late getting in tonight. I don't need to show up with baggy eyes from champagne."

"One glass won't give you baggy eyes. Please." He turned on his little boy's smile. "I'm not teasing you, Belinda. This really is a special occasion for me. For us." He reached out to caress my cheek, but Asima growled at him from the safety of my arms.

He drew back. His glare mingled disapproval and annoyance.

Though I didn't want champagne, Cavanagh's persuasion

weakened my resolve tonight. I was susceptible to any kind of alcohol and usually abstained, but . . .

What would it matter?

No. The Voice that had served me well in the past told me not to drink.

Still, I hated to disappoint Cavanagh.

I wavered. Oh, why not go ahead and give in? I could have one glass.

Cavanagh had that effect on me.

Asima made the decision. When my housekeeper came into the kitchen and took her from me, the elderly bulldog made such a desperate lunge from Marguita's arms that her head hit the bottle on the edge of the counter.

It fell and shattered.

Champagne and splintered glass sprayed all over the tiled floor.

Marguita and I screamed.

Cavanagh turned absolutely livid. He started toward Asima to jerk her up. "That damned dog ought to be shot!"

"Cavanagh!" I stepped in front of him before he could catch her collar. "Don't you dare!"

My outrage pierced his fury. He said no more. I hastily removed my sweet Asima to the safety of the bedroom. She whined softly and staggered when I put her down. "Are you hurt? It's a wonder you didn't break something. You're too old to be pulling stunts like that."

I felt her shoulder and legs, but everything seemed all right.

"You really are bad," I told her. She licked my face, and then cocked her head as if about to speak. I couldn't help but laugh. "You know it, too, miss. Why can't you leave poor Cavanagh alone? You know he doesn't like you."

When I came out, Marguita had already started clearing up the mess in the kitchen. I found a safety pin to conceal the tear in Cavanagh's pants. By some miracle, none of the wine had splattered onto the georgette silk of my Vera Wang dress so I didn't have to change. In the foyer, I pulled on a long evening coat preparatory to leaving.

By then Cavanagh had regained his composure. "I wanted tonight to be a special celebration. That's why I brought the champagne." He came up behind me and caught me around the waist. "I have an important question to ask you."

I stiffened. "Cavanagh, we're going to be late."

Cavanagh, curse him, wouldn't be deterred. When I pulled free, he took my hand instead of my waist and held it in both his. "Belinda, darling, you've got to know by now how I feel about you. I love you. I didn't think it possible to feel this way about anyone before I met you. Now I'm lost. I've not forced the issue because I know you're old-fashioned. But I'm tired of bringing you home and leaving. I want to make love to you, go to sleep with you, wake up beside you. I want to marry you. Will you?"

No!

The shriek inside my head made me gasp, but he took my response in stride. "This can't be unexpected. We may not have known each other very long, but I'm certain we belong together. You must have felt the same thing I've been feeling these past weeks."

Say no!

His proposal was lovely, obviously rehearsed. I had no intentions of marrying Cavanagh, but somehow even with The Voice urging me, I couldn't come out bluntly and say so.

I wanted to. The Voice wanted me to. But somehow I couldn't say the word.

I stalled. "You're wrong. I didn't know. This is . . . this is a complete surprise to me." I pulled away. "We've only known each other a few weeks. I don't think we should rush into anything. Marriage is such a big step. I'm not sure I'm ready." I hated myself for the lie. I didn't want to marry anyone, especially not Cavanagh with his resemblance to Gareth. The one thing I knew for sure after the past weeks was that he could never replace Gareth.

He was insistent. "I'm sure enough for both of us. You care for me, you know you do."

Tell him no!

"Of course I care for you, and it's sweet of you, but I really don't think I'm ready for marriage with anyone." Why couldn't I tell him I had no intention of marrying him? Why couldn't I say "no way" in my usual forthright fashion? Instinct wasn't behind my procrastination. My mouth simply wouldn't obey my mind.

At that particular moment in time, I truly could not turn Cavanagh down.

His lips tightened at my evasiveness, an uncomfortable reminder of his mother. He stepped back. "All right. You don't have to give me your answer now. When you're ready, we'll pick out your ring. I'm in no hurry. Think it over, Belinda. We belong together. I believe that with all my heart. "

Relieved, I capitulated, promising to think it over without understanding why.

I wouldn't marry Cavanagh. It would have been kinder to tell him so at once. The Voice told me to refuse him, and I should have. Where this compulsion came from was a mystery, this urge to let him have his way when I knew deep down inside that I absolutely did not want to marry him and that I would never marry him.

Come to think of it, it was a mystery why I always let Cavanagh have his way.

I didn't particularly want to go out with him, but I could never seem to tell him I had other plans. Never in my whole life had I been so indecisive. What had happened to me? Could it be that I was falling in love with him and didn't realize it?

No!

I relaxed. The Voice was certain about that even if I wasn't.

"I'm going home next week," Cavanagh murmured as I thrust pearls through my ears in front of the mirror over the console. "The family's having our yearly reunion. I'd really hoped to announce our engagement to everyone then."

Our reflection made us look like a well-matched couple, but the sight of him next to me, the feel of him close to me, was alien.

No, I wasn't falling in love with him. "I told you, Cavanagh. I can't say yes. Not now. I'm not sure enough of what I want."

He yielded gracefully. "I won't hound you, but will you at least come home with me for our family conclave? I know they postponed the shoot you were going on next week because of that factory explosion, so that means you're free. And Mother asked particularly that you come. Everyone in the family's eager to meet you. Say you will, Belinda."

I wasn't uncomfortable in Cavanagh's arms, but he aroused no passion in me. At his words, however, a picture of Slumber Mountain formed in my mind. Restless urges coalesced.

Why not? Why shouldn't I go back? Back to the place where I'd been given two hundred dollar bills before being shown the door. I could face Eleanor and Cavanagh's family and all the rest of the Warwicks without flinching. I was someone of importance now. I had shaken off the background of poverty and ignorance and risen far above the scab of humanity that they'd once considered me.

The unbidden thought came: Gareth told me not to get involved with the Warwicks and Cavanagh had called it a family conclave. All the Warwicks would be there.

Gareth himself might be there, whispered another small, knowing part of my mind.

So what? If I met Gareth, I could face him without embarrassment. I could show him how far I'd progressed from the homeless waif he'd pitied.

Even when he'd come to New York, I was obviously still poor little Lindy Rand to him or he would never have abandoned me as he had. Now I was successful. Everyone knew who Belinda was. If I wanted to, I could throw a couple of hundred dollar bills at him. Casually, of course. As if he were a servant.

What a pleasing thought. I wouldn't stoop to his level, but how tantalizing to know that I could if I wanted to.

For a moment, I saw Gareth's face instead of Cavanagh's staring back at me from the mirror. Serious as he had been the last time I saw him. Annoyance melted.

Come back, Lindy. Come back home, urged something inside me. Was it The Voice or was it my heart putting words to what I wanted?

"Please, Belinda." Cavanagh leaned over so his mouth was against my hair. "Come home with me."

The image of Gareth disappeared.

Cavanagh stood beside me, not Gareth. How could I think of going home with him? The only thing such a trip would accomplish would be to make Cavanagh believe I cared for him. And I didn't. Not that way.

Pulling back, I picked up my evening purse. "We'll see."

Avoiding the truth again. No matter how I tried, I couldn't outright refuse Cavanagh anything. Maybe I should talk to Dr. Lebersten about the problem. "I'll think about it."

"Good." He looked at me doubtfully. "Are you ready? Do you need to do something with your hair?"

"No." He didn't like my hair pulled severely back, but tonight I didn't care.

As Cavanagh held open the door for us to leave, Asima began to bark from behind the bedroom door. The darling dog was fearless when it came to protecting me, even when I didn't need protection. At least she'd saved me from the champagne I hadn't wanted.

Too bad I couldn't save myself from Cavanagh's proposal. How would I ever get up the nerve to tell him I didn't love him and would never marry him?

As it happened, that same night I met Gareth Warwick again and afterward, my irritating inability to refuse Cavanagh anything became a problem of the past.

CHAPTER EIGHT

AFTER THE PLAY, as Cavanagh and I stepped from the theater and headed toward the line of waiting limousines for the one he used in the city, something caused him to lag behind. One moment he was beside me, the next he was not. I waited for him to catch up but no matter how hard I searched, I couldn't see him anywhere.

How irritating. I was anxious to get home and to bed.

The exiting crowd buffeted me until I sought shelter in a secluded corner behind some columns on the front of the building. An unseasonable cold wind hit without warning. Annoyed with Cavanagh for disappearing, I pulled my coat tight and put my chin down to fasten its three large buttons.

When I buttoned the last button, I raised my eyes to find myself face to face with Gareth Warwick.

There was no warning, no preparation.

We stood not ten inches apart, me so astonished that my mouth fell open.

This was no illusion, no wishful thinking. Gareth actually stood there before me in jeans and a safari jacket that made him look casual yet somehow dangerous.

A tendril of excitement mingled with fear and wound itself around my heart.

I couldn't speak. I could hardly breathe.

He was so close I could smell the spicy cologne that brought back waves of rich memories. The way he'd fallen into the canoe on top of me, the way he'd held me when the white cat and his aunt had frightened me, the way he'd invaded my dreams and turned them into erotic fantasies before dismissing me with a word of thanks and two hundred dollars.

And the way he'd come to New York to make sure I was safe and toured the city with me as if we were old friends. The way he'd wiped the tears from my face before we'd fallen into bed.

And his gentleness. Ah, his gentleness in bed as he caught my hair in one hand and stroked my skin in the other.

Five days together, every second spent with him emblazoned in my mind despite the intervening years.

His features were still classic but older, the character of his face fully defined in carved lines of jaw and brow. A slight frown of perplexity marred his forehead, perplexity mingled with the impersonal approval men give to any beautiful female.

He didn't recognize me. He'd forgotten everything I'd been holding precious in my heart.

To hell with him.

I wanted to tell him who I was. I wanted to throw my name at him and taunt him about how far I'd come. I wanted him to know that this person in front of him that he found so attractive was the same person he'd dismissed as insignificant after she'd hauled him out of what could have been a watery grave.

This was the same person he couldn't bring himself to look in the eye when he'd flung down two hundred dollars as if I were a hired servant. Flung them onto a table rather than risk contaminating himself by putting them into my hand and giving me a simple thanks. This was the same person he hadn't even intended to see when he came to New York.

The same person he'd callously left after . . .

Heat reached my face.

Gareth's frown disappeared as my indignation grew. A smile took its place, turning up the corners of his mouth and crinkling the corners of his eyelids. "Lindy Rand." Laughing eyes studied me, the previously impartial approval turning distinctly personal. "I like your hair pulled back like that."

Rancor fled. "Hello." That was all I could manage. Simply by calling me by my old name, he'd reduced me to the insecure girl I thought I'd left behind forever.

My heart melted. He had meant no insult with his money that night. As for leaving me, so what if he hadn't bothered to keep in touch over the years? I shouldn't expect more from him than he could give. He had warned me he wouldn't be back for a long time. I wasn't one of his close friends or even anyone who belonged to his crowd. He had no reason to write or call, apprise me of his whereabouts every week.

He had sent me gorgeous spikes of lavender, though. And Asima, my sweet guardian.

Resentment forgotten, I opened my mouth to tell him how glad I was to see him, and then put out my hand. Almost touched his face.

"Gareth?" Cavanagh appeared out of nowhere.

My hand dropped.

Cavanagh, focused on Gareth, didn't notice. "Oh, hell, it is you. I didn't believe it. We thought you were still in Australia. What are you doing here?"

I wanted to consign Cavanagh to perdition even as I saw

Gareth's face become a blank slate. Without moving his head, he raised his eyes from mine, looked over my shoulder at his cousin.

"Cavanagh." His gaze slid from Cavanagh to me and back again, absorbing the fact that we were together. He smiled but only with his lips. "It's been a long time."

He was thinking that Cavanagh and I were a couple—and he was disgusted. I went hot with embarrassment and cold with pain. Something inside me tightened and quivered so that I felt I'd explode.

I'd never be good enough for the Warwicks. Gareth didn't want me, but he didn't want his cousin to have me either.

As if sensing my uneven emotions, Cavanagh closed in and took a possessive hold of my arm. Gareth noted the movement and narrowed his eyes as if he disapproved.

Of course he disapproved. Warwicks shouldn't be seen with someone like Lindy Rand.

My impulse to deny my relationship with Cavanagh passed. I even leaned onto his arm a bit. There was no reason the celebrated Belinda shouldn't appeal to a man like Cavanagh.

Eat dirt, Gareth.

"What are you doing here?" Cavanagh repeated, pushing a little forward as if to break into Gareth's aura. I wondered if he suspected how Gareth affected me.

"I might ask you the same question, cuz." Gareth's mild tone belied the cold face. "Except I guess I know the answer. I hear your father hasn't given up on his schemes so I suppose you're courting backers."

"Actually, I've been courting Belinda. I'm going to marry her."

Gareth didn't miss my start. The swift laughter in his eyes broadened his mouth, his lovely mouth that I'd forgotten could be so tempting. My nipples hardened inside my dress as desires I'd thought dead resurfaced.

"Tying up loose ends, eh? Has Belinda agreed?" Gareth directed his question at Cavanagh but his gaze melted over me like warm butter.

"No," I managed to mutter. I cleared my throat. "I mean, I've not made up my mind. Not yet." He needed to understand that it was my decision as to whether or not I married Cavanagh. That at least one of the Warwicks thought I was worthy enough to admit to that charmed family circle.

Cavanagh hugged me against him. "You will. She will," he said to Gareth as if to reassure himself.

No, I would not. I knew, looking at Gareth, that the only man I could possibly love physically or emotionally was as far out of my reach as he'd been years before. Despite my change of fortune, despite my veneer of sophistication, he saw me for what I was: insignificant and tarnished and unworthy. And I knew without being told that I'd never be able to overcome that image in his eyes.

The tiny bud of joy blossoming at the sight of him shriveled. Somewhere, sometime, without understanding why or how, I'd put Gareth Warwick on a pedestal as my ideal, and no other man could live up to my expectations. That was the real reason I wasn't attracted to any of the available men I'd met. The only reason I'd kept seeing Cavanagh was his resemblance to Gareth.

While Gareth didn't think of me at all.

"We're going home next week," Cavanagh added. His hand squeezed my shoulder possessively.

I wanted to scream and sling it off but forced myself to keep smiling.

"Mother wants Belinda to meet the family. I don't suppose you'll be there since you don't seem to care about coming home anymore. How long has it been? Eight years? Nine?"

"Ten if you're counting. But this is a special gathering of the clan, isn't it? Laying out the future of the mountain, aren't we? Getting ready to vote shares, I hear. My shares included. I'm old enough to cast my own vote now. Why would you think I wouldn't be there?"

Cavanagh's hand tight on my shoulder froze. "You're coming back to Slumber Mountain?"

"What do you think?" Gareth's smile was lazy. Had it been anyone else, I would have thought it unpleasant. I was glad it wasn't aimed at me. "With this being a once-in-a-blue-moon affair, and with the decisions the family has to make, I think I ought to be there. In fact, since I came into my inheritance just this year, I rather think I must be there. To protect my interests. Who knows? There might be an alternative plan for the mountain the others might like to hear about before they vote on your father's designs."

Cavanagh, still intent on Gareth, had forgotten he held my shoulder. His grip tightened until it hurt. "So you plan to fight it. Just like your grandmother. After all these years. I would have thought you'd have grown up, but you haven't changed a bit."

I wrenched away from his grasp.

Neither Gareth nor Cavanagh, caught up as they were, noticed.

Gareth kept showing the smile that wasn't a smile. "Did you really think I would change? Someone needs to point out the shortcomings of your father's project. Since Grandmama's not alive to play devil's advocate, I guess I'm elected, poor substitute that I may be."

Cavanagh kept himself as tightly leashed as Gareth. "We'll see you at the mountain, then, cuz. If you actually do find the time to make it down to Lassitan, that is. If I were you, I'd take the next few days to think about it. Come along, Belinda. The car's waiting."

His words may have sounded threatening or I might have read too much in them. It was hard to tell. I let him take my arm.

Gareth didn't seem worried, but his eyes didn't swerve from Cavanagh's. A man I hadn't noticed came up. He was big and had a competent air about him I recognized from the security guards hired for many of our shoots.

Gareth had a bodyguard.

He hadn't had one the last time I'd seen him. Why did he feel the need for one now? I was too busy puzzling over that to resist Cavanagh pulling me toward the limousine.

Gareth's gaze slid past Cavanagh to me. "Oh, you can pretty much count on my making it, cuz. It's good to see you looking so well, Lindy. Take care of yourself. Warwicks are sometimes dangerous. But you know that by now, I expect."

The last glimpse I had of him showed shuttered eyes and twisted smiling lips, as if he enjoyed some joke not shared with Cavanagh and me.

Later, in the comfort of the car beside Cavanagh, I felt cold. I'd wanted to stay and talk with Gareth, use my honed conversational skills to make him look at me as a man looks at a woman.

I wanted to be with Gareth instead of Cavanagh. I wanted Gareth to be putting himself out to entertain me as Cavanagh was doing.

The story of my life. Wanting more than I had. "If wishes were horses, we'd all be covered in horseshit," Gram used to say. What would she think about me longing for one Warwick while being courted by another?

Gareth.

I wondered if the same indulged boy lay beneath the man's facade, or if he could possibly have matured into the man I had fantasized so long ago. What was wrong with me, that someone not encountered in years, a man I'd had one brief interlude with, could turn me upside-down?

Face it, we'd hooked up and parted. That's the way these things went. No matter how brokenhearted one of us might be.

As we rode, I listened dispassionately while Cavanagh told one of his funny stories that never failed to amuse me. I laughed, but tonight it was from politeness. My heart and mind were elsewhere.

Gareth had come back, and the few minutes in his presence was enough to cleave whatever mental restraints kept me silent instead of telling Cavanagh I didn't want to see him again.

I could tell him now, I thought as I watched Cavanagh gesture in the middle of an anecdote. I could tell him to go away and never bother me again. I could say it without a second thought.

I was tempted. The words were on the tip of my tongue, ready to slide out.

Only one thing stopped me. If I sent Cavanagh away, I couldn't go back to Lassitan and Paladins Rest with him. Back to the Warwick gathering where Gareth had promised attendance.

What I did next should have made me ashamed. But I wanted desperately to see Gareth again, so desperately I thought my throat would strangle from sheer longing.

Somehow I regained control, but I deliberately used Cavanagh. When he asked again about me visiting Slumber Mountain with him, I agreed.

It was wrong, but I played halfway fair. "I'll go back to Lassitan with you, Cavanagh, but please understand. I don't love you. I won't marry you. I'll never marry you."

No hesitation, no wavering. No problems saying those words tonight.

They made no impression on him.

"It's a woman's prerogative to change her mind," he teased. He believed I didn't mean what I said.

"Cavanagh, I don't love you and I won't marry you. Please don't think anything you say or do can change that. Besides, I've been alone so long, I doubt I'll ever marry."

Strange how easy the words came out now that I had seen Gareth. And as easily as I could tell Cavanagh the truth, my new freedom also let me lie. "I like my life the way it is."

He waved an impatient hand. "Let's not worry about the future now. As long as you're coming home with me, Belinda. That's enough for the moment. That's all I ask."

His blithe disregard let me accept his invitation without too much guilt. Gram might not approve of my using him as a ticket to Paladins Rest, but I hardened my heart. For another chance to see Gareth, I would go to hell itself.

So I laughed at Cavanagh's stories and dismissed him at my door with an ease never summoned in the past. My problems with telling Cavanagh no were over.

Seeing Gareth had dissolved one spell. Too bad that left in its place was a much more binding one.

CHAPTER NINE

AT THE END of October, the woods outside Lassitan were rich with reds and purples and golds and greens. As Cavanagh and I drove through them, the beauty of nature's colors struck me anew. I had missed being home most during autumn.

Then Slumber Mountain jutted up before us. The jewel-toned leaves covering its sides gleamed in golden sunbeams, making me catch my breath and ache with unexpected longing.

For Gram? For my dead father? For my lost childhood? I couldn't say. I knew only that I had forgotten how lovely autumn was at the mountain and how happy I'd once been there. The sight of the towering peak brought back all the good memories. Moisture crowded my eyes but never puddled.

Successful women don't cry at trivialities.

We rode past Gram's house half hidden behind the purple plum trees. Exhilaration faded.

I was home again, home at the foot of Slumber Mountain, but I was here with a man I didn't love and there was no Gram to meet me and hug me and draw me into her little house.

The realtor I used in Lassitan had rented Gram's home to a Hispanic family. Two children, little more than toddlers, played in the yard with sticks. How far removed I was from these children, from the child I had once been. A long time ago, before my father had died and my mother had taken me away from Gram, I had been happy to play with sticks in the dirt, too.

Cavanagh noticed me looking toward Gram's house and slowed the car. "Did you want to stop? Look around your grandmother's house before we go up?"

"No. There's no need. Smith Woods Realty oversees the tenants. There's nothing there I want to see. Not anymore. Not since she's gone."

The car moved by and the house disappeared from view.

"Do you never think of selling the house and land?" Cavanagh asked.

Once I had hoped Gram and I would sell out and move to the Ozarks. Now, I wavered. The house was all I had left of her. "Not really."

"I know an investor who'd give you a good price for it."

"As long as I rent it, the upkeep doesn't cost very much. I might as well keep it, at least for the time being. Aren't these leaves marvelous? I miss the hills most of all in the fall, I think. The rest of the year I can make it all right. But in autumn, it's harder."

"If you ever do decide to sell—"

"I won't. Oh, look at that red maple grove."

Cavanagh drove with practiced ease up the mountain. I tried not to think of the last time I had negotiated this same winding road. The giant tree branches had made dark arches over the headlights, and Gareth in the seat beside me had chattered nonstop.

To hide his disquiet over what had happened on the yacht. He'd known something was wrong but not what. Not till later.

Now in daylight, the trees in their festive garb seemed innocuous and welcoming.

Daylight also let me clearly see the large dogs loitering around the gate. Mastiffs or some other large breed. But well-trained. They eyed us as we passed but didn't bark. Perhaps they recognized Cavanagh's Audi. Or, remembering their silence when I'd taken Gareth home years ago, perhaps they could sense a Warwick.

When we arrived at Paladins Rest and parked in the same underground garage and rode up the same glass elevator I recalled, Eleanor met us in the lobby. She was painstakingly dressed in sedate lounging pants and tunic that reminded me of a Stella McCartney set. Her hair was now steely gray, but her carriage was as stately as ever.

To my surprise, she swept down on me with a loud shriek and hugged me as if I'd been her long lost daughter. "Belinda! I'm so thrilled you could come."

I mistrusted her welcome but not due to any lack of warmth. She would have made Miss Manners proud. The nagging suspicion she could turn on a person as easily as she could embrace her made me wary. I'd learned a long time ago to trust my instincts.

While Cavanagh took care of getting our luggage upstairs, Eleanor gracefully relinquished her hostess duties to a relative hastily introduced and dismissed. Then she led the way to a quiet corner where a console table held drinks and small finger foods, and set about putting me at ease.

As she poured pale liquid from a crystal pitcher, she asked about my career and told me how she had followed it and how much she had admired my advancement through the years. "I always knew you'd be successful, Belinda. Anyone could see you had so much potential. In spite of all the setbacks in your early life, I felt you had the drive to succeed."

Setbacks? She didn't know the half. "I was lucky."

Ice cubes tinkled against crystal as she handed me a cold shaded glass dripping with evaporation.

"Oh no." She contradicted me with that unworldly certainty typical of the Warwicks that was so unnerving. She poured herself a drink with that same assurance. "It was destined. One can't change what is destined to be. You had that spark in you, Belinda, that ambition to better yourself. And there was something else. The aura of Fate's blessing about you. I saw it the moment I met you. That aura told me you'd do well in anything you undertook."

Right.

She led the way to a couple of chairs and we sat down. As she lifted her glass to drink, she aimed calculating eyes over the rim.

I had never before noticed that her eyes weren't dark like the other Warwicks, but were rather a greenish gold.

Cat eyes. Witch's eyes.

Idiot.

From the vast lobby at our backs, the murmur of speech and soft laughter and occasional happy squeals drifted to our ears as milling Warwicks greeted one another. A few people had been here for several days, Eleanor informed me, but most, like Cavanagh and me, were arriving today. There were already twenty or so adults, but no children in evidence.

From Cavanagh, I knew that this was a business meeting. A crucial one, he had said. The Warwicks were discussing the family's various companies and their own futures.

And Gareth had indicated some sort of vote was to be taken that he was determined to participate in.

So far as I could tell, I was the only one not related by blood or marriage to the Warwicks although Eleanor, I suspected, was sizing me up as a prospective daughter-in-law. Her attentions would have been intimidating had I been in love with Cavanagh. Since I wasn't, I took her probing questions in stride. The frightened little girl of ten years ago had long gone. I didn't worry overmuch about Eleanor's opinion.

There was only one person whose opinion I cared about.

My only fear was that he wouldn't show up.

Tiring of my noncommittal answers to her questions about life in New York, Eleanor resumed the role of perfect hostess. "I do hope you'll enjoy your visit with us. Tell me, is Paladins Rest as you remembered?"

"It's lovelier than I remembered. Of course, I only saw it once and then briefly."

"Do try the lemonade," she urged, noticing I didn't drink from the glass I held. "It's made from true lemons grown in our greenhouse, not those hard yellow things they sell in the grocery stores."

I eyed the amber liquid distrustfully, recalling what had happened the last time I'd been offered refreshments in this house. After imbibing Eleanor's tea, I'd broken a cup and ran away with my tail tucked between my legs and my heart haunted ever after by memories of Gareth Warwick.

That was stale history. I was older now and wiser, and would pit myself against anyone, including a Warwick. After ten years on my own, I was confident of my capabilities. After this meeting, if I had my way, it would be Gareth and not me, whose life would be upset.

And if I didn't have my way . . .

Well, I had to get over him sometime. As Gram would say in her forthright way, "You won't do it any younger."

With Eleanor watching me, I had to drink. I lifted my glass. "To Slumber Mountain."

Eleanor responded in kind.

"Oh, this is good," I said spontaneously after taking a tiny sip. "Marvelous. In fact, this whole place is marvelous," I added, trying to divert her attention from my still-full glass. "The house, the grounds. Everything's not only lovelier that I remembered but it's also larger. Usually when you return to an impressive place, it seems smaller. But coming here is just the opposite."

She beamed.

"So this is Belinda," said someone behind me.

"Jeffrey." Eleanor's cordial expression turned radiant. "I was wondering where you'd got to, dearest."

The man emerging from the crowd of Warwicks was about my height, with a stocky build. His forehead was flat and wide, and he had a smashed-in pug nose.

I would never forget that nose. Or that night of filmy-garbed Warwicks.

My glass shook as I fumbled to set it down.

Don't lose your head, I told myself. There was a logical explanation for this man figuring in that strange dream ten years ago. He might have been a figure in passing that night, a face or a photograph glimpsed on a table. I couldn't have conjured him up out of thin air to appear in that vivid and impossible fantasy where I had given myself over to Gareth for use in some archaic ceremony before he made love to me so beautifully.

This Jeffrey stood alive and alert and full of confidence, nowhere near as sinister or disturbed as my dream had portrayed him.

"Belinda, this is my husband, Jeffrey Tansey." Eleanor swelled with pride.

This man really was the Jeffrey of my dream. There must be a logical explanation, though. Hadn't I heard him mentioned after I waked from that ridiculous dream? Yes, he must have been the one I'd overheard quarreling with Gareth. Other than Gareth himself, everything about that episode so long ago was vague.

Beads of sweat felt cold on my upper lip.

Years-old local gossip drifted back, in the midst of murmuring pleasantries and shaking Jeffrey's hand, about how the Warwick women always kept their name when they married, and passed it down to their children.

One more reason people in Lassitan thought the Warwicks strange. There was no place for a matriarchy in this society. In our backward little north Georgia town, men were the rulers. They were the mayors and the county commissioners and the bankers and the owners of retail stores. Only the Warwick women held any power, and that was due to the wealth they so generously distributed.

"Belinda says the house looks larger," Eleanor said to her husband. "I was about to explain the changes we've made."

"*You*'ve made, dear. You were the one visualizing and then wrestling with the contractors and architects." Jeffrey Tansey turned to me. "Eleanor was in interior design before we moved back here after Annora was—"

Eleanor grew rigid.

He covered his lapse by rushing on. "Eleanor redid most of the house and then she took up a new career as landscaper. She did away with the hedges inside the courtyard and expanded the herb garden. Then she moved the rose garden out front. That's what makes the house seem bigger."

I didn't miss the little break. Right after Annora, the matriarch of the Warwicks and Eleanor's sister, was killed, Jeffrey Tansey had intended to say.

So Eleanor had taken over the house and did all her improvements after the fire.

Jeffrey patted his wife's hand affectionately. She looked at him adoringly.

They were a mismatched couple in appearance. Despite the old adage about how opposites attract, his blunt, ugly features alongside her carefully groomed elegance seemed out of place.

The children of such a union must feel strange not to carry their father's name. What kind of blow would it deal to the fragile male ego of the father? How had Jeffrey Tansey coped with having his wife continue to be known as a Warwick, watching his child brought up as a Warwick?

Obviously, just fine from his eager recitation of Eleanor's achievements. "She's redone the approach to the parking area and moved the greenhouse closer to the lake. She's also put in a rock garden on the drive side. And the pool she made the center of the courtyard is magnificent."

My appreciative murmur made Jeffrey glow as he put his arm around his wife's waist.

Eleanor herself shook her head modestly. "You're embarrassing me."

"Why? It's all true." He said to me, "Eleanor was worried about returning here to live. She thought she wouldn't have anything to keep her occupied, but she was wrong. She's planned and coordinated everything inside and outside. And done it all by herself because Cavanagh and I have been busy with our own development plans for the past few years. She's done a wonderful job, don't you think?"

I agreed politely.

"Drink up, Belinda," Eleanor urged. "Don't wait for Jeffrey to stop talking, or you'll get awfully thirsty. Jeffrey loves to talk."

"Not that you don't," Cavanagh teased his mother as he rejoined us. "I'll have some of your lemonade if there's extra."

As Eleanor served her son, I sipped at the pale liquid.

It tasted good, but I couldn't be sure there was nothing but lemons and water and sugar in it. I'd better make one glass last. A repeat of my last visit might get me thrown out before my reason for being here arrived.

No one noticed my cautious swallows.

Jeffrey returned to his wife's achievements. "Eleanor's put a lot of energy into her work but she's loved every minute of it."

Eleanor started to demur but Cavanagh said, "You know you have, Mother. Before Aunt An—Before we moved back to Slumber Mountain, you were already talking about changes you'd like to see made. So don't go moaning about how hard it's been when you're the one who wanted them."

Eleanor spread her hands in defeat. "All right, I have enjoyed it. Now if you and your father can finally get this excavation and water project underway, I intend to settle back and watch you two slave awhile."

"Things should start moving quickly now." Jeffrey turned to me. "Has Cavanagh told you any of the details?"

"Not really."

"Belinda's not interested in project details," Cavanagh put in quickly, forcefully. "I'm trying not to drive her away with shop talk, Dad."

"Oh." Jeffrey looked surprised, and then cagy. "Right."

Eleanor smoothed over the rough spot. "Yes, we women don't want to be bored by a lot of stupid technical terms, do we, Belinda?"

Eleanor and Cavanagh and Jeffrey were hiding something from me. "Only when they concern construction of a more comfortable brassiere."

The three of them laughed at my stupid joke, trying to make me a part of their group by their too-ready acceptance.

Cavanagh's parents didn't seem to care that I hadn't had a privileged upbringing. They did and said nothing to indicate they were upset at him for bringing me down. In fact, they were more than gracious to me, and I knew why.

Their misinterpretation of my and Cavanagh's relationship couldn't be helped though. I had told Cavanagh emphatically that I had no intention of marrying him. If he hadn't seen fit to inform his parents, that wasn't my fault. I'd set my course and would follow it through.

Headstrong, Gram would have snorted. I could hear her as plainly as if she were here. "That stubborn streak of yours gets you in trouble every time, gal."

I didn't care. As Cavanagh and his parents talked, I answered their occasional questions and darted glances toward the elevator.

The one I sought didn't come.

Then, as I shifted the lemonade glass into my free hand, The Voice came.

I don't want to do this.

The words popped in my head as clearly as if someone had spoken them behind me.

The hairs on my neck stood up. Heat saturated me. No animal, that.

Gareth was here, he had to be.

My stomach curled up into a knot and my heart seemed to be on the verge of flying. I wondered that Cavanagh and his parents couldn't sense my excitement.

"Jeffrey's an engineer and enjoys figuring out solutions to all my design problems," Eleanor was saying. "I decide what I want to do and he works out how it can be done. The roses beside the rocks as you come up the drive are set in drilled-out boulders filled with topsoil. I made him help me last year because when he and Cavanagh start building the park—"

She stopped in midsentence, looking toward the elevator. Her smile died. For one brief second, her expression reflected the meanness I'd surmised lay within.

I knew who she saw.

Before I turned my head, before I found the face that had floated in my dreams, I knew.

My flyaway heart grew lighter and near to bursting. The one reason I'd endured this trip in Cavanagh's company had arrived. I'd known he was close by without seeing him. I'd known it, mind and body, with no evidence to convince me other than what lay in my heart.

And here he stood.

The anticipation that had filled me all day overfilled my heart.

Jeffrey and Cavanagh looked at the doorway, too.

"Gareth." Jeffrey couldn't hide his dismay. "I didn't expect him. After all these years, I really didn't think he'd come."

Wooden-faced, Cavanagh got up. "You should have known he would. I told you what he said in New York."

Gareth, smiling and—refuting the words in my head—at ease, stopped to speak with several Warwicks. They seemed as stunned as Jeffrey Tansey. No one seized his hand and wrung it or hugged his neck or jumped up to approach him, but there was a certain deference in the body language as the crowd slowly parted to let him through.

"Gareth," they murmured to the ones around them. "It's Gareth come back home. What do you think of that?" Others greeted him as he passed. "It's been so long, Gareth," or, "We wondered if you'd come this year," or, "Where have you been hiding all this time? We'd given you up for lost." No one mentioned being happy to see him.

In the same safari jacket and jeans he'd worn in New York, Gareth continued his progress. Despite the frequent pauses, he remained intent on the same course he had chosen from the elevator, coming straight as a drawn line to our group.

Straight to me.

His cool eyes met mine briefly before sliding away to Cavanagh. The expression in them was that of a stranger.

"Aunt Eleanor." He kissed the cheek she stood to offer him.

"Dear boy." Her warmth belied her unkind expression of moments earlier. "After so many years avoiding us. I can't believe you're really here."

"Ah, but I told Cavanagh I would be here." Gareth glanced toward his tight-lipped cousin who hadn't moved his stare off Gareth. "Didn't he relay my warning?"

"Gareth." Jeffrey Tansey, standing beside his wife, pushed forward to offer his hand. "It's good to see you."

"Why do I doubt that." The drawl was not a question. "Oh, I know. You won't want me here making waves, pointing out how irresponsible your plans for the mountain are."

For some absurd reason, I chose that moment to realize that Eleanor was at least half a foot taller than her husband. Taking in that fact was probably why I didn't notice, until disapproval pinched Eleanor's face, that Gareth had rebuffed Jeffrey's outstretched hand. He stood with a faint contemptuous smile, making no move toward his aunt's husband.

Then, with a hauteur I wouldn't have believed he possessed, Gareth turned away in an unambiguous snub. His eyes brushed me.

Several of the waiting Warwicks sighed audibly.

Cavanagh, to my left, clenched his hands. Like his mother, he was angry. Unlike her, he didn't restrain himself. He did keep his voice low. "That's uncalled for, Gareth. My father has devoted over half his life to this family."

Soaring brows rose before Gareth looked back over his shoulder. "Devoted? I know of nothing to support that statement, Cavanagh. Your affection blinds you to facts."

"Gareth." Eleanor kept her temper. "We've all discussed this and we came to a decision. Jeffrey has simply been the one who—"

Jeffrey Tansey bit his lower lip. He looked as unhappy and ill-at-ease as he'd been in my dream.

"—worked long and hard to bring the project to fruition as we envisioned it," Eleanor finished, calling after Gareth.

Gareth whirled. "As *he* envisioned it. Your husband instigated this development from the very beginning, Aunt Eleanor, and you know it. He's pushed it and propagandized for years until he's worn everyone down with his arguments. But there are a few of us not easily worn down, and we'll all be here this year. I won't make a scene unless I'm provoked. Keep your husband away from me if you don't want to provoke me."

Mine was the quick intake of breath this time. Eleanor kept her perfect composure. Gareth again turned away but was caught by a couple of Warwicks.

As he greeted his relatives, I waited patiently for him to speak to me. I drank in his appearance, the intensity of his face, the strength in his shoulders, and wondered what his reaction would be to my presence. If he was as cold to me as he'd been to Jeffrey, I didn't think I could bear it.

At last he looked over to where I sat erect on an upholstered Georgian chair chosen instead of the loveseat.

I preferred to sit alone.

From three feet away, he stared at me long and hard, with such a dispassion that I thought he failed to recognize me. "Lindy," he said finally.

I'd forgotten how low he spoke, what a delicious blend of southern drawl and northern precision and foreign enunciation made up his accent.

"I see Cavanagh was successful in talking you into coming. Bringing you like a lamb to the slaughter, eh?"

I blinked. "Cavanagh asked me to come, yes."

Gareth waited.

At the suspicion of a curl to his top lip, I was compelled to add something, anything. "Naturally, I jumped at the chance to see Paladins Rest again. And meet all the Warwicks."

"Did you? Are we to expect an interesting announcement, then?"

I had no idea what he meant and told him so.

"I'm trying to discover if Cavanagh has beguiled you into an agreement yet."

An agreement? Ah, an engagement. "No." I was happy to set him straight. "No, he hasn't." Aware that the eager denial had given me away, I quickly added: "Not that it's any of your business."

At the same time Cavanagh said, "Not yet," so that we spoke together.

Heat flooded my face.

Cavanagh went on, "Belinda and I have discussed it and she's thinking it over. I'm confident she'll agree in time."

I opened my mouth and closed it again. Gram had instilled some manners in me so I would not call Cavanagh a liar with everyone here listening. No matter how much his words made me simmer, I'd stay quiet. For now.

Puzzlement replaced Gareth's disinterest. Then he shrugged, distaste plain for all to see. "It's her choice, of course. Have you saved my rooms for me, Aunt Eleanor? Or have you assigned them to someone else?"

For some reason, this caused his aunt to gasp. "Gareth, you know those rooms will always be yours, for as long as this is your home."

"Ah, I forgot. That was in the original will, wasn't it? Lifetime possession to my line. Something not easily glossed over." Despite the guise of indifference, Gareth's look was so powerful that I could feel the anger biding, bubbling in him.

I didn't understand what it meant, whether it was directed at me or at something I'd done.

There was no reason he should be angry with me. I may have

used Cavanagh to get here but I'd told him Cavanagh meant nothing to me.

"I'll take my bag up, then." He added to a couple of Warwicks coming hesitantly to help. "Thanks but don't bother. I remember the way."

My gaze followed his back. His body had changed in the past ten years, becoming taller and more mature. His shoulders, wider than I remembered, were set in a certain way that reminded me of the boy I'd found in the woods crying. And of the teenager who'd been devastated and tried to hide it.

No one in the room had welcomed him. Not a woman had hugged him, not a man had jovially clapped his shoulder. No kisses for the prodigal in this group.

He might stand in the midst of his family, but he was as much of a stranger here as I.

The most fanciful image came to my mind, an image of a valiant warrior in a circle of barbarians. Outnumbered but unyielding. Sure in his quest despite being condemned.

The idea was ridiculous, and I laughed at my stupid imagination. But nevertheless that was how I saw him.

I couldn't let him go away feeling himself still alone. "Gareth!"

The three people beside me started. His name from my mouth trilled over the quiet murmuring and whispers.

I didn't care.

Gareth paused, but it was a full five seconds before he turned. In that time, I berated myself for speaking out.

But I'd had to.

I couldn't let him go away thinking everyone in this room was against him. His family might have politely greeted him, but intuition told me he felt isolated.

From twenty feet away, Gareth's wary eyes met mine. Behind the icy mask lay remnants of the hurt and grieving boy who had lost his grandfather and later his parents and sister.

My heart bled for him, with a maturity and understanding not possessed ten years before.

All conversation had stopped. The Warwicks looked at us and waited. Self-conscious, I wished myself anywhere but here.

Too late to back down.

"I'm glad to see you again, Gareth." My voice sounded very tiny in the large living area among the silent Warwicks, but it didn't falter. "I think it's good you've come home."

Gareth smiled then, a crooked smile that wrenched something deep inside me and let me know I had done the right thing.

"That's kind of you, Lindy. But I would have been happier to see you far outside this particular gathering."

He turned, shoulders level, back straight. The tap of his shoes on the marble staircase filled the atrium.

What could I do to free myself of the spell he had put on me? What had I done to make him dislike me so much that he didn't want me in his family's house?

CHAPTER TEN

FROM THE OUTSIDE, one would have no idea how large Paladins Rest was. Only inside did the myriad of rooms and long hallways communicate the vastness of the mansion.

"I've put you in the Blue Bedroom," Eleanor said as she ushered me into a spacious room with pale blue walls and antiques of golden oak.

She remained distant as she had been since my impulsive greeting to Gareth. Maybe she was rethinking my suitability as a future daughter-in-law. I hoped so.

"What beautiful draperies." At the French doors, I fingered the blue flowered print adorning the adjoining window. "I love the pattern."

Eleanor thawed a little. "I found the material at a little shop in Cremona. I knew right away I had to have it."

"It's very unusual but it suits the room. You've pulled everything together so well." I moved over to the old-fashioned chifforobe with its hat mirror surrounded by ornate curlicues matching those on the bed and chest. "It fits the furniture perfectly. You must have spent a lot of time choosing each piece for everything to mesh like this."

She unbent further. "I tried to give each room a personality. After we moved back, I redid all the downstairs and most of the upstairs rooms. Except for—" The beginning rapprochement fled. Coolness returned. "Except for my sister's suite. That belongs to Gareth as her only surviving heir. Naturally, I wouldn't dream of touching it."

No? Cynical me. I bet she dreamed of it a lot, just lacked the courage to do anything about it. "You did a lovely job with this room. In fact, the whole house is wonderful. I'm so happy I can be here to experience it. Thank you for inviting me."

"We're glad you could visit." Eleanor unexpectedly hugged me. "You can't believe how much I've looked forward to having you here. Ever since Cavanagh said you'd agreed to come."

The warmth was probably bogus, but I gave her the benefit of the doubt and said the right things.

At last she stepped back to leave. "Jeffrey and I are right up this hall from you while Cavanagh's a few doors down. I'm afraid there won't be anyone to make beds or fetch extra towels and soap for you.

We Warwicks don't like interruptions or strangers around when we gather for one of our meetings, so most of the staff are off this week. Only the kitchen people are coming in. If you need anything, let me know."

From where I stood the open bathroom door displayed a rack of thick towels and pretty baskets of toiletries. "I'm sure you've thought of everything I could possibly want, Eleanor. I'll be fine. Thank you."

Another lie. I wanted only one thing, and that one thing was something Eleanor Warwick couldn't provide.

She paused at the door. "Dinner's at seven so that gives you over an hour to freshen up. Cavanagh did tell you that we'll be dining formally this week?"

I nodded.

"Good. Silly in this day and age, but it's one of our customs no one seems able to do away with. I suspect we don't want to." With a last complacent smile, she slid out and closed the door behind her.

By myself, I took off company manners and relaxed.

The Warwicks house wasn't a typical family home. It was more like a hotel. Eleanor and Jeffrey lived there all the time, but my years in Lassitan had taught me most members of the family came in and out at different intervals. Only occasionally did the entire clan convene. When they did, this place offered ample room to house them.

The mansion was a large pentagonal structure. Each outer room had windows with views of the town or lake while the inner rooms overlooked the courtyard.

My bedroom was an inner one. I could step onto a minuscule balcony and see other balconies far across the way. Down in the middle, neat herb gardens grew like spokes of a wheel radiating from a large five-sided pool echoing the lines of the house. A stone fountain boasting cupids and goddesses and myriad streams of water, jutted from its center.

As I stood watching the spray, I couldn't push aside a touch of claustrophobia from the position of my room. Had Eleanor put me in this particular one to make sure I couldn't escape?

Don't be stupid. So far, she and Jeffrey had been the kindest people in the house.

Having been warned by Cavanagh and again by Eleanor that dinners were formal affairs at Warwick reunions, I chose a black beaded dress to wear downstairs. Ready well before seven, I saw no need to wait for Cavanagh. Maybe that was why I'd hurried to dress.

Or maybe I hoped to run into Gareth and have a chance to speak to him alone.

Since I had to pass Eleanor's room to get to the elevator, I was quiet. No reason for her to know her son wasn't taking me down.

Her door was ajar. From behind it, an argument built.

"It's not my fault nothing's working. I've done everything you said."

Cavanagh. My steps slowed. Why was he so resentful?

His mother soothed him. "We know that, dear."

"I tell you, I've tried, but your advice hasn't worked. For weeks, I've tried everything I know to sway her. It's Gareth. He's done something, said something to her and turned her against me. You saw what happened today, the effect he has on her. He's totally distorted my intentions, twisted everything I've said. She's besotted with him."

"Cavanagh, really. When would Gareth have had the chance to say anything to her?"

"I don't know, but I tell you he's managed to influence her so that she's doing exactly what he wants. He's bewitched her. That's the only explanation."

I stopped to eavesdrop. What were Cavanagh and his mother arguing about? Who did they think Gareth had bewitched?

Me? Not when I'd seen him exactly twice in the past ten years.

Then painful realization came. I cursed silently. They were talking about a girlfriend. Of course Gareth would have a girlfriend by now. He was an attractive man, with all the needs and desires of any other male. He'd never remain as unattached as I'd done for all this time. Why had that never occurred to me?

I didn't want to hear any more and started walking again.

Cavanagh pressed, "You know it's true, Mother. If we don't face the problem now and do something quickly he'll—"

She cut him off. "Hush. I won't have anything said right now. There's no need. The family knows Gareth has deliberately stayed away and is overly emotional. He'll find it hard to get any of them to side with him." Her voice lowered. "This is what you must—"

I left them, their words growing faint and indecipherable, an aggrieved note in Cavanagh's tone that sounded suspiciously like whining.

What was Gareth doing that had set Cavanagh so on edge? More importantly, who was the woman and what relationship did she share with Gareth?

My upbeat mood had fled. I was behaving like the stereotypical lovelorn woman, chasing after a man who couldn't care less about her.

"Get yourself together, girl," I muttered. "You don't need a man. You've done all right up to now without one, haven't you?"

So Gareth had a girlfriend.

The sun would still shine. The earth would still revolve.

My heart might break, but life would go on.

Not mine. Not here. I would eat dinner tonight and tomorrow I'd fake a phone call to get me out of this enchanted castle and away from the cause of my being here. No need to humiliate myself any further.

"Serves me right for forgetting my place." I blinked back tears and used the mirror by the elevator to straighten my hair. Blue eyes were clear. No pink streaks in the whites.

Satisfied my unhappiness wasn't apparent, I reached for the button and felt his presence.

I didn't have to look to my side to know he was there. Our hands ended up almost touching on the elevator button. My right, his left.

Ringless. At least he wasn't married.

"Gareth."

"Taken to talking to yourself, Lindy?" His wonderful pale face disclosed nothing. "I can understand why you'd rather talk to yourself instead of your boyfriend. Cavanagh never was very entertaining unless he could talk about himself. Where is he anyway?"

"Cavanagh?"

Boyfriend. Could he be jealous? Intuition told me that deeper currents than I suspected existed ran through this family. Could jealousy explain Gareth's anger when we'd met earlier?

No, that was wishful thinking. I'd told him myself I wasn't going to marry Cavanagh. Still, there was something in him and in the overheard conversation I didn't understand.

"Cavanagh's a friend. Nothing more." I lacked the courage to ask about his girlfriend.

He turned his head, looking down the hall in the direction from which I'd come as if gauging the distance or . . .

His hair, straight and coal-black, was pulled back and tied in a short ponytail that brushed the collar of his dinner jacket. He stood still. He might almost know Cavanagh and his mother were talking about him, almost be listening.

Prickles rose. Was he listening to their conversation?

My wayward imagination again. But the prickles didn't go away.

The elevator opened quietly, empty in spite of the houseful of people. Gareth gestured for me to go inside. As the doors closed, he stepped in behind me and leaned over so that his mouth was next to my ear.

He didn't touch me.

He was very careful not to touch me.

I noted that care and a knife twisted in my heart. Despite my changed appearance and the week we'd shared, he couldn't bear to touch me. New York might never have been.

"Why did you come here?" he whispered, so close I could feel his breath and hear the simmering anger. It astonished me.

"What do you mean?" He should have noted the changes in me, seen that I wasn't the same poor white trash I'd been ten years before. He shouldn't question me so accusingly.

"You ought to have stayed away. I warned you back in New York." His words were brutal, shot out like machine gun fire. "You had a choice. If you don't mean to marry Cavanagh, you should have stayed away, stayed out of this whole business."

"I don't know what you mean. Stayed out of what business? Why do you think I shouldn't be here?"

My stomach fell.

From the imperceptible lurch of the elevator starting down, I told myself fiercely. It wasn't fear. I wasn't afraid. Nor was it hurt at his unexpected attack. Why should I care whether or not Gareth Warwick wanted me here?

His breath stayed warm on my neck though he maintained a discreet interval between us. I saw the smooth skin on the side of his face, unblemished by so much as a whisper of a beard. It looked as soft and creamy as a girl's. I saw the aristocratic lips open, wanted nothing so much as to follow the subtle bow with my fingertip.

He didn't care about my feelings. "You don't fit in with Cavanagh and his crowd, Lindy. You aren't like them. If you stay, they'll be the ruin of you, just like they're trying to ruin the mountain. Go away so you can keep whatever's yours safe."

A terrible cold crept over me. "What do you mean, Cavanagh's crowd? They're your family, too."

As if against his will, his hand that had been hovering near my lower arm, reached out and touched me. Inch by agonizing inch, it slipped up my bare skin until he held my shoulder, kneading it as if he wanted to blend it into his flesh.

Heat from each finger spread through my body like a laser cutting through to my heart.

Everything came back to me, all the smells and tints and exhilaration I remembered about him. Banked coals of longing stirred despite my fear.

I possessed little knowledge of this older Gareth. I didn't know what kind of clothes he preferred or his favorite foods. I didn't know if he read classics or popular fiction. I didn't know if he listened to rock or classical music. I didn't know if he rented old movies or went to see the latest thrillers.

I knew nothing except that I needed him. In some elemental, instinctual way I couldn't fathom, without him I was incomplete.

He wasn't perfect—I knew that—but to me he was and I wanted him, body and soul. The sickness at the bottom of my stomach came from knowing how much I cared for him and how little he thought of me.

His hand squeezed my shoulder painfully. "They may be my family," he said in the same low whisper, "but every family has its opportunists, Lindy. You don't belong in the same world with Cavanagh and his parents. You oughtn't be here. You're out of your depth. Way out. Go home before you get hurt."

My head whirled, my lungs could hardly breathe. With his warning, he rejected anything I had to offer him. He didn't want me here, didn't think me good enough for his family.

Oh, he'd put it politely enough, saying he didn't want me hurt. But I'd been around wealth long enough to know how people like the Warwicks twisted the truth around so that you felt you had no choice except to do what they intended you to do all along.

Well, it wouldn't work this time. I wouldn't leave until I was good and ready.

As if aware of my resistance, Gareth tore his hand away from my shoulder and stepped back, putting as much distance between us as he could. The elevator doors opened as soundlessly as before, and we found ourselves in the midst of laughing, chattering Warwicks awaiting dinner.

We were both breathing hard.

"It would be easier all the way around if you'd go back home," he said to the back of my head as I stepped out in front of him. So quietly that no one else could hear.

"I have no home," I said dismally, and knew that it was true. Despite my success, despite my prosperity, despite my fame, there was no place in the world I could call home. Home was a haven, where you could be comfortable with those people you love and they in turn could be comfortable with you. My last home had been with Gram and she was dead.

I had no one in the entire world.

My heart felt as if it were broken into bits all that evening. Deep down I had always known that because other men sought me out or found me fascinating, didn't mean Gareth Warwick would. I had no reason to hope for that at all. For all I knew, he was involved with some other woman. From what I'd overheard Cavanagh and his mother say, he probably was.

So that night I went through the motions, my training in hiding emotions serving me in good stead. With Cavanagh by my side, I meandered down the buffet line. Place cards seated us together at one of the large tables arranged in a U shape in the great dining hall, Cavanagh on my right. I ate dabs of food I later didn't remember eating, drank water only, smiled at those around me, and talked with vivacity. I laughed at jokes I didn't try to understand and listened attentively to anecdotes that bored even their tellers.

I was the perfect houseguest.

Gareth sat at the head of the U. I didn't look at him, but every once in a while, I'd catch a wisp of conversation and realize it was about him.

The gist was always the same: "Why do you suppose he came back now?" "What does he intend to do?" "Surely, he doesn't still blame Cavanagh for what happened that night."

The Warwicks were as disconcerted with Gareth as I was.

After dinner, he disappeared with several others.

Eleanor tightened her lips and ushered the rest of us into the back of a huge living area. Cavanagh begged off. I tried to—I wanted to go upstairs and mope—but she wouldn't have it. "No, no, some of the family are entertaining us tonight. You don't want to miss out on the fun."

Following the others to the rear, we arrived at a huge pipe organ. It gave a gothic touch to the elegant surroundings.

Eleanor, dressed in a medieval style that became her, noticed my amazement at the pipes reaching up to the ceiling. "It was incorporated into the original house in eighteen fifty-seven. By some miracle, it was saved out of the old house that burned around the turn of the last century. As a matter of fact, it was the only thing that survived. My grandmother had the parts restored and replaced here. It has eight hundred pipes."

Her enlightenment left me speechless. Why would anyone want such a monstrosity in their home? It belonged in a church, or a museum.

As I searched for tactful words that wouldn't be a lie, Eleanor preened. Thank goodness she took my silence as admiration. I finally cleared my throat. "It's enormous. Can it be played?"

"Oh, yes. It has a very mellow sound. We'll have a recital later this evening. You'll find that some of the family are quite gifted musically."

To escape her, I wandered over under pretense of examining the instrument more closely.

She followed me. "I used to hate this place." She swept an arm to encompass the house, in a wide gesture that made her bell sleeve billow. "I left home as soon as I could. For years I only returned for family reunions. When my sister died, though, someone had to move in and care for it. So Jeffrey and I volunteered. Once we came, I found I was glad. I belong here, I think. I feel that the house wants me here."

When her sister died. The night of the fire. "You were here the night I brought Gareth home, the night your sister died on the boat."

Her lips tightened. "Jeffrey and I and most of the family had come for a business meeting. It was scheduled the day after the fire but of course was cancelled when so many of us perished." She turned her profile to me. "Those next few days were total chaos."

A delicate white lace fan displayed on the wall next to a rapier gave an excuse to pause. "How did the fire start?"

It may have been my imagination, but I thought Eleanor stiffened. She answered easily enough, "They were never sure. Something about lanterns and faulty wiring was the final verdict, I believe. A terrible accident."

"You and Jeffrey weren't on the boat." I made my words unconcerned, not accusing.

Eleanor's forehead creased anyway. It relaxed after a sharp inspection of my innocuous face.

Perhaps I should go into acting as Ruth wanted. "You were both very fortunate."

"Yes, I suppose we were. I wasn't feeling well. I'd caught a cold somewhere. And Jeffrey wanted to go over notes for the business meeting the next day. He was presenting a new project. He'd hoped to start on it that fall."

"But Cavanagh was there? On the boat, I mean."

"Yes."

I didn't imagine her withdrawal. "You must have been relieved he wasn't hurt."

"It was a miracle, I'm sure." She quickly turned to greet some relatives and when they moved on, gave me a glib explanation of who they were.

Later, no matter how I tried to return conversation to the fire, she evaded my efforts.

Soon after, as Eleanor had predicted, we were treated to an organ recital by a musical Warwick. Fascinated by the eccentric people, feeling I was in a draculean movie, I didn't realize how late it was until the party broke up about midnight.

Cavanagh walked me back to my room.

"Call me if you need anything, darling." He kissed me without warning and I let him. I don't know why. I didn't enjoy it. I suppose I was still in shock from Gareth's forceful rejection and wanted to assure myself I was desirable. Or perhaps I was afraid of being sent home, being sent away from Gareth. Or perhaps I no longer cared.

For whatever cause, I let Cavanagh kiss me, and endured the old tainted feeling afterward.

Perhaps Gareth was right in his assessment of me. Perhaps I was white trash as he hinted. Perhaps I ought to go back to my own kind of people as he asked.

When I closed the door on Cavanagh, I took a shower, trying to cleanse myself of the kiss and the depression it engendered. Afterward, I put on a black silk gown I'd bought to wear instead of my usual pajamas—hoping that it would have a chance to seduce someone—and lay down on the soft, high bed. Above me, the dim blades of the overhead fan lazily circled.

Sleep didn't come. My heart ached too much. In my new never-to-be-admired gown, I went to the window and parted the curtains and looked out at the courtyard.

Gareth stood beneath me, in the middle of the garden beside the pool. Opening the door quietly, I stepped out onto the shadowed balcony. Spying on him might be unseemly, but I couldn't stop myself.

I was bespelled.

From overhead, the moon cast its beams, bathing him in a sheen that turned his dark hair and dinner clothing silver. He looked like the pagan god of that long-ago dream I'd experienced in this same house, bright and pure and illusive.

I watched him as he stood at the pool's edge, staring down into the water as if searching for something.

A downstairs door opened, its creak loud in the quiet night. Yellow artificial light spread beneath me where the reception area lay under my room.

Gareth turned his head toward the figure coming out.

Eleanor. I recognized her flowing dress from dinner. When she neared him, she said something.

Her sympathetic murmur drifted up but I couldn't make out the words.

Gareth shrugged, but I couldn't hear his reply either.

She put her arm through his, talking earnestly as they made a leisurely way back to the house.

I froze on the balcony, wondering if they would see me, wondering if I should call out.

No. I pressed back into the shadows, unwilling to make my presence known.

Eleanor was too engrossed in what she was saying to glance up as they approached the house, but her words floated up. "We must stand by our duty to the family, Gareth. Times have changed. You may not feel the same as the others, but you must go along with the majority."

"Duty to the family? Not everyone in the family agrees with you and your husband, Aunt Eleanor."

"It might as well be everyone," she said sharply. "Who doesn't agree? Old Alonzo, who's half blind and nearly senile? Young Artemesia, who's barely out of adolescence?"

Alonzo. I knew that name.

"Alonzo may be forgetful, but he isn't senile. Don't underestimate him. Or Artemesia. She's more intelligent and mature than you give her credit for. They both understand we have an obligation to the mountain, to the people around it. What Jeffrey's proposing will destroy it and perhaps the community around here, too."

"Artemesia." Eleanor paused, stopping Gareth, too. "Did she call you back here? Is it because of her you've come back?"

"Because of her and Alonzo and others like them. Several have been in contact with me, Aunt Eleanor. I'll say it again. Everyone doesn't believe the same things as you and Jeffrey."

They began strolling again. I saw the whites of Gareth's eyes flash in the moonlight as he passed under my balcony. Almost as if he knew I was there all the time, as if he wanted me to witness this conversation. Perhaps this Artemesia was the woman Eleanor and Cavanagh had been discussing. Perhaps he wanted me to know he was taken.

Jealousy pounded at my temples.

"Gareth, things aren't like they were a century ago. The world is different from what it once was. The family has to change with the times. We must seize this opportunity to be leaders for the people around us."

"People don't change," Gareth said. "There'll always be some who scrabble for money and power. I know that. But I never thought Warwicks would do it. Using someone the way Cavanagh's doing is despicable."

They passed under me, out of view but not out of earshot.

"That isn't why Cavanagh's brought her here. He's in love with her, Gareth."

"Then he should be doubly ashamed."

Me, they were talking about me.

"Go away, Gareth," Eleanor said urgently, unknowingly echoing the words Gareth had said to me earlier. "Go away from here now, this very night. Leave it to Cavanagh. He does love her, he wants to make her part of the family. She loves him, too. She's all but said yes."

My mouth opened in protest but closed without a sound.

Eleanor was wrong. I didn't love Cavanagh. I'd agreed to nothing nor was I about to.

"I won't go away, Aunt Eleanor. I ran away once but not this time. I'm still a Warwick and now I control Grandmama's shares. She'd want me to do what I think is right. Besides, what if Cavanagh's wrong? What if Jeffrey's scheme turns out to be bad financially as well as ecologically?"

"It will be neither. Not with the family united behind him. We can take every precaution to see the mountain isn't unduly damaged. We *will* take every precaution. United we can't fail."

"The family won't be united, Aunt Eleanor. Can't you understand that?"

His weariness made me ashamed of my petty jealousies and anxieties. He needed comforting, healing. What had happened to the confident boy I remembered? The cool reception from his own family couldn't explain his despair.

Eleanor didn't let up. "If they're divided, it's because of you. You've said something to her, haven't you? Cavanagh says . . ."

My ears strained to catch her fading words.

"Something happened that night between you and her, didn't it? That night she picked you up out of the lake. Something we never knew about. That's why she's so friendly to you now, why she holds back from Cavanagh."

Eleanor was accusing Gareth of . . . And wasn't she right? Wasn't Gareth the reason I couldn't love Cavanagh?

"No." Gareth sounded more tired. "I swear to you, Aunt Eleanor, that I did nothing wrong that night except bring her here. That night when our world collapsed and your son saw his chance and took it. That night I asked her to bring me home, to my sorrow, and entangled her life with ours. And now Cavanagh has his claws into her."

Eleanor gave an incoherent cry. "Gareth, please, don't do this. Not to Cavanagh, not to yourself. Cavanagh's a good man."

"He may be. I'm trying to believe that." The door creaked open. "But if you think what he's helping Jeffrey do to the mountain is good, you have strange ideas about good and bad."

The door clicked shut.

In the ghostly moonlight, I leaned back against the balcony doors and looked up at the night skies. What was happening? Why did Gareth dislike Cavanagh?

A cloud covered the moon and left only the stars for light. Five of them were unusually bright. Directly overhead, they stood out among the others in a thin double triangle. They seemed vaguely familiar, though I couldn't possibly have recognized them since I never had much interest in astronomy.

I never had much interest in anything except Gareth Warwick. If only there was some way I could help him. Some way that didn't involve leaving here as he asked.

Beginning to think I was truly bewitched, I went back inside.

CHAPTER ELEVEN

HANDSOME IN A long-sleeved knit shirt and jeans that revealed powerful thighs, Cavanagh showed up at breakfast the next morning in high spirits.

"Okay, people," he announced as we finished eating around the large tables of the dining hall. "The vans are waiting and the boat's ready to cast off."

It was too bad I didn't feel about Cavanagh the way I felt about Gareth. Things would have been so much simpler.

But I couldn't. Gareth had spoiled me for anyone else. If only he would realize I'd changed, that I was worthy of him.

Too bad my shrink wasn't here. She would have told me that there was safety in craving something I couldn't get. Maybe that explained my preoccupation with Gareth. I wanted him because I knew he was unattainable.

"Is everyone ready?" Cavanagh asked as he stood beneath the arched doorway. "You know how Dad's a stickler for schedules. We don't want anyone to get left behind."

"Is it that time already?" several of the Warwicks asked. Engrossed in laughing and talking among themselves, they'd paid little attention to anything else. Now they began recalling jackets and hats and scarves in their rooms still to be fetched. "We're not ready yet. Let's hurry!"

I laid down my napkin and pushed back my chair without enthusiasm. "I need to get my sunglasses."

About half the family had elected to enjoy a boating tour of the autumn leaves outlining Lake Lassitan's miles of shoreline. The antique yacht was gone, destroyed by the fire. Cavanagh had been so excited in describing its replacement, a three story houseboat specially designed for the lake, that I had agreed to go on the luncheon trip. Even if it wasn't the original yacht I'd once envied, at last I would see the Warwicks' floating home firsthand.

So after years of imagining and wishing I could board their fabled water home as a guest, the time had come. And I didn't care.

Gareth had been absent all morning. After his and Eleanor's disagreement, I doubted he planned to go with us. My day would be wasted. If I faked that phone call, I could leave. There'd surely be someone who could take me to the airport.

In my room, the idea of pleading a headache gained momentum.

No. I'd already put in an appearance at breakfast. Cavanagh would detect the lie at once. Besides, it didn't make much difference where I was. I was going to be miserable regardless.

Sunglasses retrieved, I started out, but, remembering from experience how much cooler the air felt on water, went back for a jacket. Apathetically opening and shutting drawers, I picked out a hooded windbreaker and folded it over my arm.

In the hall, I saw him coming this time.

My skin began its tingling long before the long, loose-limbed figure rounded the corner. A large white cat—much larger than I recalled—sidled along behind, trying to be inconspicuous. Gareth paused for a fraction of a second, as if the sight of me made him want to reverse directions and go the other way.

The cat stopped, too.

I fiercely willed Gareth to come to me, willed it so hard my nails dug into my palms under cover of the folded jacket.

In the end, as if my desire had forced him to continue, he walked down the hall toward me. Slowly. Reluctantly. "Lindy."

Falling into step, we headed toward the elevator. "Hi, Gareth." I wanted to say something, anything to keep him near me. I could think of nothing.

His wariness was so apparent that I nearly screamed.

What did he have to be afraid of? I was the one hurting. Hurting for a kind word, a smile, anything that signified some sort of regard.

Oh God. I was as bad as a dog, waiting for its master's pat.

What did it matter? I was fast losing my pride where Gareth was concerned. "Are you going on the houseboat?" was all I could come up with.

He gave me a sidelong cautious glance, gauging whether to answer frankly or prevaricate. "I thought I might."

Maybe he didn't want to come if he found out I was going. Maybe I should hedge the way he had.

No, the honesty he always compelled drew the words out. "I'm looking forward to the trip. For as long as I can remember, I've wanted to see the Warwicks' famous boat."

We reached the elevator, but he didn't punch the button straightway. "About what I said last night, Lindy. I was out of line. I didn't mean to hurt your feelings. I was trying to warn you. Some of our family are . . . Some of them can be cruel. I'd hate for you to find it out firsthand."

"Warn me? Is that what you were doing? Then you were being very kind." I put on a bright smile for his benefit. No way would he learn that he'd made me feel low and contemptible and unworthy. "But I'm not that sensitive. I can take care of myself."

His eyes crinkled up and his lips twitched, and he gave the delighted chuckle that I recalled. "Liar. You haven't the slightest idea of what I'm talking about." He unexpectedly changed the subject. "Are you going to ride down to the boat with Cavanagh?"

"Everyone's going together. They said something about vans."

"Don't go with them. Come with me."

"All right." Not one moment to even pretend to think. Not one thought for Cavanagh or the other Warwicks. They didn't matter. Gareth was the one who had enticed me here, the one I wanted to be with.

As if calibrating the elevator's passage before pushing the call button, he surveyed our surroundings and belatedly noticed the cat hiding behind a fern stand. "Jacinth. You can't come today. Stay here."

The white cat, licking a paw, cocked his head as if to say: "Are you talking to me? Surely you're not talking to me."

He yawned daintily, and then gave us his profile, but continued to survey us from the corner of his eye.

"Ah, the old ignorance is bliss theory. Is he the same cat I met the last time I was here?"

Gareth looked puzzled, and then laughed. "I had forgotten how he scared you the night you brought me home. Yes. He's thirteen years old and still incorrigible." The cat casually stretched and started toward us again. "I mean it, Jacinth. Stay here."

Jacinth set his bulk down. I could almost see him glowering. "He minds well for a cat."

Gareth raised a cynical brow. "He puts on a wonderful front."

The elevator came to a whispered stop, empty as it had been the night before. We got in as a noisy group emerged from the other end of the hall. When Jacinth made a last minute lunge, Gareth's nimble foot held him off. The doors closed.

Another second and we'd have been surrounded by Warwicks. Ebullient, I blessed my good fortune that we'd missed them, that he'd wanted me to ride with him, that I was alone with Gareth in an elevator dropping toward the garage underneath the house.

"Timing," he said, almost as if he'd read my thoughts. "Timing is ninety-nine and nine tenths percent everything."

"And the other tenth?" I asked, pleased that he had thrown away his depression. How easy it would be to reach out, put my hand through his arm as if he were a friend.

"Luck, darling Lindy. Pure luck." He smiled a real smile for the first time, a crooked joyous smile, as if he'd come to a decision and thrown his cares away.

We looked out the back of the elevator toward the lake below. Happiness welled inside me. "I've never thanked you for Asima."

"You didn't need to. I hope she's been a good protector."

I remembered the smashed champagne bottle. "The best."

As we exited the elevator in the underground garage, several Warwicks looked at us curiously. They were used to seeing me with Cavanagh.

"I ought to let Cavanagh know I'm going down to the boat with you."

His smile fled. "He'll know soon enough."

I didn't ask how. All the common courtesies drummed into me by my father and grandmother, all my sensitivities to others' feelings, fled underneath Gareth's spell. I was with him. It didn't matter whether or not Cavanagh was upset. My only regret was that I'd chased Gareth's smile away.

He hustled me into his car, a little two-seater convertible that looked like a vintage model and probably was, and we drove out into the sunshine.

"Shall I let down the top?" he asked as we started down the mountain. "Your hair's pulled back so it won't blow."

"I don't care. Whatever you like." It was strange not to have an opinion after having made so many decisions on my own over the years, but I honestly didn't care. I wanted whatever Gareth wanted.

He wanted the top down and pulled off the road to get out and take it off. I put on my sunglasses, not just to hide my eyes from the brilliant sun. They might reveal more to the man driving than was wise.

When he got back in, he flashed a quick grin that displayed perfect teeth. His eyes were crinkled, alight with mischief.

My heart turned over. In that instant he was the little boy I'd first met in the woods. I started to ask him if he remembered that summer.

Before I could, though, he spoke. "Put on your jacket, pretty Lindy. I'd hate for you to catch cold."

He drove fast and competently, the clutch and gearstick extensions of himself, so smoothly did he operate them. I put up my hood to keep my hair from tangling, and he threw me another sideways smile as if he shared my joy in the rush of the wind, the feel of the car hugging the pavement, the warmth of the October sun beating on our shoulders.

His hair that had been tied at the nape of his neck for dinner the previous night blew free in the wind. It flowed back in a straight veil.

The image of him beside me—shifting gears so easily, grinning into the wind with pleasure as he drove, his hair black streamers around his face—burned itself into my brain, adding to the few other good memories hoarded from the past.

What I felt was doubtless sexual attraction, so intense as to be undeniable. Perhaps it bordered on obsession. If he had stopped the car and kissed me there on the side of the road, I would have done whatever he asked. Made love in the car or on the road if he'd wanted.

Nothing I'd ever experienced had prepared me for this. Most of my life I'd had to be controlled and passionless, putting needs before wants. Today, for the first time, I recognized that everything I'd achieved was nothing compared to what I desired.

Gareth Warwick was at the center of my desires.

The hunger for him grew so acute that I was afraid to look his way, even from behind the protection of my sunglasses. Instead, I kept my eyes on the scenery beside the road, trying to admire the bronze and red and flame leaves as we breezed by.

He shouted over the roar of the motor. "Isn't this great? There isn't any other place in the world as beautiful as this mountain."

I laughed, recognizing an opening given to a pretty woman by an interested man. "What about Colorado?" I teased, recalling that strange moonlit ride up the mountain in Gram's truck when I had driven and he had talked nonstop. "Or Switzerland? Or some of your other old stomping grounds? Isn't Slumber Mountain rather commonplace beside them?"

He shook his head. "This is home. Don't you feel it?"

I did feel something, but years of denial had left their mark. Never show your vulnerabilities. Never admit your needs. "I've seen hundreds of places more beautiful than here and I'm sure you have, too."

His smile fled abruptly. He gave me the curious sidelong look that made me feel he was judging and finding me wanting. The brief comfortable interlude was gone.

Another test failed.

I should have agreed with him, admitted how the hills with their colorful array moved me to tears.

Everything I'd ever learned about dealing with men had deserted me.

Fool.

We were the first to arrive at the houseboat. I climbed out before he could come around to help me, so he retreated a good two feet away. He looked me up and down. "Do me a favor. Take off your shades."

I hesitated, unwilling to reveal myself so completely to him yet. When I did comply, I put on a mannequin's blank expression.

He studied me, forehead wrinkling.

The old inferiorities returned. "What's wrong?"

Dark eyes briefly flickered on my face. He gave his laugh that started off as a chuckle and ended with a peal, and took an involuntary step forward. "Not a blessed thing. You're beautiful, Lindy, too beautiful for cousin Cavanagh."

"I wish you'd stop bringing up Cavanagh," I said crossly.

He took another step forward. "I wish I could. I know who you remind me of now. One of Alfred Hitchcock's heroines. All cool and sophisticated on the outside."

My heart pounded. "They weren't that way on the inside."

"No, not on the inside. But they were actresses. How do you feel on the inside, Lindy?"

I forgot my fear of revealing my weakness to him. I reached out and took his hand. Heat made my fingers tingle as I drew him closer. "Not cool." Then I was in his arms, arms that wrapped around me with agonizing slowness.

Why did he take so long in tightening his embrace? Was he afraid he'd hurt me? Or was it that he didn't want to hold me?

No such compunctions or uncertainties restrained me. Hang-ups were nonexistent. I caught him around his neck and pulled him to me. The blood coursed through my fingers, my lips, my breasts, my hips, everywhere we touched. My body felt swollen to bursting as we kissed.

A squeal of tires came from the main road. A minivan turned onto the paved driveway leading to the graveled parking lot. We jumped apart. Like mine, Gareth's chest rose and fell. A mixture of conflicting emotions raced over his face.

"I wish you were different," he said thickly, looking at me in a calculating way foreign to everything I knew of him. "I'd like to think you didn't care and I could hate you and then all this wouldn't matter."

He must have seen the pain in my expression and felt ashamed because he reached out as if to touch me. He stopped, his hand inches from my cheek. "It's no good," he whispered, and his misery was almost more than I could bear. "I couldn't hate you properly no matter what."

Nausea welled. "Why . . . why should you hate me at all?"

"Because you're so damned superficial. Because you don't care."

"That isn't true. I do care."

"Belinda, there you are! Cavanagh's been looking for you." A Warwick looked inquisitively from Gareth to me.

"She rode out with me," Gareth said brusquely. He was back to the man I didn't know. "Let's go on board, Lindy."

He started to take my arm but changed his mind and drew back. In the end, he gestured for me to go before him over to the boarding ramp.

He didn't touch me.

I felt numb, the way I'd felt ten years before when he'd tossed his hundred dollar bills onto a table as if I were a servant he no longer had use for.

Superficial. He thought me so superficial he didn't want to touch me. All right, I supposed I could be considered superficial, but why should that make him so angry? Was he angry because he wanted me while simultaneously despising me?

Superficial. Was I superficial? If I wasn't, how could I convince him of it?

"Captain Owenson," Gareth greeted an elderly man in navy tee shirt and faded jeans as we boarded. "You're still with us on the new boat. I thought maybe you'd have retired."

A grin spread over the face of the older man as he recognized Gareth. "Heck no. Not me. Got a long time 'fore I have to think of retiring."

They spoke for a few minutes as I stood quietly and tried to compose myself.

"No way we could rebuild the yacht after the fire," the captain told Gareth. "The heat was so intense she burnt down past the waterline. You left town right afterward, didn't you? Never came back so you never saw her after that night."

"No." Gareth sounded unduly curt. "I didn't come back. I didn't want to see her." Something like a shudder started, was brought under control. "Take us on a tour, will you? I'm sure Lindy's interested in the layout. Most people are."

Was that a gibe? A reminder that I was one of the ordinary people?

He didn't look at me. I tried to appear relaxed as we followed the captain. Inside I remained numb.

The houseboat was bigger than Gram's entire house.

The front of the main deck was open to the skies but overlooked by two more decks rising from the rear. The open part, where little tables dotted the sides, was large enough for dancing. A big enclosed area adjoined with more tables and a wet bar. Then came several small rooms with sofas and chairs, tables and lamps.

"The next deck up has a sun room taking up half of it with a large bunkroom and bath kind of like a dorm in the other half. We put young people in there when the big house gets full-up. On top of that deck is the pilot's room and a smaller sun deck," Captain Owenson said, pointing upward. "You can go up if you like, but I thought we'd finish the rest of this deck first and go down."

We agreed and continued walking through small rooms on the main deck.

Somewhere I saw a full bath before we reached a storage area for rafts, water skis, fishing rods, and other water paraphernalia. It was a relief to finally step onto the small rear deck boasting such necessities as two jet skis and a barbecue grill. Over the back rail, winched up out of the way and ready to be lowered into the water at a Warwick's whim, hung a Ski Nautique.

The houseboat was a big floating playhouse. A toy of the wealthy as the yacht must once have been.

The captain looked at me expectantly. "What do you think of her, missy?"

"She's lovely. Much bigger than I'd thought."

He laughed. "Wait till we go below."

Gareth said nothing but looked a little white. This must be the first time he'd been on the lake since the deaths of his family.

I wanted to take his hand, but he stayed well away from me.

The opulence continued below decks. A fully-equipped kitchen with microwave, dishwasher, freezer, trash compacter, and twice the cabinet space of my apartment.

We interrupted the work of people dressed in navy tee shirts and faded jeans like the captain's.

A man stirred a large pot on the stove while two women set out stacks of dishes on the counter. One, sixtyish and chubby, looked up as we entered and put on a big smile.

"You'll remember Peg Cartrell," the captain told Gareth as she approached.

"Peg!" Gareth's delight was as obvious as the woman's. "Do you still make those fried peach pies?"

She hugged him without self-consciousness and pointed to a platter piled high. "Spent all morning making 'em just for you, honey. Boy, it's good to have you back. Place ain't been the same since you left. Don't you ever go off like that again." She squeezed his arm affectionately.

I knew how she felt.

The captain led me into the bowels and the boat's bedroom section. Each of them boasted king-sized beds with bright quilted bedspreads and matching curtains over the double portholes. Each also had its own bath with shower. One had a small sitting area.

"When the house is full, the younger families sleep on board. Then sometimes the Warwicks let performers at the County Arena stay here whenever they're in town," the captain told me when I wondered aloud who used them. "We've had all kinds of rodeo stars and famous country singers on board. The motel in town's okay but most of 'em like the boat better."

I turned to ask Gareth if he'd ever slept on the old yacht, but he was gone.

The grizzled captain picked up on my disappointment. "He went back up. I 'spect it's hard on him, being back on the lake after what happened to his folks and all."

I thought of Gareth's set face. "Was he all right?"

The captain paused a moment as if deciding how much to confide. "He will be. He's always been self-sufficient, you could say. Depends on hisself instead of anybody else. The Old Lady used to comment on it when he was a little fellow. She worried, afraid he was too trusting. But she knew he had that independent streak and figured he'd make it all right. It come in handy after the accident, too."

Then, as if afraid he'd said too much, he turned abruptly. "Come on, you can go upstairs if you like, missy. Sit in the sun with the others."

The very top of the boat was strictly a lounging-sunning deck, with chairs and recliners and more tables.

Some of the crew were putting out cushions and blankets since the wind was chilly. Two couples conversed in low tones on one end.

I found a chaise on the other end and sat down with a blanket, alone and forlorn.

So I was really on the Warwicks' boat.

Hard to believe.

Any other time my situation would have been fascinating. Any other time, soaking up the sun, snug in a blanket as the wind hit me in the face while the majestic boat plowed through the autumn waters, would have been my idea of heaven. Any other time I would have been euphoric admiring the leaves of scarlet and gold and russet that lined the steep hills around the lake.

Not today.

Gareth thought I was superficial.

To top off my misery, as I brooded, Cavanagh bounded up the steps and jumped on me. "Why did you go off with Gareth like that? How could you do that to me? What the hell were you thinking of?"

It was wrong to go without telling Cavanagh. I had known it when I agreed to go but hadn't cared. And I was in no mood to mince words now. Not while dealing with Gareth's rejection. "I'm not your property, Cavanagh."

"I brought you here to the mountain."

"I can leave when we get back to the house." I might as well go. Nothing was turning out as I'd hoped.

My words sobered him. "Oh God, Belinda."

Lying back, I put an arm over my eyes.

He picked up my other hand where it rested against the plaid blanket and put it to his lips. "I didn't mean what I said. I'm so crazy with jealousy I can't think straight. Don't leave. I don't care what made you do it, what he's said to you. He doesn't love you, Belinda. All he wants is to take you away from me."

I removed my hand. "I'm not yours for him to take away." How many times did I have to reject Cavanagh?

"Please don't go."

So I agreed to stay.

Not because of Cavanagh's apologies and pleas but because of Gareth. Because despite his contempt for me, I couldn't bear to go away from him.

"Go on back to your family, Cavanagh. I'll doze here in the sun." And work on this heartsickness.

He reluctantly stopped huddling over me and left me free to watch Gareth when he came up. I heard his odd, low laugh and opened my eyes to see him in the midst of several people along the far rail, talking and listening and making himself agreeable.

Later, I followed his dark head as he insinuated himself into another group, and then another, his presence animating them as it had the first.

Almost like a politician trying to get elected to some office or another.

Under the benign sun, I tried to forget my problems by puzzling over what was going on within the Warwick clan. Most of them, except for Cavanagh and his parents, seemed to be warming up toward Gareth.

Cavanagh and Gareth seemed to be setting themselves on opposite sides for some unknown purpose, and most of the family were taking Cavanagh's part. The rift might be over this water park Cavanagh and his father planned, or maybe something more. Like control of the family's wealth?

Anyway, Cavanagh wanted to do one thing while Gareth wanted to do another, and so far Cavanagh was winning. That couldn't be why Gareth disliked him, though.

What I had to do with their quarrel baffled me. I'd told Cavanagh I didn't love him. I'd told Gareth, in words and by coming with him today, that Cavanagh meant nothing to me.

My assurances seemed to make no difference. Gareth might have brought me to the houseboat, but he ignored me now.

Throwing back the blanket, I walked to the rail. No one would miss me if I jumped in.

CHAPTER TWELVE

OF COURSE, I didn't jump.

I did lean over the rail and watch the waves below, thinking about the yacht devastated years ago. This boat was decked out for a party, too, the way the yacht had been that night. The only things missing were the twinkling lights. Maybe daylight cruises didn't need them.

Back then, I'd envied the Warwicks their yacht, their lives. Today, I didn't. My life was proof that material things didn't bring happiness.

"It isn't the same as the old yacht. I cried when it couldn't be saved after the fire."

A woman had come up, so quietly I hadn't noticed. No, not a woman. A young girl I vaguely recalled from dinner the previous evening.

"I'm Artemesia Warwick." She offered a hand. "We met for just a moment last night before the recital."

"Oh, yes, I recognized your face but never got your name. I'm sorry. There are so many of you."

Artemesia. The one mentioned in Gareth's conversation with his aunt.

I looked at her with more interest. Was Gareth involved with one of his relatives?

No, he couldn't be interested in a child like this. She couldn't be over twenty.

But she boasted the creamy complexion and long face of the Warwicks. Her glossy black hair flowed straight and free to her shoulders, and would have fallen into her face had she not pulled the front strands into braids caught up at the back of her head. Anyone would have deemed her beautiful, with her straight nose and full lips and clear eyes.

Innocent eyes.

Hard for any man to resist. Perhaps Gareth preferred girls like this, trusting and untainted and young as I had never been at that age.

My stomach lurched to think of her and Gareth as a couple. Go back to the tragedy. "What caused the fire?"

"Some lanterns strung around the railings, the fire inspectors finally decided. They shorted out near the middle area of the main deck. With the oiled wood, the fire spread before anyone realized what was happening."

"How awful."

She smoothed her slacks over curvy hips. The khakis were fitted but not tight. Understated. Classy. Like her. "Yes, it was. It seemed like a nightmare. One minute people were laughing and dancing under the pavilion, and the next they were screaming and . . . Oh, stars. It was terrifying. Most of the people who died were trapped down in the salon. They were discussing a meeting they were to have the next day at the house. Arguing, really. Anyway, they didn't have time to get up from below."

"You were there when it happened?"

"I was nine, the only child there except for a few older kids like Cavanagh and Gareth," she said matter-of-factly. "My parents were taking me down to Disney World after the business session. Downstairs everyone got in an argument about the meeting the next day. My father got all red in the face, he was so angry. That's how I remember him still. My mother sent me upstairs to stay with the older kids hanging out up on deck. I just got there when the fire blazed up behind me. Someone pushed me into the water and that saved my life. My parents were trapped with the others in the salon. The top cabin collapsed on them. I lost them along with both my grandparents."

Whether she and Gareth were together or not, her straightforward recital made me warm to her. I knew the heartache of losing a loved parent. "I am so sorry."

Artemesia gave a tiny shrug but couldn't hide her pain. "I've gotten used to it. Luckily I had my mother's parents to go to. They and her sister raised me. There were a lot of Warwicks lost that night though."

"How can you bear to come back here?"

She looked out to the lake waters, the chop foamy in places where the small waves broke. "How could I not come back?" She turned back with a blinding smile. "This is our home, the mountain and the lake. This is where we draw our strength. We're more vulnerable on water, but we can't give in to our fears. We have to try to overcome them. Our family's always been as close to the water as we are to the mountains, but some, like me, never master our fear of it." She squared her shoulders. "So I have to keep trying. Facing one's fears is always better, don't you think?"

"That's what everyone says."

Unless one also had to face a reality that was unbearable. I had run away from my hell.

As had Gareth. After the fire, he had run and stayed away for ten years. Why had he chosen this particular time to come back? He'd said it was business but did Artemesia have something to do with his return?

What a strange family these Warwicks were. I wished I were not so attracted to them.

To one of them.

I lacked the nerve to probe Artemesia about Gareth so we stood quietly for a while, watching the shoreline.

Finally, tentative fingers plucked at my sleeve. "Look, I oughtn't ask, I know, but I can't stand not knowing. Is it true you've agreed to give up your claims to the mountain?"

"My claims to the mountain?" I pivoted to stare at her. "I don't know what you're talking about."

A tiny frown creased her perfect brow. "You do know what Cavanagh and his father want to do to Slumber Mountain, don't you?"

Ah, the development Cavanagh was planning. "Cavanagh's told me something about a water park here. I suppose Lassitan could use the money it would generate."

"Water park!" Two spots of color flared in her cheeks. "The water slide and resort come later, much later, after they've destroyed the mountain."

"Destroyed it? I would have thought the mountain would be part of the attraction."

"Ha! Once they get through cutting it down, there'll hardly be a mountain." Anger stained her white skin down to the neck of her blouse. "The old trees will be chopped down, the streams will be diverted, and they'll have to build a concrete mountain for their slides. When that happens, when the mountain is leveled, all the nearby towns around it will lose their souls."

Her words disturbed a chord in my memory.

I had once sold my soul.

No, that had been a dream. Only a dream.

When I failed to speak, Artemesia's words tumbled out. "Oh, stars, yes. They intend to eventually put in a golf course and a hotel and shops, and later on, condominiums and an office park. But the mountain itself will be gone and Lassitan as we know it will be gone, too. This spot will be exactly like all the other tourist attractions in every other part of the country. Oh, please, don't let it happen."

I shook my head to clear it. "What does this have to do with me?"

"They can't do anything without you agreeing. They need your rights."

Dark eyes looked at me expectantly, the pleading in her face changing to doubt and then uncertainty. "You don't know anything about what Cavanagh and Jeffrey are planning, do you?"

"Apparently not." Whatever she was talking about, I had nothing to do with Cavanagh's ventures. Although leveling the mountain was unthinkable. Was it even possible?

Maybe. But certainly improbable. Artemesia's imagination was working overtime. Her age meant she felt things more deeply than an older, more experienced person.

She touched my arm. "Gareth said you didn't care, that you were going to give Cavanagh the rights and there was nothing we could do to stop you unless your conscience kicked in."

"Gareth?"

"Yes. He . . ." She bit her lip. "I'm sorry. I shouldn't have said anything. He told me not to bother you, that we couldn't talk you into something you might regret later. He said you had to make the decision yourself."

I had no rights to the mountain. Even if I did, I wouldn't give them to Cavanagh. I wouldn't give anything to Cavanagh.

How could Gareth believe I didn't care about the mountain?

Slumber Mountain had sheltered me throughout my childhood, giving me comfort in its strength and rugged spirit. Even when Pop died and life turned bitter and my mother dragged me off to distant parts, the memory of it helped me cope. And afterward, when I ran away, I'd come back to it to heal. Gram's home beneath the mountain had been my refuge.

"Gareth told you I didn't care about the mountain?" I curbed my fury. "What exactly did he say about me, about the mountain? What rights does he think I have?"

My tone drove her back. She shook her head uncertainly. "Never mind. Please forget I said anything. Gareth was right. I shouldn't have brought it up."

"I want you to tell me why—"

But the chance to question her evaporated when Artemesia rushed away like a frightened child and I watched her go, smoldering as I considered what little I did know.

Jeffrey and Cavanagh wanted to destroy the mountain and then turn it into a tourist attraction. Destroy it by leveling it. Why would they go to such extremes? And what did I have to do with any of this?

Nothing made sense except that whatever Cavanagh and his father planned, Gareth was against. At least that explained the tension between the men. The family must have taken sides, too. Most of them against Gareth, from the looks of things, and today he was openly lobbying to change their minds.

That explained why he was working the Warwicks like a southern politician at a gospel singing.

Over the houseboat railing, the mountain jutted, silhouetted against the clear blue sky, trees covering its bottom, the Warwicks' home barely seen on its top.

A passion rose in me. "Our mountain," my father had told me long ago. "We can see it and touch it and always be a part of it, Lindy, no matter what the Warwicks or anybody else does. So long's we have our part, they can't take the mountain from us."

As the boat glided on, the craggy bulk gave way to the point that stood upright like a sentinel standing guard over the lake. I did indeed feel a certain affinity with the mountain. How horrible to see its proud shape taken down, to have buildings snaking over its acres, tourists driving over crisscrossed roads.

Still, what did Cavanagh's project have to do with me?

And what did Gareth think I was going to give Cavanagh that was so upsetting to Artemesia?

Any rights I had in the mountain proper were purely spiritual. My puny acres at the foot couldn't stand in the Warwicks' way if they chose to clear-cut or grade or build water parks all over its surface.

I could ask Gareth. Make him tell me what he thought I had that could stop the depredations.

The ache in my heart dulled a little at this legitimate excuse to approach him. Maybe once he knew I hadn't promised anything to Cavanagh, he'd change his mind about me.

* * * *

CAVANAGH, BALANCING A cup that steamed invitingly, found me back in my lounger. "I brought you some hot coffee. I thought you could use it."

His manner was appeasing though I was the one in the wrong. I was the one who had gone off with Gareth without letting him know.

Gareth who'd kissed me and then said he wished I was different so that he could hate me. Gareth who'd brought me here and abandoned me at the first opportunity.

The other small groups had gone down to the main deck, and Cavanagh and I were alone. I took his proffered cup. "You're right. It's cool out here."

"Drink it up. It's black, just the way you like your coffee."

No, I didn't like it black. I drank it black. Cavanagh had never bothered to discover the difference.

There was a restrained note of excitement about him. He had a paper in his hands that he folded and unfolded nervously. "It'll warm you down to your toes."

The cup was hot and I was comfortable enough under my blanket without the coffee. "I'll let it cool a moment."

Past Cavanagh's shoulder, I saw Gareth gallop up the metal stairs to the upper deck and come toward us. Breathing hard, he stopped in front of us. He also held a cup.

I schooled my face, not wanting to show him how glad I was to see him, how his accusation of superficiality had stabbed me.

"I brought you some tea," he told me, much as Cavanagh had done a few moments before.

"Thanks, but your cousin had the same idea." I held up the coffee.

In less than a second, Gareth had taken the cup and thrown its contents into the water below.

"You—" Cavanagh turned white with rage. His hand trembled as he crumpled his paper and stuffed it into his pocket.

I was as shocked. "Gareth! Cavanagh brought that coffee to me."

Cavanagh took a step toward Gareth. His hands had balled.

"From the bottom of the pot." Gareth darted his sidelong glance at Cavanagh, his own free hand fisting. "It would have been bitter."

Something passed between them.

Cavanagh was the one to yield. He stepped back, exhaling noisily. "Don't you think it's time to let up, Gareth? People already think you're a mental case."

"Only the ones favoring your father's scheme." Gareth offered his cup to me. "This tea's freshly brewed. Licorice, the kind you like. It'll taste better than Cavanagh's coffee."

He remembered that I liked licorice tea.

Still, he'd barged in here when he'd ignored me all morning. "I don't want tea." Sorry when I realized how petulant the words sounded, I attempted to gloss them over. "What I really want is lunch. Isn't it about that time?"

Both men looked at me, as dispassionate as the people who watched me on the runways and assessed me like I was a commodity to be bought and sold.

My heart sank. Were my supposed rights in the mountain what this rivalry was all about?

Gareth was wrong if he'd told Artemesia I could stop Cavanagh and his father from developing the mountain. I had no power to stop Cavanagh or any other Warwick from doing whatever he wanted with Slumber Mountain. Surely they couldn't believe I might lay claim to the mountain. Was that why Gareth had asked me to ride with him?

"It certainly is about that time, Lindy." Gareth's distinctive drawl ended the uneasy silence. "Lunch is being served even as we speak."

The three of us went down, the tension as thick as cottage cheese and not nearly so appetizing. On the main deck, Gareth smiled coldly. "I'll leave you with Lindy, cuz. I'm sure you'll take excellent care of her." He turned to me. "Don't forget, you're riding back with me."

Another moment and he had blended into a small group of Warwicks to resume campaigning.

Tight-lipped, Cavanagh led me to the buffet table. When I exclaimed over the lunch menu, he was too preoccupied to respond. He was probably brooding over his run-in with Gareth.

Spotting Jeffrey, he said, "Help your plate and sit down, Belinda. I need to tell Father something but I'll be back in a minute. Save me a place beside you."

Lunch looked superb, with chicken fingers and crabcakes and shrimp cocktails along with various other dishes such as country-cooked green beans like Gram used to make and fresh homemade biscuits not normally associated with catered food. I lingered over the sweet potato pie but with regret, passed it over. A tiny helping of green beans with a few boiled shrimp and a slice of tomato looked lost on the plate.

Another part of my career I hated: always having to watch my diet. I'd stint at dinner to pay for the grease-seasoned beans.

Each table held a crystal vase of fresh flowers on a pristine cloth set up for two or four people. Choosing an empty one with four chairs, I played with my food to make it seem I was eating as much as everyone else. The blue lake waters with the gray ring of mountains and colorful leaves made a glorious backdrop.

If only Gareth could be across from me, lunch would be perfect.

But I was stuck with Cavanagh. I wasn't upset that he'd abandoned me because I dreaded the opportunity for an intimate talk with him that was long overdue.

I don't love you, Cavanagh, and I never will. I hope we can always remain friends but I will never marry you. It was easy to practice the speech in my mind. Telling Cavanagh in person would be a different story.

Various Warwicks alit at the other tables, but Cavanagh didn't return nor did I see his parents anywhere.

Not until I'd drunk half the freshly brewed coffee—and salivated to the oohs and ahhs as the adjoining table consumed large pieces of the sweet potato pie—did The Voice come.

Unexpected. Clear. Angry.

No-o-o-o . . . Too cold . . .

I froze, listening for more.

Nothing.

Perhaps my shrink was right. Perhaps The Voice did come from my imagination.

No. My skin prickled. The words had been clear.

Something must be wrong.

I completely forgot about the sweet potato pie and other surroundings.

That Voice was the intuition my grandmother had called a gift. The words were not my imagination no matter what anyone might say.

I strained but heard nothing else. Yet The Voice was clear.

Someone or something needed help.

Where was Gareth? If I heard The Voice again, I would tell him. Never mind that I wanted it to stay another of my secrets.

I couldn't see him.

Cavanagh appeared, tense and serious, and put his filled plate on the table beside mine. He sat down without looking at me, hesitated before picking up his napkin.

Like he knew something was wrong, too.

The inner Voice flared suddenly, faintly, unmistakably. *Come back. Help me.*

The words were familiar.

I searched the group around us but still couldn't find Gareth.

Come back. Like Gareth had called ten years ago.

With unjustified certainty, I knew what had happened, and my heart hammered.

The Voice came from Gareth. He was in the water behind us.

I shot up so abruptly my chair fell backward.

Cavanagh's napkin paused in midair. "What's wrong?"

I had to weave through tables before getting to the boat's enclosed area. Behind me, I heard Cavanagh push his chair back.

He caught me by the elbow and swung me around. "Belinda! What is it?"

I shouldn't tell him. Instinct warned not to. But I had no choice. "Cavanagh." *Stay calm, be reasonable.* "Gareth fell off the boat."

He stiffened.

Shaking off his hand, I hurried toward the back.

He raced after me, came up as I entered the small salon area. "Don't be ridiculous, Belinda." He seized my upper arm, not gently. "How could Gareth fall off the boat? Someone would have seen."

When he wouldn't let go, I dragged him along with me. We went through the first room and into the main salon. Several people sat on the sofa and chairs, plates in their laps and drinks on the end tables. "I don't know, but he's in the water."

"Belinda, stop it." He spun me to a halt. "You're hysterical."

Conversation ceased as the diners turned startled faces toward us. I didn't recognize any who might help me and turned to Cavanagh.

"I tell you Gareth's back there in the lake." Fear kept my words even. My teeth grated together. "We have to go back."

"Someone's in the lake?" A Warwick's husband, blonde and sturdy, responded to the anxiety in my voice. "Who? What happened?"

Cavanagh exploded. "She doesn't know what she's saying! She's been eating out front, for God's sake! How could she possibly know Gareth fell into the water?"

I wrenched my arm away and rushed on. Behind me, people argued as to whether or not someone had fallen.

Bursting out of the storage room onto the back deck, I leaned over the rail and scanned the lake we'd just cruised. The water was greenish-gray, almost black. I searched desperately through the foamy waves for a dark green sweater.

I'll never find him.

Then . . .

As on that night ten years before, his face showed up first, white between the waves and aimed in our direction.

"There!" I pointed as Cavanagh and a few others crowded out to fill the small area. "He's there. We have to go back."

There were no more objections. A tall Warwick took charge. "Let down the Nautique. It'll be quicker."

In a moment, the ski boat had been lowered into the water carrying two crew members and the Warwick who'd ordered it launched.

Cavanagh, when I glanced at him, surveyed me with narrowed eyes. In them lurked uncertainty and something else he could not hide.

Hostility?

I retreated a step. For one wild, uncontrolled moment, I sensed he would have left Gareth to die. That he was angry with me for showing everyone Gareth was in danger.

Remorse crowded out panic. Jealousy was eating at Cavanagh. I had been honest with him from the beginning, but I had never gone far enough.

I had to make him realize I would never marry him. Never.

"Cavanagh." I put out a hand.

He turned on his heel.

No more than I deserved. I bit my lip and went to lean against the rail.

The Nautique shot over the waves and reached Gareth. The

ponderous houseboat slowed to a stop. No one on the back deck spoke as the crew members on the Nautique pulled Gareth from the water. Gareth was conscious. We could see him talking to the other Warwick.

The ski boat seemed to take forever to turn around and reach us, but finally, occupants still inside, winches lifted it up to its normal berth on the houseboat.

I sagged at the rail. My stomach unclenched. No cause to throw up now. Gareth was safe.

The crewmen clambered out and turned back to help Gareth and his relative down. The people around us began to chatter.

". . . can't understand how it happened," a woman said.

"Gareth is volatile, always has been," a man responded. "I wouldn't put it past him to jump in and then tell us someone pushed him. He tried to say that before, didn't he?"

"Aren't you prejudging him?" cut in a familiar voice. Artemesia was challenging her relatives. "Would Aunt Annora have left all her holdings to Gareth if she'd thought he wasn't capable of looking after them?"

"Eleanor says he's degenerate."

"Eleanor!" Artemesia dripped scorn. "Eleanor's completely besotted by Jeffrey and Cavanagh. She hates Gareth, always has."

"Artemesia," the woman said patiently, "Gareth left us after the accident. He ran away and didn't come back until now. He couldn't have cared about his heritage and the family or he'd have stayed in touch. He would have been learning how to manage the assets, learning how to keep us strong. Cavanagh on the other hand—"

"Is a sneak, if not worse." Artemesia fairly sparked. "Doesn't it seem strange that Gareth, the only one willing to challenge Jeffrey's decision to go against our traditions, everything we've stood for, suddenly falls off the boat? Just like what happened ten years ago when my father and others spoke out against harming the mountain during the meeting. They died. And if Belinda hadn't realized Gareth was gone today, he'd have been left in water cold enough to kill him. Don't any of you wonder how it happened?"

"He never came back after the fire," the woman murmured stubbornly.

"Maybe he was afraid to come back. Have you ever thought about that?"

Someone gasped, the rest stared at her. Artemesia made an exasperated sound and whirled on her heel.

One man started to say something to the woman who had borne the brunt of Artemesia's anger but noticed me listening.

He shrugged and smiled. "Artemesia's young. The young take things to heart."

They also see things older people can't, I almost said.

No, this wasn't my family or my fight.

But Artemesia's empassioned outburst revived doubts about Cavanagh.

He'd been insistent that I was mistaken about Gareth being in the water, and he'd tried to keep me from getting to the back of the boat.

When Gareth stepped onto the deck from the berthed ski boat, he didn't blame Cavanagh or anyone else. He answered questions quietly, giving assurances that relieved the Warwicks. "No, no, I'm fine. Just a mishap. I'll be okay once I get some dry clothes and warm up."

He would have said if Cavanagh had pushed him. Of course he would have.

I slumped in relief. I hadn't realized how afraid I'd been.

My relief was short-lived when Gareth's eyes sought out Cavanagh in the crowd. But despite his level glance, he made no move or accusation.

He looked away only when Artemesia touched his arm. "You have to get out of those wet clothes."

"I guess I'd better find some more then."

"Belinda told us you were in the water," she said to him as he started down the stairs leading to the bedrooms. "She made us stop for you."

"Did she?" He paused, looked back at me. "Thank you, Lindy."

He didn't sound appreciative though. He seemed as remote as ever.

Face it. I was fooling myself. So I'd woven a fantasy in my sleep, made him into some hero of mythical proportions. He wasn't. Gareth was just a rich snob who looked down on me. He'd used me in New York to while away the days, and then left when he got tired of playing. I wasn't anyone he could respect.

Superficial, he had called me.

Maybe he was orphaned like me, but that was the only way we were alike. He didn't care whether or not he hurt someone. He didn't merit pity or love or anything else.

A shame I couldn't convince my heart of that.

At the dock, as we prepared to disembark, Cavanagh found me. "Ride back with us. Don't go with Gareth." He leaned closer. "You don't know what he's like."

I'd always treated Cavanagh with careless indifference. He might be in love with me, but I couldn't love him. Today was the first time I suspected any kindness toward him was wasted.

He continued pressuring me. I wavered.

From my last glimpse of him, Gareth would rather not have my company going back up the mountain. Maybe it would be best to go back with Cavanagh. I prepared to yield gracefully, if reluctantly.

Before I could open my mouth, a familiar drawl came. "It's rude to leave the dance with anyone except the person who brought you." Gareth stepped between us. "Lindy, are you ready to go?"

Happiness, crazy unadulterated happiness, shot into my heart and head. "Thanks anyway," I told Cavanagh, despite his dismay.

"Belinda—"

"Wants to go with me. Isn't that right, Lindy?" Dressed in the crew's uniform of long-sleeved navy pullover and jeans, Gareth looked dangerous.

Elation fled.

Superficial. That was how he viewed me. Part of me was angry. Part was piqued.

Choosing Cavanagh would wipe the assurance off his face. But I couldn't.

Get me within two feet of the man, and my pride was in shreds.

"I'll ride back with Gareth, Cavanagh." My mouth was dry. "Thank you for offering though."

Gareth managed, somehow without touching me or Cavanagh, to shepherd me down the ramp to the bank.

CHAPTER THIRTEEN

BEFORE HE CLIMBED in, Gareth put the top up on the sports car.

I was glad.

The carefree mood of the morning had muted to pensive as I came down to earth. Illusions long cherished regarding him must be abandoned. Sooner or later I'd have to face the truth: he cared nothing for me. He was playing with me for his own ends.

Sooner or later I'd have to go away and forget him.

But not yet. Not yet.

I looked over at him as he drove, his smile erased as if he too had lost the gaiety of the morning.

He had lowered his window halfway, and the wind rushing in ruffled his hair. In an effort to keep it out of his face, he pushed the flying strands back behind his ears.

On the side of his forehead exposed to me, a darkish mark showed in the hairline. A beginning bruise.

I made a sound.

He looked toward me, startled, and then realizing what I'd spotted, hastily ran his fingers through his hair to free it and conceal the telltale sign.

"How did you get that?"

He kept his eyes on the road, took his time answering. "When I went into the water."

"Did Cavanagh do that? Is that what happened? He hit you and threw you into the water? He did, didn't he?"

"Don't worry about Cavanagh," he said coolly. "I turned my back. It won't happen again."

My breath deflated. Until now I had convinced myself Cavanagh had nothing to do with Gareth's fall. I'd pretended he couldn't be callous enough to hit Gareth and leave him in lake waters too cold for a man to survive.

"You could have drowned. You ought to file charges."

"Against my own kin?" The corner of his lips visible to me tilted up. "I don't think so."

"He tried to kill you."

"No. Not really. His temper got the better of him. I'll take care of Cavanagh. He's jealous." The enigmatic glance flickered toward me, and then away. "Artemesia says Cavanagh hasn't told you about the mountain. She thinks he lied to the family when he said you were prepared to sign a quitclaim deed. Is that true?"

"A quitclaim deed? For what? The mountain? What does the mountain have to do with him trying to kill you?" The thought of Gareth dying drove everything else out of my mind. "What does the mountain have to do with me?"

He concentrated on the road, almost like he was making up his mind about something.

Wanting desperately to insure he made it up correctly, I chose my words. "I'm not about to do anything for Cavanagh. I liked him once, but I'm not sure I feel that way anymore. If he would hit you, his own cousin, then I don't like him at all."

He grinned at me before looking back at the road. Not the ironic distant smile, but the boyish grin that turned my heart. "You really have no idea what's going on, do you?"

"I could have told you that from the beginning if you'd bothered to ask."

"I was afraid to ask. At first I thought you'd hooked up with Cavanagh. And then I was afraid you were with him because you were an investor in the scheme. I didn't want to hear you say you'd agreed to his proposal."

"I haven't agreed to anything."

"I didn't know that."

"Now you do. Did you really think I'm the type person who'd be interested in developing a water park and resort village on the mountain?"

He took a long breath. "That isn't the entire story. The resort village will come later. Afterwards. Once—" He licked his lips. "Lindy, what I tell you is private."

"I can keep a secret."

His expression softened. There might even be a hint of pity. "I know."

He couldn't know about the shameful secrets of my past. If possible, my body went colder than when I realized Cavanagh had thrown him off the boat. I'd told no one about my stepfather except my psychiatrist.

No, Gareth couldn't pity me. He didn't know. My secret was safe.

"Tell me," I said brusquely.

The car went around a curve. "Years ago, my grandmother, while excavating for the swimming pool, discovered a mineral inside the mountain."

"What kind of mineral?"

He inhaled, blew out slowly. "A different kind of mineral. A new one. Have you heard of tsavarite garnets or maybe tanzanite? Or moissanite?"

"Jewels?"

"Gemstones, yes. Found in only one place, hence their value. Grandmama discovered a different stone in Slumber Mountain, in colors ranging from white to black and every shade in-between. It has the hardness of a diamond and is as bright as a diamond. But it isn't a diamond, not according to the analysis. It's something else. Something never recorded."

The necklace from Cavanagh. The brilliant pink pendant that I had never worn.

I told him about it, how its touch repelled me. "Cavanagh didn't tell me what it was, but I can't wear it."

Because it had been torn from the mountain. No wonder I'd felt ill when Cavanagh had fastened it around my neck.

Gareth nodded. "There were some pink gems in the ones Grandmama pulled out. She hired experts to examine and research them. The consensus was that the material is something unknown. That makes it something that could be immensely valuable if it were marketed properly. As far as we know, Slumber Mountain has the only lode."

"And Cavanagh wants to develop it."

He downshifted before braking at a stop sign. "His father was the first one to agitate for mining. Grandmama decided against it but after she died, Jeffrey's been working on the others. There's going to be a vote soon. Looks like it'll be close."

"You're against it."

"The lode runs through the core of the mountain. The only economical way to remove the stones is to quarry out huge chunks. Like strip mining." His mouth tightened. "Jeffrey would destroy it simply for the wealth to be had."

I glanced involuntarily up toward the proud mountain peak looming above. How horrible to see its beauty destroyed to make jewelry for a woman's—or man's—vanity. "I still don't understand what this has to do with me."

"I'll have to go back into history a bit. Do you care if we make an unscheduled stop?"

With him? "Of course not."

He turned the car into a road leading into a lakeside park. Being a weekday and the autumn of the year, the parking lot was deserted except for one empty boat trailer attached to an SUV.

Gareth drove around the SUV toward a section fronting the

water. "I couldn't go into all the details at the house. Not with all the little ears around."

"I understand." I didn't. Not really. But nothing mattered except I was with him and he was talking to me like a friend.

When he parked in a sunny place overlooking the point, I laid my head back against the seat. The blue sky held fleecy white clouds. A red truck pulled a boat in and started backing down the ramp. The trailer went sideways, and the driver had to pull up and start all over.

I watched the truck and the clear sky and the sun-strewn lake ripples, thinking of the mountain but conscious of Gareth beside me.

His eyes were on the truck, too, and he was also thinking of something else. "When the Cherokee territory got parceled out in the early eighteen hundreds—"

I roused myself to murmur, "Trail of Tears, somewhere about eighteen thirty-seven or thirty-eight." Gram being part Cherokee had interested me in their removal.

"Smart girl. That's when the Cherokee were moved out. The lotteries actually started earlier."

"While the Cherokee still lived here?" I tried to imagine how I'd feel to see my home given away to strangers. "How awful."

"Life isn't always the way it should be."

"No," I said sadly. "Sorry. Go on."

"Our family didn't enter the lotteries, but we bought most of the mountain and the surrounding lands from people who did. A man named Larkin Lightfoot drew five hundred acres. His holdings ran from below the river to the top, part of it going directly up the middle of the south side. It was the only accessible route to the peak. He refused to sell because he was married to a half-Cherokee who'd always lived here."

"Good for him. So he kept his land?"

He watched the waters sparkling, but a smile played on his lips. "My family didn't want all of it. Just the part on the mountain."

"I'll bet they managed to get it."

"Did I say you were smart?" He gave his curious abrupt laugh. "We did get it but not in an, um, entirely legal manner. I'm sure the Lightfoots were discouraged from using the land that the Warwicks wanted. Don't ask me how. I don't know and I don't care."

"I think you're lying. I think you know exactly how."

His laugh boomed out.

I laughed, too. I could pretend for a moment he was the person I had fallen in love with. I could pretend that he didn't despise me, didn't look down on me for my superficiality or anything else.

He shot me a mischievous glance. "Maybe I do know, but it's

unimportant. In any event, the Lightfoots left that portion of the property alone. Gradually, through the years, we Warwicks laid claim to it. Finally, at the turn of the century, we got the county to cut a new access road that divided the Lightfoot property into two parts. The part where your grandmother's house stands and the part that's on the mountain."

He stopped expectantly.

I thought I knew where he was going but . . . "I come into this how?"

"Because, my dear innocent," he said patiently, "your grandmother was the descendent of Larkin Lightfoot and his half-Cherokee wife. Research says you are his only legal descendent."

"Really?" Exciting though it was to hear the history of my father's family, I had reservations. "When did you find this out?"

"A few years back when Jeffrey was doing a title search on the land so he could begin to mine it. When he found we didn't have rights to the whole mountain, he discovered your grandmother did but she wouldn't sell or . . . To make a long story short, Jeffrey needs you to sign a quitclaim deed relinquishing any ownership, including mineral rights, that you could legitimately lay claim to in the mountain. There isn't a financial institution in the world that will back his development plans until the title is absolutely sudsy squeaky clean."

I digested this in silence.

Cavanagh and his father wanted me to sign a quitclaim deed. Gareth wanted me not to.

That was the reason Cavanagh had come to New York. That was the reason Gareth was spending time with me now.

"Was this why your family argued the night of the fire on the yacht?"

His face clouded. "Yes. Grandmama was adamantly against the project, but Jeffrey had talked some of the others around, and they were pushing to go ahead. Her death put everything on hold. Her cousin Alonzo was sole trustee of her shares and he refused to do other than what Grandmama had wanted. He held Jeffrey off by simply not making a decision. The trust ended when I turned thirty last month. Her assets are being dispersed."

I was beginning to understand. "So how does it stand now?"

"Jeffrey's promoted his scheme for the past ten years. He thinks he has the votes to start mining. But even if that's true, he still needs your quitclaim deed."

"And you?" I needed to hear it from him. "What is it you want from me?"

"What do I want?" He put his hands behind his head and leaned back in his seat and looked out at the wind-chopped lake. "They'll be willing to pay you a lot of money if you sign."

I impatiently lifted a hand. "I have money. What is it you want me to do?"

He turned to look me in the eye. "Suffice it to say I don't want the mountain brought down to a pile of rubble and then rebuilt as a water park, no matter how computerized and how top of the line and how good for the local economy it might be. I don't want Slumber Mountain destroyed and a resort village built up over its ruins. Do you?"

That in a nutshell was why he had invited me to ride with him today.

I couldn't let him see how much I cared what he wanted, what kind of power he had over me. I couldn't go through his rejection again.

What I could do was use the unsuspected weapon he had handed me.

He didn't let me mull for long. "Will you sign a quitclaim?"

I shrugged. "Maybe."

Study the alternatives, I told myself. As long as I put off a decision, Gareth would talk to me, stay close to me. "What do the rest of your family think?"

"Many of them are for it, but they've been lobbied so long by Cavanagh and his parents, they don't know if it's a good idea or not. I'm making inroads, but it's hard." He removed his hands from behind his head and cranked the car. He looked tired.

"Artemesia is on your side."

"Yes. And others." He left the car in neutral, faced me over the gearshift. "You won't sign your rights over to Cavanagh, will you?"

Of course not, I started to say.

But once he had my promise, would I see him again? Or would he go away, look at me as if I were a stranger? This could be an advantage. If I had time enough, I could change the way he thought of me, make him see the woman I had become rather than the contemptible waif I'd been.

Other men wanted me. Why shouldn't he? A smart woman would seize the opportunity to try out her wiles.

"I'll talk it over with you before I do anything drastic. I'll promise you that much."

He put the car in reverse. "I guess that'll have to do, then, won't it?"

When we started out, he didn't seem nearly so tired. My answer had satisfied him.

The drive home was better than I'd expected. When a deer flashed across in front of us, barely missing our car going up the mountain, we were able to share the shock and chatter about our close escape as if we were friends.

Perhaps, I told myself, he's beginning to like me.

That was all I wanted.

CHAPTER FOURTEEN

AT DINNER THAT night, I wore a Nicole Miller rose-colored embroidered taffeta that brought out the color in my cheeks and set off the blue of my eyes. Since I'd worn it before and garnered lavish compliments, I assumed Gareth would be suitably impressed.

No such luck. One day I would learn not to anticipate Gareth Warwick's reactions.

He did smile and speak to me with undeniable warmth as he stopped for a few minutes when he came into the dining hall. But then he went through the buffet line and took his seat at the head table. His earnest conversation proved he'd forgotten my presence, forgotten I existed.

Still working to garner votes.

His hair was parted and left loose, so that the dark strands concealed the hairline. I would have liked to push them aside and examine his forehead, see for myself how bad a bruise had been left. I was still undecided about what to think about his accident.

Cavanagh had hit Gareth. They'd almost come to blows before so this shouldn't be so surprising. And he might not have seen Gareth fall overboard. He wouldn't have deliberately left Gareth in the water to drown, no matter what animosity lay between them.

Cavanagh might be angry with Gareth for standing in the way of his father's plans, but he wouldn't do that. Not to his own cousin.

I stole a glance at Cavanagh on my right. He watched Gareth as closely as I did.

Gareth had all but admitted Cavanagh was responsible for the bruise, but he'd also said Cavanagh hadn't meant to kill him.

No, Cavanagh wouldn't kill his cousin.

I laid down my seafood fork. Neither he nor Gareth would ever admit what had really happened. If only I could read minds.

After dinner Gareth's efforts didn't stop when we went into the back area that held the organ. He fell into step with yet another group of Warwicks. Cavanagh had me go on ahead while he lingered with his father. Both stayed well away from Gareth.

Tonight a different quartet of musical Warwicks were set to entertain. They brought out an oboe, a flute, a lute, and a full-sized harp to lull us into lethargy with soporific instrumentals.

At least the organ wasn't moaning out its gloom and doom airs.

Was every evening here spent listening to competent but not expert musicians?

Looked like none of the others shared my dismay. I chose a comfortable chair against the wall and hoped I wouldn't go to sleep.

Gareth didn't pretend to listen. He was hard at work across the room, cornering one group and then another, laughing and joking. Persuading.

At the other end of the room, Eleanor and her husband were doing the same thing. Cavanagh watched them but took a seat beside me. He had little to say and looked as tired as Gareth had earlier.

We didn't discuss the afternoon. I started to ask if he had thrown Gareth in the lake and left him to drown, but I didn't. If he had, he wouldn't admit it.

When he got up and brought us drinks, I thanked him politely and pretended not to notice how quiet he was. I was glad he didn't talk. I didn't want to learn that he had deliberately tried to kill his cousin.

There's no proof, I soothed my conscience. Gareth wants to leave it be.

The truth was that I didn't want to confront Cavanagh. Even if he did have another strike against him.

Had he deliberately sought me out to get me to sign over any rights to property on the mountain I might claim? Had he set out from the beginning to use me?

Everywhere I turned, people were using me. Sponsors, photographers, magazine editors, my agent Ruth, and Cavanagh. Even Gareth had turned on the charm when he found I hadn't agreed to sign Gram's property over to Cavanagh.

I'd hoped when I got to this point in my career I would have it made. I'd planned to use my wealth to thumb my nose at everyone and what they thought.

Fat chance. It hadn't happened. I might as well accept that it never would.

Not with these dormant feelings for Gareth Warwick emerging.

He's a man, I told myself. You've dealt with men before. Gareth isn't any different.

Except he was because I loved him.

Impatient, I took a sip of the drink Cavanagh had brought. The tiniest hint of rum and several exotic fruits made up a concoction that tasted extraordinarily bland. I took another sip, and found the mixture quite flavorful. "This is wonderful. Thank you, Cavanagh."

He smiled at me, a sweet smile almost like Gareth's.

Hmm. Could the drink be more potent than it seemed? Did

Cavanagh mean to use it to make me sign a quitclaim deed? Memories of his coffee came back, the way his hands had twisted a paper. A paper that could have been a deed.

How fanciful. One thing was certain, though. I should never have allowed Cavanagh to get close to me, to touch me, kiss me. I should never have encouraged him to think I might love him.

Whether he'd meant to leave Gareth in the water or not, I was afraid that like his mother, deep down inside, under that amiable exterior, Cavanagh hid another personality.

One controlled and calculating.

His eyes, like his mother's, occasionally cold beneath their luster, gave him away. He had hidden motives that I hadn't known about, maybe other motives that no one knew about. I would do well not to trust Cavanagh.

I didn't trust Cavanagh, but even he wouldn't drug me with his family surrounding us. The drink in my hand looked innocuous, and it tasted all right. Two sips wouldn't be enough to hurt me. Of course not. Maybe a little more . . .

The music was quiet and soothing. I was tired. My breathing grew even as the harpist executed a lengthy interlude of unbelievable intricacy and dexterity. I needed to close my eyes.

No! I jerked awake.

I couldn't go to sleep. The Warwicks would snicker amongst themselves about how the poor ragamuffin couldn't appreciate good music. Worse, what if I snored? They wouldn't forget that either.

My head was way too heavy for my neck. I could hardly hold it upright. Maybe if I leaned back.

I tried to stay awake, but my eyelids kept drooping . Perhaps if I closed my eyes.

Just for a moment.

* * * *

LOUD WORDS PUMMELED me. Shouting, rude voices hurt my ears and shocked me out of a peaceful black void.

People argued over my head, but my eyes were glued shut.

No way was I going to pry them open and see what they were fighting about. If whoever was shouting would hush, I could go back to sleep.

"He doesn't want to admit he's wrong."

"That isn't true. All I'm saying is we have to think carefully about changing our code."

That was Gareth. He sounded quite close.

I tried to wake up to see how close, but my eyelids refused to budge.

"Jeffrey is right. The good we could do must be taken into consideration." That was Eleanor. I recognized her regal tones.

"What good?" Gareth's heartfelt cry made me jump. "Can't you see that in the end it means destruction?"

"Not if we use the mountain's force correctly."

Some more Warwicks chimed in. "We could do away with sickness."

"We could put an end to all the destructive weapons mankind has developed."

"We could clear up pollution."

Gareth laughed harshly. "How? By giving this kind of power to one man? And what will keep him from misusing it?"

"Not one man." Eleanor spoke again. "We are the Custodians. We'll all share in making the decisions."

Silence. Someone took a deep breath.

"All right," Gareth said. "Let's think about this logically."

His hair would be falling into his face and his long hands pushing it back impatiently. I wanted to see him. Again I tried to open my eyes.

That fruity punch had put me to sleep. So delicious. Had I finished it?

Gareth went on, "Suppose a group of people can wield this kind of power without being corrupted themselves. How do you plan to control it?"

"United we'll be strong enough." Eleanor radiated certainty. "All of us together can handle it."

"If you believe that, you've been misled." Gareth remained reasonable. "Why were we given the task of guarding the mountain's spirit if it could be controlled? Don't you think we'd have discovered before now how to harness it if there was a way to do so safely?"

Eleanor again. "We've gone over this thoroughly. The pool above the seat of power will filter the magnetism so that the mountain's spirit will vent from its bed with less force. Our united minds will attack it, diluting its strength when it comes through the mediary—"

"Through Lindy, damn you! Call her by her name!"

What had I done that merely speaking my name brought out such anger in Gareth?

Not that I cared enough to protest. This apathy was rather restful.

Gareth calmed. "She has a name. Say what you mean, Aunt

Eleanor. Harming an innocent woman who never hurt us is surely not part of our code."

Was he worried about me? I should have been soaring, but all I could summon was a vague interest. I struggled to open my eyelids, but they remained glued tight.

That damned drink.

If I ever woke up, I'd never accept another drink from a Warwick.

"Belinda won't be harmed." That was Cavanagh.

A female Warwick soothed, "She's the mediary, Gareth. She bears the mark. She would be here regardless. There's no reason to think she'll be harmed more by attempting this deviation than if we carried through with the original ritual."

"You've been brainwashed." Gareth's calm made him all the more convincing. "Jeffrey Tansey's grandiose ideas caused half our number to be killed ten years ago in the fire, and he'll be the cause of others' deaths tomorrow night if you do this."

Eleanor flared back, "Jeffrey had nothing to do with what happened. And simply because he has high ideals doesn't make him wrong! It wasn't his fault that certain members of the family forced an unnecessary contest. It wasn't his fault some died. He wasn't even there."

"An idealist can be as dangerous as a criminal." Gareth sounded weary. "Jeffrey's schemes started this division among us."

"Division?" Cavanagh asked. "Most of us here are in agreement. Do you refuse to do it, Gareth? Shall I challenge you for the right to be the conductor?"

A hush pounded the air.

I lay with shuttered eyes, wondering what they debated, why it mattered so much, what I had to do with any of the Warwicks' business.

"As you will," Gareth said finally. "I can't stop you."

"By the goddess, perhaps I shall!"

The silence pressed.

Then different people exclaimed softly until Eleanor's strained voice said, "Cavanagh, please. Gareth, don't make it come to that. Join us. This is our last chance for another century to test our theory. Once we harness it, we could do away with wars and starvation. Even disease."

"How? By becoming dictators ourselves? Because that's what would happen, Aunt Eleanor. You know it's true. Once we get in a position to force everyone else to obey our mandates, we'd be worse than the scourges we want to abolish."

"The boy's right." The quavering voice sounded familiar. Ah, the old man of my previous dream ten years before. What had they called him?

"Alonzo, spare us your homilies," Eleanor snapped. "We're well aware of your opinions."

Alonzo. Of course. Gareth's grandmother had named him trustee of her estate. In life. Maybe he was trustee in this dream, too. Would he wear those filmy robes this time?

I wanted to giggle but couldn't.

"We must adhere to our code," Gareth said.

"Those opinions bind us to rites originating in the dark ages," Cavanagh scoffed.

"But they've been tested and proven. They've never failed us in the past," Gareth countered. "That fact alone is deserving of consideration. Besides, Lindy may refuse to act as mediary. She has that right. Will you force your wills upon her, too?"

"We'll settle that. Now. Here," Cavanagh said. "We'll let her choose. Mother, wake her up."

I heard the swishing sound of silk and smelled, as in that other fantastic dream years ago, roses. Cloying, heavy roses, reaching out to drench me in their overpowering odor. Then fading, becoming delicate, soothing.

"Belinda," Eleanor said beside my ear. "Belinda, open your eyes."

Now my eyelids moved. I no longer wanted to giggle.

The Warwicks gathered around me in a circle two and three and four people deep.

Sure enough, dress clothes of dark suits and colorful party dresses had given way to those white gauzy garments that seemed to float.

When had they found time to change clothes?

Never mind.

They were enchanting. A group of real life fairies gathered round to stare at an oddity.

Me.

Despite my profession, I detest being stared at. But here I indulged them. I could endure these stares with perfect tranquility because this was a dream.

Gareth stood slightly to the side, alone, while Cavanagh waited behind his mother. They were handsome men, both of them, evenly matched in height and weight.

For a moment, with their hair falling down past their jawlines, they reminded me of gladiators in some Roman emperor's court, waiting to see who would win the right to vie for the prize. Or perhaps prehistoric priests, waiting for a sign to tell which sacrifice the oracle would choose.

Imagination again. From the drink. I'd have to remember . . .

Both men watched me unblinkingly, Cavanagh with too-bright eyes and an excitement he didn't bother to hide. Gareth with tight lips and shuttered face that told nothing of his feelings.

Darling Gareth.

The little boy had worn that same face, grief for his grandfather hidden behind the mask until my coaxing made it spill over so that he could cry in my arms.

Love swelled, filled my heart.

That was why I could never forget Gareth. I had loved him as a little girl and I loved him as a woman. How clear dreams made everything.

"Belinda," Eleanor crooned.

She stood right beside me. I tried to look, but my eyes wouldn't focus properly.

"It's all right, dear, you don't have to wake up completely. You're going to be given a great opportunity tomorrow night, an opportunity few people are offered. We need to know whether or not you will take it."

"An opportunity?" I was dull, couldn't understand. My throat felt scratchy and dry.

"Yes. Don't speak, dear. Not yet. Let me explain. You remember our last little bargain, don't you? I kept my word, didn't I? You've been successful. You've become famous. You've made more than enough money to last you the rest of your life, haven't you?"

It was true.

"Do you remember how you felt?" she whispered. "That night when you loaned your soul to the mountain? Do you remember how wonderful it was?"

I did. I'd wanted to stay there forever, but Gareth had made me come back.

Gareth.

I wanted to be angry with him, but I couldn't.

My love for him was a sickness that devoured me. I would do his bidding, give him whatever he wanted. One day I would have him or I would lose him, and until then I was doomed to this limbo, a place where waiting had become a habit.

Eleanor cleared her throat. It sounded as dry as mine. "You do remember. I can tell. No, you don't need to try to speak. Not yet. Right now, I want to ask you a favor. I can't bargain with you as I did before, Belinda. This time your word will have to be freely given, without coercion or bribes. You're attuned to the mountain, attuned in a way that few people can ever be. You've been into its depths, joined its soul. Tomorrow night, the mountain is going to try to destroy itself. If it succeeds, it will destroy everything on it and in it and around it."

She went on, conjuring up scenes of mass destruction.

Flumes of lava, plumes of steam, raging fires, and crashing rocks. Beautiful tall trees tumbling like broken Popsicle sticks. Green shrubs overrun by the hot stream. Squirrels, deer, raccoons, and all the wild creatures that had been a joyous part of my childhood, running for their lives.

And Lassitan, the town. Destroyed house by house. Screaming people trapped inside their homes. Parents trying to protect their children as they ran toward shelter.

Not even the lake would be safe from the molten horrors the mountain would loose.

The potential destruction came to vivid life in Eleanor's description.

My body jerked. I tried to sob, but couldn't.

"You understand, don't you? You don't want all that to happen, do you?" Eleanor asked.

Such horror? Of course I didn't.

"You can stop it, dear," Eleanor purred. "Since you're attuned to the mountain, you can channel its destructive rage so that it can be used to advantage. We intend to capture its power and harness it so that it will help mankind rather than destroying everything in its path. To do that, we need your help."

Gareth rasped, "Save the propaganda, Aunt Eleanor. Give her the choices."

Eleanor inhaled and exhaled in displeased gusts. "We need you regardless, Belinda. Either to harness the mountain's force or to channel it back into the rock before it destroys itself and everything around it. You must be here so that we can complete the ritual and control the power. Will you do your part?"

I looked at Gareth, trying to see what he wanted me to do.

"Tell her the choices." He kept dispassionate eyes on me.

Eleanor huffed, but her hand stroked my hair. "You can stay and join with the mountain's spirit to save it, or you can do nothing and go back to your life. I don't think you can choose to do nothing, can you? You have too much compassion. You care too much."

Gareth might want me to refuse Eleanor, to choose to do nothing about the havoc to come. But if I did, I'd be sent away and never see him again.

Besides, I couldn't leave the mountain. It offered no rage. Only peace.

Anticipation stirred as I relived the stone encompassing and sheltering me. What I wouldn't give to feel that peace again.

Gareth might be afraid for me. Or maybe he was annoyed that the rest of his family joined with Eleanor in wanting to use the mountain for good.

I must be as superficial as he charged because I didn't care which side of the Warwicks won whatever it was they struggled over.

But I couldn't stand by and allow the mountain to destroy itself and the town around it. And I wouldn't willingly leave Gareth.

Once before I had run away from life to lick my wounds with Gram. This time I would fight for what I wanted.

"Yes," I murmured. "I'll stay."

"I knew we could count on you." Eleanor sounded satisfied. "Cavanagh, take her up to bed."

"No!" The strength of my reply surprised even me. "Gareth."

Cavanagh's face darkened. He took a step forward. Had it not been a dream, I would have been afraid.

"I told you," he said to his mother through clenched teeth. He whirled to address the others. "Gareth bound her. He bound her to himself when he bound her to the mountain ten years ago. He pretends to be so very good, so very ethical. Yet he's bound an unprotected soul because he wanted her himself."

The Warwicks gathered around us gasped.

Not Gareth. He gave his strange chuckle. Then, as if he could not contain himself, loosed peals of outright laughter.

The others turned, one by one, watching him as he laughed like a madman.

The laughter floated crazily up into the high-ceilinged room. Each peal hit the rafters and splintered.

I was the crazy one. How could I see a sound?

The peals vanished when Gareth stopped laughing. "Bound her to me?" His lip curled in a twisted smile. "No, Cavanagh. You're far off the mark. I've never bound her to me, knowingly or not. Her will is too strong to be bound to any person. I could barely bring her out of the mountain when she merged with it. You have my oath she is not bound to me."

"Then why is she so resistant to—?" Cavanagh bit his lip.

"To what?" Gareth prodded. "Is that why you've been trying to feed her Eleanor's potions? Did you intend to bind her to you while she was insensible?"

"Cavanagh wouldn't do such a thing," Eleanor cried.

"Yet you believe that I would? Do all of you believe that of me?" Gareth looked around the group as if gauging their faces. "Never mind. I tell you again under oath that the only time I bound her, I bound her for the mountain. Even then I nearly lost her. None of you understand the strength of her character."

His relatives' faces told nothing. He shook his head. "My oath is all I can give you."

"That's enough for me," one of the Warwicks said, and the others murmured agreement. "She's got the mark. She's doubtless guarded against such things."

"I'll take her upstairs." Cavanagh started forward.

Gareth forestalled him. "She asked for me. Until tomorrow night is past, I'm still the conductor."

Cavanagh ceded his place to his cousin, however unwillingly, however angrily.

Gareth strode over, stared down, and reached out for me with gentle hands. "All right, Lindy. You've made your choice. Rest now."

A great sweetness fell over me, a contentment like that I'd felt inside the mountain.

After he lifted me, I remembered nothing.

* * * *

I AWOKE IN the Blue Bedroom with my black nightgown on, no clue as to how I'd gotten there. The clock said three-thirty, but moonlight flooded my room and made it bright as day.

What had happened?

I was listening to awful music. Then Cavanagh had given me a drink. I hadn't wanted it, but it tasted so good I'd taken a couple of sips. Or more?

Oh Lord, no. I hadn't gotten drunk. Please, no. I closed my eyes.

But I must have, because another one of those strange dreams had befallen me.

What had Cavanagh put in that drink? I shouldn't have drunk any of it.

It was this house! This house and all the eccentric people surrounding me. They were driving me crazy.

Why had I ever come back to this place?

I relived the moment in my dream when Gareth had reached out for me. I had been so thankful that he and not Cavanagh would be the one to put me to bed.

My eyes flew open. Had he?

Had I dreamed of Gareth reaching for me because he'd actually carried me upstairs? Had he undressed me, put on my nightgown, laid me between the sheets?

Calm down, calm down.

No. Surely not.

Cavanagh would have gone ballistic at the idea of Gareth putting me to bed. Eleanor must be responsible. Not even Eleanor, annoyed with me as she was for not favoring her darling son, would let a man undress me.

Fully awake, I got up. My mouth tasted funny.

Creeping onto the balcony, I viewed the serene courtyard and the large center pool. The fountain's spray glistened in the moonlight, but the pool water was dark, so dark as to make me shiver.

Where was Gareth's room situated?

He'd come down the hall from that side where any one of several balconies might be his. If he had an inside room which he might not. But if he did, there were no lights, no way to distinguish behind which door he might be sleeping.

What a fool I was, to be out here mooning over a man who probably wished me to the devil. He had to be disgusted if I'd gotten so drunk I couldn't find my way to bed.

All his opinions would be confirmed. I was superficial, unintelligent, and a sot to boot.

Like my mother.

My stomach threatened to upchuck. Holding it, I bent over. Why couldn't I learn? But there had seemed so little rum in the concoction Cavanagh had brought me. The drink had seemed so harmless.

I slid down to the floor of the tiny balcony, my knees beneath the nightgown drawn up to my chin, and my arms wrapped around them.

If I could see Gareth, I could explain to him that I didn't normally drink too much—hardly ever drank at all—and never ever passed out at dinner parties. If only I could find him, tell him I had no intentions of signing that quitclaim deed over to Cavanagh.

That had to be what brought on that horrible dream, the rivalry between Gareth and Cavanagh as to the future of the mountain and surrounding land.

There was no other reason for such strange dreams.

In the white of the moon, I laid my chin on top of my knees.

Then, drawn by some unknown force to look up at the night sky, I found the five stars in the pattern of two perfect isosceles triangles standing tip to tip, with one star acting as a point for both. From the time I'd noted the stars earlier, they had moved closer together.

Almost as close as the five moles on my wrist that I unconsciously fingered.

In the courtyard, movement. Two figures strolled to the pool. At its edge, they looked into its depths and murmured.

Jeffrey and Eleanor.

Jeffrey was shorter so when Eleanor took his face between her hands, she had to bend slightly. I could see her mouth move but couldn't hear what she was saying. When she finished, Jeffrey's shoulders drooped. She spoke directly into his face, more urgently than before. He straightened and nodded unenthusiastically.

Whatever she wanted, he was agreeing.

She patted his cheek. Then they embraced and started back to the house, his arm around her waist and hers around his shoulder.

The middle of the night was a strange time for Cavanagh's parents to be awake and out in the courtyard. When they were gone, the moon and stars shed a pale glow on the empty courtyard, turning the fountain's spray into silver as it fell into the pool.

After a while, I came in and went back to bed.

CHAPTER FIFTEEN

TENSION CRACKLED THE next morning.

Planning to walk in the woods after breakfast, I'd dressed in jeans and my favorite blue shirt. I picked up a windbreaker as an afterthought, and then went downstairs, braced for curious or hostile stares. The dignified Warwicks could sneer or snicker because of my drunken debacle of the past night. I would hold my chin up and pretend nothing was amiss.

Strangely, there were no comments or knowing glances. No one acted any differently than they had the day before.

Then I found out why.

Their focus was elsewhere. The strain showed in the hushed tones of the Warwicks at their different tables and in Eleanor's distracted greeting.

Pouring some coffee, I got a piece of plain wheat toast and found a corner. Preoccupied Warwicks around me nodded but went back to their private murmurings.

Jeffrey, forehead creased, added to the tension when he came in. "Has anyone seen Cavanagh?"

"No." Eleanor couldn't hide her unease. "Not this morning."

Other Warwicks shook their heads. The faces turned toward Jeffrey were blank, not inquisitive or knowing. The air fairly vibrated.

Whatever was going on had nothing to do with me.

Jeffrey went out of the dining room, presumably to look for his son.

I was more interested in Gareth's whereabouts.

Pride forbade me to ask about him, but after breakfast, a surreptitious search revealed he wasn't in the living area or the game room or the library. When I walked past the bookshelves though, I saw him in the courtyard.

He was watching the koi in the pond. Alone, for once.

Donning my windbreaker, I rushed out the library's French doors to where he stood and plunged into a nervous apology. "Gareth, I'm afraid I got a little high last night."

A smile lurked in the back of his eyes. "Did you? Really? No one noticed."

"I didn't disgrace myself?"

"No." He pretended to think. "Unless you're talking about your bending Alton's flute with your foot before you pushed Marianna's head through her harp strings."

I hoped he was teasing. "They were quite good. But terribly tranquilizing."

"They were terrible, period. Although there are certain things one can't say to family. I think everyone forced to listen to them would have cheered if you *had* attacked them."

"Did you—How did I get to bed?"

"Artemesia sat right behind you and saw you nod off. She got me to help her walk you up. Nobody else noticed."

He grinned at my relief. "But to fall asleep in the middle of Weiss. My, my. It'll be a long time before any of our musicians ever play for you again." He clucked solemnly before his mouth twitched. "Lucky you."

Glad he was upbeat, I fell in beside him when he started back to the house. "I'll apologize to them."

"Don't you dare. You'll just encourage them. Besides, I told you no one noticed when we left. That included the musicians. If you can call them that."

He hooked his thumbs in his jeans pockets. Was it to make sure he didn't have to touch me? My warm glow faded. He still treated me like a pariah.

"I enjoyed hearing them play."

"Don't bother to lie." In a quick subject change, he said, "I understand you're all set to leave tomorrow. Have you had a good time here?"

"I . . . Yes." Except for getting what I came after.

That thought led to another.

What had I come after?

Go ahead. Admit it.

Gareth.

He said, "I hope our problems here didn't affect your visit."

"The problems between you and Cavanagh?"

He gave a quick sidelong glance. "Actually, they're more between me and his parents. I can't fault Cavanagh for being loyal to his mother and father. In any event, you should never have been brought into our quarrel. I'm sorry you were."

A slow burn began at the base of my stomach. "Do you get to New York often?"

"No. The last visit was my first in nearly ten years. I've been . . . busy."

"Come see me."

"I thought you were going to retire at the end of the year." His ironic half-grin twisted his mouth. "I can't come and see you in New York if you've left town for the Ozarks, can I?"

A rock made me stumble. He caught me, righted me, just as quickly removed his hand.

The Ozarks? I hadn't told anyone about my plans to quit modeling except for David, my agent's husband and financial advisor. David wouldn't reveal client information to anyone, though. That would be unethical.

But he was as awed by the Warwicks as everyone else.

I got back in step with Gareth's strolling gait. "I'm not sure whether or not I'll retire. I don't know where I'd go if I did."

"You could come back here."

What did that mean? "I could. I have good memories of here, of Pop and Gram. But Lassitan has changed so much, with all the second homes being built and the new people moving in. It wouldn't be the same."

I waited for him to speak, to ask me why I didn't mention my mother, to say he'd come to see me if I returned home. To say he'd like me to come back.

He slowed down. "You've changed, too. Perhaps you're right to stay away. The past is the past."

Alonzo Warwick came out and called to him.

"I have to go." As Gareth left, he spoke over his shoulder without looking back. "Your stepfather's dead, Lindy. He burned to death in an automobile accident shortly after you went to live with Ruth and David."

I whimpered, froze in my tracks. All the sickening memories so carefully put away came back to torment me. How did he know about my stepfather? No wonder I disgusted him. How long had he known?

How did he know?

He heard my whimper, whirled, reached me in two steps, and took my shoulders. He looked me in the eye with gentleness devoid of pity. "Things like that are never the victim's fault, Lindy. You've put what happened behind you. Your mother's dead and he's dead. It's time to let it go."

The same thing my shrink had been telling me. The same thing Gram had tried to tell me.

A sound, part sob, part strangled gasp, came out from a deep hole inside me.

My loss for words didn't bother Gareth.

He kneaded my shoulders, and there was no aversion in his fingers, only kindness. "Let it go. The past doesn't matter. Only the future. And that you can try to arrange. Sometimes it even works out the way you want." Then he fell back and with an unconcerned, "I'll see you later," left me to join his older relative. The white cat appeared from nowhere to jump up into his arms and be carried off.

Blindly, I sat down on a bench that overlooked the lake in the distance, soaking in his words, wondering how he'd found out, how he'd known. How long he'd known.

Wrapping my arms around myself, I tried to warm the cold that pulsed through me.

I was seventeen years old again, scared and defenseless and worst of all, engulfed in that dirty feeling that wouldn't go away.

"He can't make you happy."

I jumped nearly as high as the white cat could spring. "Cavanagh!"

The last person I wanted to see at this moment.

And I didn't need his accusing words on top of Gareth's bald statement. "Don't sneak up on people like that. And why would you say that to me?"

"I know how you feel about Gareth. You don't even try to hide it." His smile, so much like Gareth's, brought out none of the yearning that Gareth's could. "He's not worthy of you. He's had his head stuck in the sand for years, traipsing about Europe and Africa with some environmental group or other. He wouldn't come back and train with the family like the rest of us. Now, after we've done all the exploration and engineering, he thinks he can come in and go thumbs down on the whole project."

"What do you plan to do?" I asked directly. "Strip-mine the mountain and turn it into a resort area?"

"The Warwicks are entrepreneurs. That's the way we operate. We make deals to make money. Just like you. You wheel and deal in your looks, your face, your body. You sell them to make people buy things they don't need and don't want. We do the same thing except that in this case, we're going to be helping an awful lot of people in Lassitan in the process. So don't look down your nose at me, little Lindy Rand."

From him, my name was a sneer.

"I'm not looking down my nose at you, Cavanagh." I almost pitied him, despite what he'd done to Gareth. "Heaven knows I'm the last person in the world to look down my nose at anyone."

His demeanor softened. "Then give me a chance to make you change your mind. I'm crazy about you, Belinda. I'd do anything for you."

He tried to take my hands, but I pulled them away and put them behind my back.

"Cavanagh, I don't love you. I've told you I don't. It would be unfair to pretend I do. I think it's for the best that I'm leaving in the morning."

"You already knew about the mineral in the mountain, didn't you?" Suspicion dawned. "What else has Gareth told you?"

"He's told me about the quitclaim deed you want from me."

"Did he also tell you why I want it? Did he say that the economy in Lassitan will boom if we do this? People around here who've never known anything but poverty will have a decent income for the first time in their lives. Lassitan will become a place on the map, a tourist attraction for the world. Did he tell you all that, or did he give you the song and dance about keeping the mountain pure and natural?"

"He hasn't talked to me about much of anything except to say you need the deed before you can go ahead with the project."

"Will you give it to me?"

Pretty blunt. Cavanagh's true colors were coming out. Now I could say the word to him without hesitation. "No."

A muscle in his throat throbbed. "In spite of what I've explained to you, how the economy, the people of this area can be lifted out of poverty, you refuse to sign a miserable little piece of paper that would let it all happen?"

"I can't sign it."

"You mean you won't."

"All right. I won't." So easy to say. There'd been no reason not to be honest before. Maybe it had taken Gareth's return to put some spine in me.

Cavanagh's calm was deceptive. "I hope you don't live to regret your decision."

He almost said something else but instead, left. His back was stiff and unforgiving.

It was a very unsatisfactory beginning to my last day on Slumber Mountain.

* * * *

EVERYONE WAS AFFECTED in one way or another by the split within the family.

Though I didn't care about the family feud, I did care about leaving Gareth. Before we were separated, I'd like to touch him, hold him. Artemesia didn't act like a girlfriend, but he might have one somewhere to explain his remoteness.

But he hadn't kissed me at the houseboat the day before against his will.

I might have instigated it, but he'd returned my kiss with as much fervor as I could hope for. What if I came up to him and put my hand on his arm and smiled up at him like a woman wanting to be kissed? What would he do?

There was nothing to keep me from finding out. Today was my last chance.

Boldly, I marched back into the house to make plans.

The hard part was getting Gareth alone. He was continually at the center of a small circle of Warwicks, still trying to get his votes for the business meeting scheduled the next day.

Finally, after lunch, I saw him going out the side entrance in a sweater, jeans, and athletic shoes.

I wouldn't demean myself by running after him. I'd wait till he got back and ambush him. Then Cavanagh, dressed in sweats, headed in the same direction as Gareth.

Perhaps I was being unduly suspicious, but Cavanagh had put that bruise on Gareth's temple.

If Cavanagh had thrown Gareth off the houseboat to drown, a witness might stop a like attempt today.

I shrugged on my windbreaker as I hurried down the steps of the deck. I had to run to keep Cavanagh in sight. After a few minutes he overtook Gareth in a secluded clearing with a steep drop-off that overlooked the northern edge of town.

I came up close enough to see Gareth stop and turn. Close enough to hear him say, "I was expecting you, cuz."

So a rescue wasn't necessary. I sheltered behind tall underbrush and caught my breath. Should I show myself or slink away before they saw me?

Cavanagh held something in his hand. "Were you? It won't make any difference."

"There are others besides me who're against this. Your father won't win."

"He will if you run away again. You've been gone so long that most of the family already believe you don't care. If you leave, they'll know it was because you couldn't stop our development."

"Ah, but I can stop it. If I get enough votes." Gareth's eyes never left Cavanagh. "And I'm close."

"You won't get them." Cavanagh raised the thing he held. I heard the dull thud as he slapped it against his hand.

A metal pipe. Cavanagh meant to attack Gareth.

No decision to make. I stepped forward. "I'm here."

Cavanagh whirled.

Gareth moved fast, reaching for and catching the lead pipe.

Cavanagh cursed, held onto it with one hand, and hit out with the other.

Gareth dodged the fist, pulled on the pipe, and kicked Cavanagh in the left knee.

Cavanagh went down and as quickly bobbed up, but Gareth had the pipe now. "Give it up, cuz. You can't win by killing off the opposition. Not this time."

I held my hand over my mouth to keep from screaming out.

Cavanagh was the first to step back. "You've always had your way, haven't you? Aunt Annora always petted you, giving you whatever you wanted. Too bad she's not here now. You'll find it's not so easy when there's no one who'll interfere."

"For pity's sake, Cavanagh. I was her grandson. Aunt Eleanor gave you as much as Grandmama gave me. If I was petted, then so were you. But you can't get your way all the time by playing rough. One of these days, you're going to have to learn that."

After a long moment, Cavanagh said, "We'll meet again, cuz." He brushed by me. "You're backing the wrong horse, Belinda. Gareth has managed to convince only a handful of the family that this development is bad."

I stood well back from him.

When he'd gone, I turned to Gareth.

He stood on some spongy lacy moss. Behind him the autumn trees gapped to show, far below, a vista of rolling fields dotted with tiny homes that looked like doll houses.

His shuttered eyes concealed more than I could ever plumb.

I stuck my hands in my pockets to keep them from shaking. "He tried to kill you."

"No. Just put me out of commission." He threw the pipe down. "It's a cousinly tradition."

I hated him being so flippant. "You have to tell someone about Cavanagh."

"I'll handle it. Forget it, Lindy."

"What if he had managed to kill you with that pipe?"

"He didn't want to kill me, just frighten me. Cavanagh's been brainwashed by his parents. He thinks he has to bulldoze people into submission."

I bit my lip. "Gareth, tell someone. Alonzo or Artemesia. Maybe that man who took the Nautique out to rescue you yesterday."

Some of the tension left his shoulders. He even smiled. "It's all right, Lindy. Cavanagh has a temper. But so do I. Forget what happened just now. Please."

I bit my lip. Maybe it was my fault Cavanagh had tried to kill

Gareth. "I told Cavanagh I won't sign a quitclaim on the property over to him."

Something flickered on his features before caution reclaimed them. "I'm glad." In his sweater and jeans, he looked very young, as young as he'd been ten years ago. His dark straight hair, cropped neatly below the collar, fell rebelliously toward his face. "What did Cavanagh say when you told him?"

"Nothing. But he tried to hurt you."

My fingers itched to push back the lock of hair hiding his bruise from yesterday. What could he do? Send me away? I was leaving tomorrow anyway.

"Lindy," he said as I moved toward him, but there was no real sharpness in his protest, only resignation.

"I want to see if your bruise is better."

"I'd rather you didn't."

"Why? Can't you bear for a woman to touch you? Or is it something else?"

"You know why, Lindy."

I swallowed, afraid I did. "It is me. You can't bear for me to touch you because of my past. Because my stepfather raped me." He'd found out and that was why he despised me.

Don't let me throw up. Don't let me be sick in front of him.

"No." He put out a hand but let it drop. "Dear God." He looked skyward, and then back at me. His words were almost inaudible. "You're right about one thing, Lindy. I can't bear for you to touch me."

I froze. What I most feared. He'd never feel anything but pity for someone like me.

Get away. Go on before you barf right here.

My feet wouldn't move.

"Not because of what happened to you," he said, louder. "I told you it wasn't your fault. And it wasn't. No, the reason I don't want you to touch me is . . . I've always had a soft spot for you. Ever since I was nine years old, when we met. Do you remember that summer? And when we were together in New York, when we . . . I almost didn't leave you. I almost persuaded myself I'd be okay if I stayed there with you. Did you know that?"

"No." The sickness receded. "And you did leave me."

"Yeah. When a hit-and-run driver ran me down, broke my arm and a couple of ribs. That scared me enough to stay in hiding like I'd originally planned. If anything had happened to me before this year, the estate would've gone to the family. The mining would have gone ahead."

My mouth gaped. "Cavanagh tried to kill you back then? In New York?"

He shook his head. "I don't think it was Cavanagh. Hired help, probably."

"Did he hire them?"

"It doesn't matter. I'm here, healthy and hardy, ready to do battle. That's all we need worry about now."

I gulped, moved closer. "Then it's all right for me to check that bruise, isn't it?"

He went absolutely still, didn't say no or yes.

The dark strands slid like silk through my fingers. I combed them back until I could see the grim mark from where the bruise began in his hair to where it ended over his ear. Tears formed. How could Cavanagh wittingly hurt his own cousin? Gareth didn't deserve such hatred.

He turned his face so that his profile was to me. His lips parted to take in a rasping breath. My hand followed, unable to stay away from his cheek.

His rigidity, his clenched hands, his tension didn't arise from my hurting him. His tension came because he couldn't stand for me to touch him.

Hot tears, for him and for myself, flooded my eyes. I had to blink furiously to keep them back. I felt a pulse in his forehead throbbing beneath my fingers and slid them down to his jaw. "You've been running scared all along, haven't you? You were so near to drowning yesterday."

All the while I wanted to say how I couldn't bear the thought of losing him when I'd never had him. I ached to kiss the bruise, comfort the hurt. "And today . . . If he'd hit you with that pipe, Cavanagh could have hurt you badly."

My hand cupped one side of his face. I leaned over to put my mouth on his bruised forehead.

"Don't, Lindy," he said raggedly. "You don't know what you're doing." He put up a hand to push me away, let it stop in midair before it reached me. Before he had to touch me.

My heart burst, but I wanted to take him into my arms.

"Gareth, I'll be gone tomorrow." Pride was forgotten. I put my other hand up and stroked his jaw. His nostrils flared. One tiny response didn't mean anything, but at least he hadn't rejected me entirely. "Surely you can stand my touching you for a few moments. Yesterday at the boat you didn't mind. Do you remember?"

His iron control exploded. "Remember? How could I forget?" Then he shook me so abruptly my hair fell into my face. "You little dumbass, every time you come around me, I lose track of what I'm supposed to be doing. All I want is to wrap my arms around you. All I can think about is holding you, getting into your head, and tearing you up inside the way you've done me."

All the time he spoke, he was pulling me down, falling with me so that I landed on my knees on the moss beside him. He caught me and twisted me in his arms, lowering me on my back so that I was trapped on his lap between his chest and his bent legs.

His knee bone pushed against my hip, hard and unforgiving. Heated lips pressed my nose, my forehead, my cheeks, my neck.

I lay stunned, cherishing each touch, not knowing what was happening except that Gareth held me and said things to me that up to now I'd only dreamed of hearing from him.

"Don't you understand?" he said between fierce kisses that I welcomed. "I can't come near you without wanting to do this." He plunged his tongue into my mouth and skimmed my teeth, tangled it with my own tongue. "And this." He ripped apart my windbreaker and pulled up the blouse, stroking the valley of my breasts above my bra with his tongue.

I was on fire, a fire I'd dreamed about and feared I'd never experience again. Every flick of his tongue, every brush of his fingers brought new tingles of desire.

"And this." He raised his head long enough to look into my eyes as his fingers slid beneath my bra and pulled it up. His head bent back, sucking at one nipple and then the other.

After a bit, he came back to my mouth, kissing me as he pushed at my jeans, forcing an entrance where his hand could slip inside and cup my rear.

I groaned, caught his hand, pulled it around. Its touch left a trace of molten gold down my hip and around the top of my thigh. His hand splayed on my belly and traced down where my open legs welcomed him. His fingers met my panties, slid under the elastic and crept into the region budding to life.

This was what I'd craved, what I'd longed for. Happiness suffused me.

He stopped suddenly and leaned back. I lay against his knees, too limp to move.

"D'you see now?" he asked, breathing still ragged. "Do you see how you affect me? I go out of my mind when you're near me. I always have. I can't control myself when I'm with you. All I want to do is make love to you."

"Then do it," I whispered, out of my head with delight and desire. "Please, Gareth."

"Not like this. Remember before? In New York? What happens if you start comparing me to your stepfather again?"

"But you made it all right."

He pushed me to the side with a mutter that sounded suspiciously like an expletive. "Then, yes. But what if rushing brings it all back? Here there's no place, no time, to do it the way I want to do it. Not for you."

I hadn't thought of my stepfather, not once while Gareth was kissing me. The man belonged in another world, another life. "It doesn't seem to matter when it's you."

"No?" He shook his head. "All right, say it works. But what happens when you wake up tomorrow and take off? Never caring what you've done to me, to my life?" He got to his feet, brushing the dead leaves away with a violent gesture.

Out of my mind with happiness, I scrambled forward and caught one of his legs to hug it to me. I pressed my cheek against the muscled thigh under the jeans.

I was quite shameless. "Don't let me go," I whispered. "Make me stay."

He remained obstinate. "You don't know what you want. You're—"

"You're wrong. I do know. And you can make me stay, Gareth. Please. All you have to do is ask. All you've ever had to do was ask. I think I've loved you since we first met, when I found you crying by the river after your grandfather died."

Absolutely shameless.

The tightness slowly disappeared, making him seem very young, very vulnerable. He was the boy I'd known twenty years ago, crying because he'd lost someone he loved. The boy I'd desperately tried to comfort.

"That was so long ago. I didn't know if you remembered or cared. I didn't know you felt that way, too." He added, whispering, "I figured you didn't even think about it. Grandmama said I couldn't go down there anymore, that your mother was too sick to look after us and I might get hurt. I would have come anyway except your father died and then we went off to London."

Too sick to look after us.

The blinding truth. My mother had been drunk. Old Mrs. Warwick had come to get Gareth and found my mother passed out while Gareth and I were down at the river by ourselves.

The reason Gareth couldn't play with me was because my mother couldn't be trusted to keep us safe.

And Pop's heart attack.

Had what Mrs. Warwick told him exacerbated a condition that we hadn't known about? Had he been worried all along about me, about my mother?

Such simple explanations for what had seemed magic.

He touched my hair with a tentative hand. "I thought you were just grateful for me getting you on with Ruth. I didn't know you cared the way I did."

From where I knelt, I looked up past his chest to see his face turned down to me, tender and soft as the boy he'd been, the boy I continued to love.

I melted inside. "You know now."

He laughed then, his funny little chuckle that soon grew into a lusty shout of laughter before he pulled me up and took me in his arms. We embraced in the sunshine on the edge of the mountain. As we kissed, a gust of wind shook the oaks around us, sent the leaves swirling down around us in a shower of gold as if to christen our newly reached accord.

I should have told him in New York how I felt about him. I'd known. I just hadn't been willing to admit it. I'd been afraid. Afraid he'd laugh. Afraid he'd turn from me in disgust.

My hand inside his shirt tingled from the intimacy the gesture entailed.

He forestalled more exploration by taking my hand out of his shirt front and putting the palm to his lips.

"Gareth, please." I couldn't go on. I couldn't frame audible words.

I wanted him, and I didn't want to wait.

He looked into my eyes, smoothed my hair back as I'd smoothed his. "I'm not prepared, Lindy. I'd promised myself not to be as weak as I was in New York. I didn't expect you to feel this way. I didn't expect this." His face glowed, the passion on it as tender as any I'd known my entire life.

"So what? I don't care."

"I do. I don't want there to be any regrets for either of us. Not today. Not later."

Mundane concerns I refused to think about. "I wouldn't regret anything. Just this once, we can skip a condom. It doesn't matter." I pulled him to me.

His body stiffened again. I caught my breath, half fearful he would change his mind and repudiate his words.

But his face remained the same, full of tenderness. "But I'd regret it," he said. "I'd regret it forever if you got pregnant when you didn't want to because I wasn't careful enough."

I tried to tell him again it didn't matter, but he put his finger on my lips. "We'll go down to town, pick up something. That'll give us both time to think. I don't go in for casual sex, Lindy. I don't think you do either."

"I don't go in for sex at all," I whispered, hanging my head. "I've never done this before, Gareth, except with you. You're the only one I've ever been able to try it with. After what happened, I . . ."

I couldn't speak. I didn't want to remember my past.

He didn't make me. "We'll go out and get something." He caressed my hair. "Afterward, we'll talk about it. Then if you still want to, we can."

Sighing, I laid my head against his shoulder. "All right. I can wait."

"Good." He was hoarse. He cleared his throat. "This way, if you change your mind, it won't be too late."

"I won't change my mind."

We walked back to Paladins Rest hand in hand. The sky above us was robin's egg blue, and the clouds were pure clumps of fluff. The leaves were vivid reds and oranges and yellows. The trees themselves were sentinels lining our way.

There'd never been a sky so beautiful or a path so resplendent.

When we reached the house, Gareth took me around to a side path. It led to a rough wooden door set in rock. "This is a short cut through to the garage. It saves climbing the deck stairs. You can wait while I change clothes and then we'll go into town. If you still want to."

"Yes."

I couldn't remember the last time I'd been so happy.

* * * *

IN THE OLD part of town, a pharmacy stood on the main street directly across from a trim Victorian house. When Gareth and I parked, I saw the house had been converted into a law office. The sign caught my eye. SPECIALISTS IN REAL ESTATE AND PROPERTY.

"I'll wait out here in the sunshine," I told Gareth, never meaning to bask in its golden light.

After he disappeared into the pharmacy, I went inside the old house. The furniture looked fresh off the delivery truck, and the newly painted walls were bare.

A receptionist put down her magazine and greeted me with a pleasant smile. "Good afternoon. May I help you?"

"I want to see about getting a property deed drawn up. Now if possible. I'm in a hurry."

She stood quickly. "Let me check and make sure Ms. Letters can do it. Wait right here," she added as if afraid I might leave.

The attorney was available. She was young, dressed in a neat suit, and looked about twenty despite her granny spectacles.

"I've only been open a week," she confided as she shook my hand. "Not too many clients yet."

"I'm glad. I'm anxious to get this done right away." I told her what I needed.

"I can't have it ready for you until tomorrow morning. I have to get the legal description and do some more research. It'll take a little time. But then you can sign it and I'll file it for you." She mentioned a fee.

"That'll work. Thank you."

My side excursion had taken all of fifteen minutes.

When I came out, Gareth stood on the sidewalk in front of the pharmacy. His hair was a dark halo in a stream of sunshine and his back was rigid as he scanned the streets.

He was probably worried I'd run away.

Silly man. Where did he think I'd go?

I crossed over, touched his arm. "Gareth." I loved saying his name.

He turned. "Lindy! I didn't know where you were. I thought you might have had second thoughts. I was worried."

I nodded toward the house. "I went in there."

His eyes traveled past me, puzzled. "A shop? Why?" Then he saw the sign. I could tell he understood by the change in his face.

What I couldn't tell was whether or not he'd planned it this way, deliberately bringing me to a pharmacy with law offices specializing in property so conveniently across the street.

Did I care? No. If Gareth loved me, he would become my refuge. If he didn't love me, what good was Gram's land anyway? "They're going to draw up a deed. It'll be ready tomorrow. I'm going to sign all Gram's property over to you. You can do whatever you like with it."

He froze, looked at me with unfathomable eyes. Then he did a strange thing. He leaned over, picked up my hand, and kissed its back in a dignified manner that seemed familiar.

No, I was mistaken. It was a courtly mannerism, an old-fashioned gesture no one else had ever used with me. By the one gesture, Gareth had raised me up to his own level. I no longer felt insignificant, tainted.

"I'll never be able to do as much for you," he said.

I tried to joke. "You don't have any land I want."

"No. I mean I'll never be able to return your trust in me. All I can do is try to make sure that you don't ever look back and regret doing this."

A cloud went across the sun.

What did that mean? After I went back to my work and he went on his way?

I waited for him to say something else, but he didn't. Perhaps he couldn't.

It didn't matter. I swallowed. If sex was all he could give me, I would take the sex.

We were silent in the car going back through the autumn vales. I barely noticed their dazzling brilliance. I didn't try to touch Gareth. Later I would be able to touch him as intimately as I desired, and I was content to wait.

I didn't know what Gareth thought as he drove. I wasn't sure I wanted to know.

CHAPTER SIXTEEN

AT THE HOUSE, an excited Alonzo waylaid us.

"Cassandra finally decided in our favor. We've got her on our side. And she has Humphrey and Eliza's proxies, too," he said to Gareth. "Come talk to her. She can persuade some of the others if she will . . . Very influential . . . Everyone listens . . ."

As the elderly man dragged Gareth off into the library, Gareth barely had time to throw a rueful glance of apology toward me. I waved my forgiveness.

I might be on my own till dinner, but afterward, he'd be with me.

As I started up to my room, Cavanagh caught me at the elevator. He didn't look happy. "Where've you been?"

Gram always preached honesty was the best policy. "I went to town with Gareth."

"He's using you."

Hearing my own doubts from Cavanagh was unwelcome. Perhaps that was why the words sprang so readily to my lips. I didn't stop to think what impression they might give, what Cavanagh might take them to mean. "Have you ever thought that perhaps I might enjoy being used?"

Cavanagh's eyes widened. "You don't know what you're saying."

I donned my coolest, haughtiest demeanor. "No?"

Brushing past him, I found the stairs and ran up them as if chased by ghosts. As the afternoon passed with no word from Gareth, I bathed for dinner.

Lying in the garden tub surrounded by potted greenery, I luxuriated in water softened by bath crystals. Afterward, legs needed shaving and repairs made to pedicure and manicure. Then I lotioned and perfumed my entire body. Once I applied makeup and piled up my hair, I teased out a few strands to curl around my face.

A blue gown snapped up from a new and struggling designer was perfect for dinner. The velveteen top fell off-shoulder while the nipped beaded waist started below my bust and ended at my navel like a medieval girdle. Chiffon flared into a flowing skirt.

Last, I put on matching sandals and jewelry. A yellow topaz bracelet circled my wrist. A dragonfly in amber hung suspended between my breasts. More yellow topaz dangled from my ears.

When I looked at myself in the long mirror on the bathroom

door, I was satisfied. The dress disguised my thin figure, and suggested curves and cleavage. The blue shade turned my eyes to cornflower, and the topaz and amber highlighted my hair.

All my preparations, all my care was because of Gareth. I wanted to be perfect for him, that he might not be disappointed.

When I started downstairs, Eleanor materialized after I pressed the elevator button. She stopped at the sight of me.

"Hello, Eleanor."

She might have been a vindictive cat waiting to spring. The accustomed sympathetic veneer was missing. "So you showed your true colors to Cavanagh. I warned him about you. I told him you were leading him on. When you find out Gareth won't control the wealth in this family, you'll crawl back to Cavanagh but he won't have you. Not now that he knows what you really are."

The truth she bared, that I had used Cavanagh to get close to Gareth, should have made me flinch. Another time such spiteful words would have crushed me.

Not tonight. Nothing could spoil tonight. "So what am I, Eleanor?"

"One of the sorry white trash who insinuate themselves into the company of people like us. You may be rich and famous, but all the money and glamour in the world can't change your origins, can they? Or your past."

She knew how to attack, Eleanor did, but her eyes frightened me more than the barbed words. They looked almost maniacal.

I involuntarily stepped back. Her hostility was Cavanagh's doing. I'd told him before we came here that I didn't love him. If his mother had believed otherwise, he was to blame. Not me.

Another of the Warwicks, one I didn't know, approached as the elevator opened.

Eleanor ostentatiously ignored me. "How pretty you look, Deidre," she cooed. "Are you going down? Do let me keep you company."

The middle-aged woman, almost as tall as Eleanor and as elegant, smiled at us.

I let them enter first. Deidre might have guessed what Eleanor had been saying or she might not have a clue, but anyone chummy with Eleanor was someone to be leery of.

"Aren't you coming?" Deidre, polite Warwick that she was, held the elevator.

After hesitating, I got in.

Eleanor's brows, soaring like all the Warwicks', drew close together. "You'd think a woman wouldn't encourage a man if she didn't mean to marry him, wouldn't you, Deidre?" Her tone was jovial but her face betrayed her.

Deidre's puzzled brows came together. "Pardon?"

Eleanor tittered. "Some people are ingrates, never understanding what they've been offered."

"And some people are simply ingrates," I said dryly.

My attack startled the other two women. We rode down in silence, an icy one on Eleanor's part, a dreamy one on mine, and an uneasy one on poor Deidre's. She kept glancing from Eleanor to me and back until the elevator stopped. Then she bolted.

I didn't blame her.

Eleanor stalked out.

Squaring my shoulders, I put up my chin before following.

Gareth came late for dinner, after most of us were seated. I had no chance to talk to him since his place was at the head table. I could see him across the room, though, and he winked at me as he sat down. I had to be glowing, but I tried not to look at him too often.

Cavanagh, on my right, said little. I was glad. The portly man on my left wasn't a Warwick, I'd learned at our first dinner, but was married to one. Across from us, Alonzo, Eleanor and the Warwick who played the lute were animated. Eleanor was gracious and charming toward them. She ignored me, even when Alonzo or the other man tried to include me in their conversation.

I didn't care. With the anticipation of what was to come later, I couldn't be anything but lighthearted.

Despite my good intentions, my eyes kept turning toward Gareth, and occasionally I caught him giving me a tiny encouraging smile. Once, as I laughed at something the lute player said, Gareth's smile widened as if he enjoyed my pleasure. His gaze swept over me like a caress.

I could hardly eat. I could hardly sit still in my chair. I wanted to be alone with him.

At some point, Cavanagh began talking to me in a low persuasive way, telling me of the benefits the mine and planned development would bring to the community. "No one else has such a gem, Belinda. Our scientists say it comes from a meteorite that crashed into the mountain millions of years ago. When people find out Lassitan's the site of a stone no one's ever seen, they'll come in droves. Lassitan will be catapulted to the list of must-see places. Lassitan will be catapulted to the list of must-see places. We intend to make over the entire town as well as the mountain to cater to the tourists. Everyone will benefit."

"I'm sure you've thought it all out, Cavanagh." His and his father's lavish plans for developing the mountain and Lassitan held no interest for me. Slumber Mountain wouldn't suffer if I had anything to do with it. It wouldn't suffer under Gareth's care.

"Belinda." He half-turned and leaned in close. "It all hinges on you. You can make it happen. You and only you."

Honesty compelled me to tell him that I was signing a deed over to Gareth, but I didn't want to spoil the night. I'd tell him later. "Talk to Gareth instead of trying to force him to change his mind. If you'd discuss it, you might be able to compromise."

"No." He sat back. "The time for talk is long over. Gareth has all but lost. I'm assured of enough support from within the family to overturn any veto he might give. Gareth won't be a factor as long as we have control of the mineral rights. But our plans all hinge on you."

Better to get it over with and enjoy the rest of the evening. I took a deep breath. "I'm sorry, Cavanagh. I've made arrangements to have a property deed drawn up giving Gareth all the property Gram left me, including any mineral rights. Whatever dealings you plan will have to go through him."

Cavanagh almost bent the fork he held, but other than that, he showed no surprise at my response. The look on his face was akin to despair. "He's using you, Belinda. He'll dump you when he gets his way. I wish you'd believe me."

My chin snapped up. "Dump me as you intended to?"

To his credit, he looked aghast. "He's poisoned you against me. You know how I feel about you. I love you."

"You made it a point to meet me, wine me, dine me. All because you needed my help. Is it any wonder I'm confused about why you spent so much time with me, why you wanted to marry me?" I brushed away his hand. "But your reasons don't matter. Not now."

We finished the meal with no further speech.

After dinner, Eleanor announced another impromptu concert in the back of the living area. Cavanagh pulled back my chair. "Come out to the garden with me, Belinda."

"No." I had every intention of dawdling and waiting for Gareth.

At the head table Gareth got up, but a little flurry of Warwicks circled him and hid him from view.

Cavanagh took my elbow and drew me toward the door leading outside.

I was getting very tired of Cavanagh. At the threshold, I dug in my heels. "Haven't we said all there is to say?"

He gripped my arm harder. "No."

I pulled back. "Cavanagh, let me go."

He propelled me forward. "One minute, Belinda. That's all I ask, just one minute."

I wouldn't make a scene. Not tonight. "I don't want—"

He dragged me outside so fast that I stumbled on the deck.

To hell with not making a scene. "Cavanagh, let me go! If you don't let me go, I'll scream."

He stopped abruptly.

I went past and would have continued beyond the railing had his grip not been so tight.

I gasped.

On the edge of the deck, I teetered, looking down at the sharp face of the mountain. Widths of harsh bare rock plunged to the bottom where riprap, the huge blocks of granite used to fight erosion, covered the lake bank. A fall might not be fatal but there'd be injuries.

Cavanagh didn't let go my arm. "Gareth's bewitched you."

He spoke calmly enough, but moonlight bathed part of his face and his expression was far from calm.

I'm not an easily frightened person, but his hopelessness scared me as much as his mother's maniacal stare had earlier.

"Cavanagh, let's go back inside."

"No." Still holding me, he drew a folded paper from his pocket. "I want you to sign this."

I had seen the paper before. "You had that on the houseboat, when Gareth took my coffee and threw it over the side. It's a quitclaim deed, isn't it? Have you had it ready all this time?"

"I wanted you to sign it in New York but that damned dog attacked me before I could explain. If you'd signed there, you'd never have had to come here, never become entangled with Gareth." The jealousy was raw, explosive. "He's interfered every time I've had the chance to ask you to sign. I knew he'd bewitch you. He's always taken everything I've wanted, everything that should have been mine. I never cared before, but I'll never forgive him for stealing you. I love you. He'll never love you like I do. If you'll sign this, we can start over."

Mad. Completely mad.

I tried to be gentle, very conscious that we were on the edge of the mountain and that nothing stood between me and the steep rock below except a flimsy wooden railing.

Best not make him angry.

"I'm sorry you think you're in love with me, Cavanagh, but I don't care for you that way. I never have. Even in New York I told you that. You remember, don't you?" He gripped my arm so tightly it began to ache.

His free hand shook out the folded paper. "Sign it, Belinda."

Contracts signed under duress weren't enforceable, were they?

Would Cavanagh holding me on the edge of the mountain constitute duress? "Cavanagh." Useless to try to reason. "No."

He pushed against me, trapping me against the railing.

"Cavanagh!" The posts bit into my back and rear.

This is how a mouse caught by a cat must feel.

"I would be sorry if something happened to you before you signed this deed," he said in such a conversational tone that I almost didn't comprehend his meaning.

"Something . . . You mean something like Gareth falling off the boat?"

"That was an accident. We exchanged words, yes, but I didn't push him off."

"Really? After you knocked him unconscious, you didn't throw him in and leave him to drown?"

"He wasn't unconscious. And no one meant for him to drown."

"Like you didn't mean to hit him with that pipe you carried out when you followed him yesterday?" No use hiding my contempt. If he wanted to push me off, he would. And I'd never have my night with Gareth . . .

"Gareth knows me. We've always fought, but I don't wish him dead. He just needs to understand this project is too far along. This afternoon was my last chance to make him see."

Crazy. Maybe he and his mother were both crazy.

"Do you think killing me will change his mind?"

"Killing you?" His hand came up to caress my cheek. "I'm in love with you."

I pulled my face away. His grip on my arm tightened. "If only you had loved me back."

He's going to throw me over.

A cat screamed.

A heavy ball of white fur landed on Cavanagh's back.

Then Gareth was there, his face black as I'd never seen. In one quick motion, he jerked Cavanagh off me and pushed me to safety. "Keep your hands off Lindy, Cavanagh."

"You've got no business interfering." Cavanagh clenched his fists. "This is between Belinda and me."

"No, it isn't. You might hurt other people, but I'm not going to let you hurt her." He lowered his voice so that I almost didn't catch the rest of his words. "For ten years, I've been trying to find excuses for you. I know what it was like growing up with your mother's needling and your father's ambitions. But no more. Not when you involve Lindy."

Cavanagh hit him.

Gareth staggered back. Terrified for him, I stepped between the men.

Cavanagh's fist came toward me. Before it could land, Gareth's arm caught the brunt of the blow. At the same time, he pushed me aside. His jab caught Cavanagh's chin and sent him reeling.

By this time, people inside had realized something was wrong and were flocking from the house. Shocked cries accompanied a general rush toward us.

In a few moments, the two men had been separated, held apart by several Warwicks and Warwick husbands. My husky dinner partner was one of them.

Eleanor, on the verge of tears, pushed to the front. "Why?" she asked Gareth, wringing her hands. "Why did you come back after all these years? Why are you doing this to us?"

"Ask your son," was his terse reply. The men holding his arms released him. He didn't look at me and I didn't speak. I couldn't. I held my hands up to my mouth to keep from sobbing.

Eleanor turned on me. "You! You're the cause of all this!"

Gareth shielded me. "Aunt Eleanor. Don't." His anger vanished, and he sounded tired. "Look to your husband if you want someone to blame."

Jeffrey looked over where he stood beside his son. His lips pulled back, baring his teeth like little white fangs. "You would blame me for your attack on Cavanagh?"

"Cavanagh attacked Gareth," I said shakily.

Jeffrey turned back to Cavanagh. As his restrainers let him go, Cavanagh shook himself like a dog. He patted his father's arm and went toward Eleanor. "Come away, Mother." He took her arm and led her away in a stiff motion that belied his calm. Jeffrey, with one last malignant look at Gareth, followed.

The rest of the Warwicks made no attempts to conceal uncertainty and disapproval and curiosity. Even pity.

"I don't think we're in the mood for a concert tonight, lovely though I'm sure it'll be," Gareth said politely to the musicians gawking with the rest. He took my arm. "Come on, Lindy."

His jaw bled where Cavanagh had hit him, on the same side as the bruise beneath his hair. A box of tissues sat on a console by the elevator, and I pulled one out.

This was my fault. Gareth ought never to have had to suffer. I ought never to have dated Cavanagh. I ought never to have come back to this cursed place. Maybe I was the one cursed. "I'm so sorry."

Gareth took the tissue from me and held it against his jaw. "It's all right, Lindy. This is nothing to do with you personally. Cavanagh's a hothead and he's under a lot of pressure from his parents. And he's in love with you. He won't bother us again."

"I thought he was going to throw me over the side." My voice shook.

"I think he simply meant to scare you into signing the quitclaim deed."

"He's crazy."

"He's . . . Cavanagh." Gareth took the tissue off, checking for blood. "And yes, perhaps he is a little bit crazy. Who wouldn't be crazy with Eleanor for a mother and Jeffrey for a father?" He smiled though his eyes didn't. "Of course, I was crazy for a time, thinking you were going to marry him. How can I fault him for feeling the same way?"

The thought of Gareth being jealous both pleased and displeased me. "I could have told you how I felt about you. I could have told you a long time ago. I think I knew that night I pulled you out of the lake. But when you sent me away with those hundred dollar bills, I was so angry with you, I wanted to kill you."

"What hundred dollar bills?" He frowned, and then his brow cleared. "I remember. Why were you angry? You needed the money. I didn't like seeing you the way you were, so worried, so tired. Money was all I could do to help you."

"You threw it down on the table as if I were a prostitute!"

His eyes widened. "Did I?" He considered. "Maybe I did. I didn't mean to. You see, I'd just found out about my parents and sister and Grandmama. Jeffrey waited till after I changed into dry clothes before he bothered to tell me about the fire, that they were dead. I don't remember how he told me exactly, but I do remember what I said to him. 'Grandmama's dead now so she can't influence the others. You can go ahead with your plans now, can't you?' He looked at me with this little smirk. As if he had thought of that long before. As if he had counted on what he'd do if—no, *when*, Grandmama died."

I sucked in my breath. "You think he planned the fire?"

Gareth shrugged but the hurt was there. "He never answered me, but he didn't have to. He didn't grieve. My grandmother and my mother and my father and my sister died that night along with a lot of other parents and children. But Jeffrey never grieved."

My heart ached. "It doesn't matter. Not now. You won't let him have the mountain."

His hurt dissolved. "No. It doesn't matter so much now."

We looked away from each other as we waited for the elevator, me aware that my face was glowing as his was beginning to do.

"Like a prostitute?"

He went back to what I'd said. "Hey, how do you know how much prostitutes get paid?"

I flushed, turned to him. "You prick."

He began to laugh and so did I.

Cavanagh's inexcusable behavior was forgotten.

The excitement banked inside me, stirred, began to rise. My breath came faster, my heart raced, my body felt unlike it had ever felt.

Other than in those weird dreams.

And this wasn't a dream.

The elevator opened and we entered. Alone, of course.

Safe behind its concealing doors, Gareth took me into his arms and drew me hungrily against him. His hands roved my back and hips, his mouth crushed mine. "I've died a hundred times this evening, waiting for this," he said against my hair.

My heart swelled. I put my lips against his neck, tasted the spicy aftershave on his skin, touched my tongue to the small cut on his jaw. I was content to be held, but only for the moment. "I've waited ten years for this."

"No longer than me, Lindy. No longer than me."

We walked from the elevator, arms around each other's waists like teenagers.

His bed was a massive antique affair, a four-poster with griffins on the top of each post holding back the canopy. A chord of memory stirred somewhere deep within me. It reminded me of something, but recollections were vague and this was here and now. There were more exciting things to concern myself with.

Gareth, a few feet away, threw his jacket onto a chair and loosened his tie. He stood in the shadows, but I felt his eyes on me as I waited.

"Take off your dress."

He hadn't turned on the lamps so I strained to see in the moonlight. His bared chest was pale as was the outline of his face beneath the shock of black hair. Stripped down to his pants, he stood motionless.

No reason to be nervous. This wasn't the first time we'd been together, and I had unabashedly chased him to get him to this point. But I was.

I wet my lips with my tongue, and then turned and walked, casually I hoped, to the doors leading outside.

Gareth's room had a commanding view of the courtyard. His balcony was twice as big as mine. I stepped out onto it and into pale light that came not from the full moon, but from the triangles of stars I'd noted on a previous night. Their orbits had brought them together, so close that their light melded together into one large orb of brilliance.

I breathed the night air and looked up at the night sky and felt the familiar craving. He was behind me. I could tell without looking that he was behind me.

His arms slid slowly, deliciously around mine. His chest warmed my back, bared by the blue dress. His naked length molded itself to mine, his face nestled against my head. "Come inside, Lindy. We've waited so long."

Time stood still. His words throbbed in my ears. He held me safe in his arms.

I hung back. "You know I'm not good at this. What if it doesn't work this time?"

"We'll try again. Just like we did before."

His kindness and patience were so apparent that I turned, slowly, agreeably, absorbing every different nuance of his body, every different touch of his body as it brushed me in each different place. My breasts tingled as he slipped his hand down my neckline to touch one and then the other. The light played on his face and shoulders, a dancing cascade of light and darkness whenever he moved. I reached out, fingered the black hair that led down to his navel.

"Come to bed, Lindy."

I let him lead me inside, into a wisp of light.

"Take off your dress." He was hoarse. "I want to see you. All of you."

My heart would surely burst. "I can't say no to you."

He lay on the bed as I unzipped the side of my dress and pulled it over my head. Beneath it, I had deliberately left off bra and panties and hose. A gossamer slip, strapless, cupped my heavy breasts and fell past my heated groin. At his encouraging smile, I pushed it down past my waist, past my hips, past my knees, until I stood nude amid the silk and chiffon debris.

He held out his arms and I walked through the starlight to him. When he enfolded me and drew him down against him, I felt the artificial barrier he'd bought sheathing his length, keeping us apart. A moment's regret that he'd insisted passed, a small price to pay for the euphoria of being with him.

We lay together, the experience not new but strange enough to both of us so that we stretched out against each other, seeking again the knowledge of how to hold one another, how to caress one another. One day such gestures would be familiar but tonight, every touch, every sigh, was new and exciting and awkward.

During our explorations, he rolled over on top of me.

I stiffened, then relaxed and shifted my hips expectantly.

He didn't enter. "It's too soon."

His hand went down, caressed me until I was half out of my mind with wanting him. Only then, when he could see I was on the edge, did he lower himself into me. What I had felt the first time with him was nothing compared to the present. As he pushed against my center once, twice, he set off my orgasm.

Not like before. Different. Harder. Wilder. More powerful.

My scream of wonder coincided with his own quiet groan, his own spasms drawing out my pleasure longer.

Afterward we lay entwined on the bed, drained. He put his lips against my ear. "I love you," he whispered. "And not because of any paper that you sign."

Happiness choked any answer. I'd been afraid I would disappoint him, that my past would have warped me so that I couldn't love him properly.

Tears threatened, were blinked back.

Everything was all right. I wasn't frigid. Gareth wasn't disappointed. "I love you, too, Gareth," I whispered back. "I've loved you since I was seven."

He laughed his low laugh. "That's when I fell in love with you, too. When you hugged me and didn't make fun of me crying, I thought you were the nicest girl I'd ever met. And that summer we played together was one of the happiest times of my life. I never changed my mind about that, Lindy. Never."

I matched his laugh.

His lips, soft and pliant, began to nibble on my ear lobe. By the time they'd moved down my neck, the old fires had begun to blaze.

"I want to know every inch of you," he told me.

For the first time in my life, I wanted a man to look at me, to know me, to touch me. So I allowed him every liberty.

He started with my head, running his fingers through my hair. "So silky, so soft. Oh, you have a cowlick here. I can see its whorl. And another there."

Then he used his tongue to follow the curve of my ear, making little noises of approval as he traced one and then the other. "Perfect. Like shells." He went on down, stroking my neck. "So graceful. I've always loved your neck." Then my shoulders, my arms. Down to the valley of my breasts, my nipples, my navel, all the while exclaiming at how perfect I was.

He skimmed down to cup my thighs and knees and calves, and then caught one foot and outlined each toe. "I always knew you'd have long narrow feet like this. Lovely. Just like your fingers." He caught my toes in his mouth and sucked on them before he moved up my legs and stopped at my pubic area. He aimed his little smile at me as if asking permission.

Never in all the years of my career had I felt as beautiful as I did under Gareth's eyes. I parted my legs without hesitation.

"Sweet, sweet Lindy," he murmured against my swollen flesh. "Let me lick you here. And here." He encouraged me, approved of me, let me know he found me desirable. Made me feel I was clean and pure.

I gripped his shoulders, enjoyed their strength. Under his gentle attentions, I felt worthy of him or any other man.

The past was not my fault. I understood that now.

That time had gone and only the present mattered. The present and the future.

When we finally joined, he kept careful control of himself, so that I could savor the new experience of having the man I loved inside me, making love to me.

My dream of years ago came back, and it seemed that I traveled through space again, up into the night skies, moving in unison with Gareth until the strange new sensations awakened in me exploded in a brilliance of rainbow lights.

"Will you stay with me?" Gareth asked later, sleepily, as he lay with his head cradled on my breasts. His fingers entangled my hair, pulling its strands around his neck. "After tonight, I mean."

"Will you stay here?" I countered, rubbing his nipple. This was the first time he'd been home in ten years.

"With you, I can."

"Then so can I." I would make my home wherever Gareth made his.

He got up, came back to the bed with glasses and a fifth of champagne. When he used the corkscrew, I giggled.

He looked up, askance.

"I've never seen a naked man use a corkscrew with so much savoir-faire before."

He lifted his swooping brows in pleasure. "You think so? Do you like the sight? Is it aesthetically pleasing?"

"I'll have to look at it a few more times to decide."

Gareth did have quite an air about him as he held the bottle under his arm and twisted the cork. When it popped—perfectly, naturally, without a busted cork or fizz all over the floor—I applauded. We emptied the bottle in bed, licking spills off one another and laughing.

I fell asleep, more content than any time since I was a child.

Cavanagh, nor anyone else, could ever have infiltrated my heart. Only Gareth could have knocked down the barriers, let me fly to the stars.

CHAPTER SEVENTEEN

I SAT ENTHRONED amidst a crowd of shrouded figures. Figures dressed in funny dark robes and hoods that shaded their faces and made them anonymous.

Only their tall slender forms and pale narrow hands gave them away as Warwicks.

Gareth might be among the group, but as in my previous dreams, the thought was a passing curiosity.

I was content simply to be. Uncaring. No idea where I was, no idea how I'd got there.

This wasn't my room at Paladins Rest nor was it Gareth's. But the surroundings were familiar from my dream of ten years ago. The griffins still hovered in flickering candlelight, their talons still held silken draperies.

The soft hangings drew back.

No human hand pulled at them. They furled back of their own accord, forming five long columns. The walls revealed were gray and hard, carved from the same solid stone as my seat.

Rock bounded five sides. In front of each of the five corners, single robed figures stood. Behind them, more hooded Warwicks lined the five walls encompassing us. Between them, a few paces toward my throne, stood others.

I sat in the center.

This group of silent, unmoving sentinels stood beneath a ceiling that had also changed from my long ago dream. Where before there had been the freedom of night sky and stars so close as to embrace me, now a glimmering glassy covering held the moon at bay.

Enthralled as a child, I gazed up.

The pool in the courtyard. We are under the pool in the courtyard.

Two figures materialized from beyond the circle, weaving through different sides of the sentinels to meet before me. The costumes they wore were loose, not robes like the attire of the others but dazzling white and short. Like Roman legion tunics except these gleamed like silk.

The circle of filtered moonlight fell on the two men. Cavanagh and Gareth.

I should have been surprised.

They stopped a few feet away.

Their hands lifted in grim salutes, first to each other and then to me.

From nowhere, two other figures appeared, hoods of their dark robes pushed back. Eleanor and Alonzo, each somber with a grave dignity I'd never suspected either possessed.

They stood on either side of me, her right hand clasping his left. Their free hands took mine so that we formed a circle.

Should Eleanor be holding my hand, hating me like she did?

It didn't matter. This was a dream.

She and Alonzo began to chant. "The goddess has sent us to guard the mountain. The goddess has sent us to calm the mountain. The goddess has sent you to carry our exhortations to the mountain. You are our mediary for the mountain. You are the one who understands the mountain spirit. You are the one the spirit listens to."

Hands dropped. They stepped back to allow Cavanagh and Gareth to approach me and kneel. Gareth cupped my right foot in his hand, Cavanagh my left.

An uneasy frisson at Cavanagh's touch faded into apathy. This was part of the dream ceremony.

Both men bowed their heads as Eleanor spoke in her normal voice. "Among the custodians, there is discord. Before we send our exhortation to the mountain, there must be none. The custodians must be in complete accordance."

Alonzo took it up. "Discord must be erased and harmony restored. Only purity, harmony, and faith can be offered to the mountain. A challenge has been issued and must be decided before this can be done. There can be only one conductor." He addressed Gareth and Cavanagh, still on their knees before my stony throne. "Plead your case and begin the contest."

He and Eleanor fell back. Gareth and Cavanagh lifted their heads.

"You have the power to do what is good." Cavanagh sounded urgent, compelling. His face was pale, his dark hair swept back. He looked me full in the eyes. His own burned feverishly.

"You have the power to do what is right." Gareth too stared me in the eyes. His were bright as Cavanagh's, shining with emotion and something else.

What did they mean? They were wrong. I had no power and tried to say so.

Cavanagh saw I would protest. "What's right is good," he said quickly.

"What's good is not always right," Gareth again rebutted his cousin. Gently, calmly.

Around us, the hooded Warwicks stood silent. Listening. Judging.

This contest was a trial of some kind that one of the two men kneeling at my feet must lose.

And to lose was to die.

With that certainty, apathy vanished. I wanted to scream out against what they were doing, tell them that I would do whatever necessary to keep Gareth safe.

My lips remained closed, my voice mute.

Silk slithered as the two men stood.

"I am prepared to do battle for good." Cavanagh's face glowed with a fanatical light.

"I am prepared to do battle for right." Gareth squared his shoulders, accepting the duty thrust upon him but not wanting it. A duty he didn't seek but must fulfill.

Broadswords appeared, tall and heavy and awkward though both men handled them with ease. In the dimness, the blades shimmered like the light of the moon.

The small room expanded. When Cavanagh and Gareth were magically transported to some far corner, we could see them plainly.

They hefted the swords, tested the weights.

This was insanity. Someone needed to stop them.

Not me. I was stuck behind an invisible screen, unable to speak, unable to move.

Unable to look away.

Cavanagh struck first.

Gareth's sword clanged as it caught the blow. And the next blow. And the next.

The tendons on Cavanagh's arms stood out. The deadly weapon swung over his head as if it were a toy. Sweat popped out on his upper lip, then his forehead.

Gareth's face glistened, too. He didn't attack but parried each swing Cavanagh made. Gradually, he began to give way.

This is a dream. The swords are only a dream. The fight is only a dream. Gareth is not in danger.

Only a dream, only a dream.

Nothing I saw was real. But why was my heart pounding? Why this fear?

What if it isn't?

No, it has to be a dream, I told myself over and over. It's only a dream.

My nails dug into my palms so deep they drew blood. I needed something to hold onto. Sliding my fingers around, I discovered hollows on either side of the throne. My hands slid inside them as easily as if they knew where to go. There were handholds. I gripped them the way I gripped the arms on a dentist's chair.

The two men continued to fight.

Water poured off their foreheads and chests. Cavanagh's teeth clenched when again and again Gareth turned aside his blade; Gareth's teeth clenched each time his sword held off the other.

This could have been a movie scene except there was no rousing music and no gallant acts of derring-do.

Two men fought for their lives. They gasped for breath and sweated. Cavanagh swung a blade that could decapitate while Gareth dodged again and again. The few sounds were those of the great swords meeting and the soft rustle when the barefoot warriors moved on the rock.

A misty silver light—from the swords or the moon?—glanced off their white garb and set faces, turned them into ghostly visions.

I clutched the familiar hollows in the rock and prayed for Gareth.

The tableau might be a dream but it seemed much too real.

At some point during the fight, the mountain waked.

I sensed it. My physical apathy gave way. My blood stirred with something akin to sexual desire. The seat beneath me trembled, the room itself became alive. Around us, filtered moonlight turned into a pure white column that fell on hooded Warwicks and warriors alike.

Wonder filled me. Warmth spread from my hands all over my body.

I belong here.

No one noticed what was happening until one of the sentinels gasped. "The stars are aligned with the moon!"

Everyone looked up. Even the two warriors paused to stare.

The five stars had passed behind the moon and were nowhere in sight. Their nimbus turned the moon as bright as the sun.

"The Awakening has started," someone said from behind me. Behind the matter-of-fact tone lay quiet panic. "The issue of the conductor is unresolved, but the mountain is already rousing. We can't wait. We must have a decision now."

Power seeped into me through the rock, from the mountain's heart itself. No longer did my sleeping giant lay tranquil and proud. Its spirit had come alive and was ready to claim its own by whatever means necessary.

Even violence.

That unearthly presence focused, took my soul into its grasp. It readied itself for the final lunge toward freedom. I heard it singing.

Out, out, out.

Eleanor had painted a dire picture of the mountain exploding and destruction following. The mountain's strength had to be turned back if her prophecy was true. Only calamity and tragedy would follow the mountain's eruption.

I should do something, but what?

The joy of the awakening power drained me. The impending destruction seemed distant, of no moment. I didn't want to do anything. I had no will to oppose it. Except . . .

"Gareth!" My cracking voice was barely audible.

Two faces turned, but Cavanagh reached me first.

I tried to escape, but the mountain held me fast.

Out, out, out.

"Don't fight it. Let it roll through to me, Belinda," Cavanagh said urgently. His hand hovered. "Let it come to me. I can control it."

"No." Gareth took great panting breaths from his defense against his cousin's sword. "No one can control the spirit. It must go back. Back into the mountain. If it escapes, it'll destroy itself and anything and everyone near it."

"It won't escape." Cavanagh bent nearer. "The others will help me take it, bend it to my will. That's why we're here."

"The mountain's spirit will never bend to any human's will, Lindy. Even you are only its mediary." Gareth, weary, still refuted his cousin. "If it escapes, it will destroy Cavanagh and anyone else in its path. You must contain it, restrain it until I can reverse it."

All the while, The Voice inside my head chanted. *Out, out, out.*

The mountain's need filled every pore, every vessel and vein, every fleck of skin on my body. Its desires became mine.

I didn't know what to do. I didn't know how to hold the power or turn it.

Maybe I didn't want to do anything.

"I can't," I tried to tell Gareth.

No sound emerged. Perhaps it wouldn't be so bad to let the mountain have its way.

Suddenly Cavanagh muttered, "I can control it." He seized my foot and the energy focused in me poured into him. He had taken it.

No. The spirit in the mountain had taken Cavanagh.

Power seeped out of my foot into him. Exhilaration rushed through me as the mountain's spirit rushed into this new receptacle.

I ought to warn him. I ought to do something . . .

Gareth started forward. "No, Cavanagh, no!"

"I can!" Cavanagh cried. "I have it! I have it!" He was incandescent, beautiful as Gareth, happy as I'd ever seen him. "You thought I couldn't do it, you thought—"

He screamed. His back arched in a horrible spasm as though hit by a thousand volts of electricity.

Gareth turned to me. "Call it back, Lindy! His hand is still on you. Take it back before it destroys him."

How? I tried to ask.

Gareth heard anyway.

"You know how." His calm reassured me. "Relax. The spirit will come back if you want it. It knows you, depends on you. Let it come back through you. Bring it back into the mountain. Tell it to come back."

I did as he said because I wanted it back. I had to have it back.

Under my craving, it began to fill me as before. I'd never let it go again.

From far away, Gareth soothed me, guided me. "That's right. You've caught it, Lindy. Now let it in."

The energy crept back, molding my arms, my legs to the rock on which I half-sat, half-lay. My body beat, pulsated.

I became molten lava, ready to explode with the joy of life. Every cell, every organ, grew ecstatic with the timeless spirit harnessed inside me.

"Lindy, do you have all the energy?" Gareth's urgency was enough to bring me out of my ecstasy. "Have you taken all of it back?"

Though I couldn't even groan, he understood. "Good. Now give me your hand."

No. "Can't," I managed to get out.

"Yes, you can."

"No!" I'd stay here where I was safe, never go back where I would be hurt.

"I know you don't want to, but you have to give it to me. Otherwise, you'll die from holding it. I can't take it from you. You have to give it to me freely. Please, Lindy. Please. I can't let you die."

He was afraid for me. His anguish pierced the fog of pleasure. I had to pull a hand out of that hollow before I became part of the mountain.

For Gareth.

All the while The Voice's chant grew to a deafening roar.

Out, out, out!

The excruciation I went through to remove my hand was indescribable, something I relive in nightmares. If anyone other than Gareth had asked me to do it, I could not have. But I loved him more than life. My trust in him was absolute.

I cried when I pulled away from the rock. When I abandoned the mountain, its screams' crescendo turned me faint and tore me apart as if I'd lost half of myself.

The Voice faded to a murmur.

When I did as Gareth asked, he held my hand tightly in one of his. The other touched my rocky seat.

The fog lifted. I could see the surroundings, hear chanting from the robed figures still in place. Drops of sweat fell from Gareth's jaw as he struggled to conduct the power back into the mountain. His tunic darkened with perspiration.

Behind his shoulder, another face appeared, a Warwick face contorted in rage. Eleanor had turned from ministering to her downed son.

"Gareth!" My warning filled the small room.

He turned his head, never losing his hold on me and the rock, as Eleanor attacked him. They struggled.

She sought to divert the power flow from Gareth to herself.

There was a sudden wind, a wailing. The filtered moonlight glimmered and became blinding. The glassy ceiling above me ripped away. Water poured down as if a hurricane had loosed torrents above us.

Warwicks screamed. Some fled, some held their places.

Still Gareth and Eleanor fought.

I could stop them. The mountain needed something. If I could help it, there'd be no need for this contest.

As Gareth held Eleanor off with one hand, I slipped out of his other and found my handhold in the rocky ledge beneath me.

There was no pain putting my hand back, not like when I'd taken it away.

Again I was filled with rapture.

Out, out, out. Back to where I belong, The Voice said plainly.

I understood.

You want to go back to the stars, I told it. You want me to send you back to the stars where you came from. And in another flash of insight: *This is what I was meant for. I can do it.*

But either I underestimated the mountain's power or overestimated my own strength. My back arched when the spirit coursed through me seeking a way out through my body.

There was no way out. Not with me bound to the rock.

Gareth, throwing off Eleanor's hand, reached for me. "No, Lindy! Don't let it take you! It'll kill you!"

I felt myself dissolving, going into the mountain, becoming part of its majesty, part of its triumph.

Understanding.

Its spirit wanted unity with all things. Unity with me. Unity with the trees, the water, the stars.

All I had to do was to give it up, allow it to become as one with its origins. I desperately sought a way to release it.

Gareth, his face stained with perspiration and blood where he'd bit through his lower lip, forced my hand up.

"No-o-o-o-o!" The scream tore at my throat, reverberated in the crevices.

He slipped his hand into its place in the mountain.

Behind him, Eleanor's crumpled form lay untended on the bare stone beside Cavanagh. The other Warwicks chanted around us.

The mountain's spirit released me, coursed through me to Gareth and back to the rock, again denied an outlet.

Out, out, out! it raged.

"I can't hold it," Gareth said, despairingly. "Too much got away. It's attracting the rest."

He didn't understand what was happening, but I did. I couldn't release the spirit but Gareth could.

Parched lips barely croaked. "Let it go. Put up your hand and let it go."

"Lindy, the mountain will erupt."

"No. I've felt it, heard it. It says it belongs in the stars and wants to go back. Only the spirit part of the mountain will leave. Our letting it loose is the right thing to do. Please, please trust me."

"She can't know what she's doing," another Warwick said, chant forgotten. "Gareth, take it from her."

Gareth hesitated.

How could I make him believe me?

"Please, Gareth." I groaned. "I understand it. If we prevent the spirit from going back where it belongs, it really will destroy everything one day. Not only Paladins Rest and Lassitan, but more."

Gareth was torn.

The other Warwicks, wide-eyed and uncertain, were no help.

"I know this, Gareth." I sobbed. "The mountain doesn't lie. You must trust me. Point it to the stars."

He made up his mind. In one quick gesture, he raised his left hand from the rock. His right hand held onto me so that the power, that unworldly and unprecedented power bound in the mountain, flowed through me into him and passed through to the heavens where it belonged.

Gareth had trusted me as I trusted him.

The room shifted. A wind howled, blew the draperies outward. The Warwicks murmured, chanting forgotten, their pattern dispersed.

They huddled in small groups and spoke among themselves and waited.

The wind extinguished the candles. A shuddering began deep in the heart of the mountain.

"I told you!" Eleanor screamed from where she had crawled to Cavanagh's side. "She came to thwart us! She intended all along to betray us!"

Her anger bounced off the joy of the mountain's spirit as it fled upward, to be reunited with the rest of the universe. Its destiny.

Gareth fell on my lap, exhausted. My trust in him hadn't been misplaced, nor his in me.

The mountain was appeased. The spirit that had abided inside it for centuries had gone home.

CHAPTER EIGHTEEN

OUT, OUT! LET me out!

The Voice woke me.

My eyes popped open to moonlight streaming through the double French windows. Its pale beams turned objects in the room an eerie white.

Where were the rock walls? Where were the robed Warwicks?

Reality slowly returned.

Gareth's room. I was in Gareth's room, in Gareth's bed, in Gareth's arms.

Happiness fled as The Voice came again.

Out! Help me get out!

Who was it? Gareth lay beside me, sleeping peacefully. He was safe. Did I care about anyone else in the house?

Of course I did. Artemesia, Alonzo . . . even Cavanagh and his parents. If any of them were in trouble, I would have to help them.

But with the exception of Gareth, I didn't normally hear humans. Most of them had lost too many natural instincts, I sometimes thought, to emit the primal fear that called to me.

Jacinth.

Of course. Cats always wanted something. With a small sigh, I got up. So many times in New York I had steeled my heart and passed by those mournful cries. I couldn't do that, not here, not if it were Jacinth or perhaps another Warwick.

Though I tried to be quiet, Gareth awoke. "What's wrong, love?"

"I don't know." I couldn't tell him about The Voice in my head. One day I would but not now. There wasn't time. "I have to go. I have this feeling. Something's wrong." I started putting on my rumpled blue dress and shoes.

After a moment's astonishment, Gareth hopped out of bed and pulled on some jeans and a red shirt. "I'll go with you."

No questions, no misunderstandings, simply acceptance of what I had to do. My eyes misted at his faith in me. "There's no reason for you to come with me. It's not even daylight."

"I want to."

As we left the room, a door opened down the hall behind us. Eleanor peered out, a malevolent sneer distorting her patrician features.

I shivered behind Gareth's back, but he had turned in the direction I indicated without noticing his aunt. There was no point in telling him.

In silence I led the way toward the spot where The Voice grew ever more frantic.

I have to get out! Out! Out!

It came from below us. "We have to go down."

He didn't hesitate. "The elevator will wake everyone up. Here. Let's use the stairs."

No questions, no complaints. I loved him.

I flew down, Gareth on my heels. One flight, and then another down the large curving staircase ending in the lobby. Then into a less ornate set of steps leading to the cavernous garage where a wild yowling met our ears.

"Jacinth!"

The howling didn't stop when Gareth called out.

Rushing toward the hair-raising sound, we found the white cat flinging himself against an outside door, clawing and shrieking in a way I'd never heard any cat do before.

Even Gareth was reluctant to approach him. "Jacinth?" he said quietly. "It's all right, Jacinth."

At that moment, the floor shifted. I clutched Gareth's arm. He leaned into me so that we held each other steady.

"What was that?" I whispered.

Gareth didn't answer but went to the door and opened it. With one last scream, Jacinth bounded outside. His paws and the door were bloody where he'd clawed the wood.

The garage, hewn out of solid rock in the heart of the mountain, shuddered around us, so gently that I thought I must be imagining it.

With mouth set in a grim line, Gareth took my arm and pushed me toward the door where Jacinth had fled. "Go outside, Lindy."

I resisted. "Why? What is it?"

"Earthquake."

"What? We don't have earthquakes in Georgia!"

"No, not normally." His hand pushed me steadily toward the door. "Go outside to the parking lot."

I went through but he turned back. "Where are you going? Don't leave me!"

"I have to wake the others."

"I'll help you!" I started toward him.

He took hold of my shoulders, fear naked in his face. "For God's sake, don't make me worry about you being safe, Lindy. I can't stay here with you and you can't go with me. Please understand."

The mountain rocked ever so slightly. I screamed and clutched him. "Gareth, come with me! I'm so frightened!"

He touched my cheek, giving me a tiny twisted smile. "You? You may have been afraid sometimes but you've always faced your fears head-on. I think that's what made me fall in love with you all those years ago. I have to warn the others. You of all people should understand that. They're my family. And my responsibility. I'll be back soon."

"Gareth—"

"If you love me, get outside and stay away from the house. If you love me, don't make me choose between your safety and my family's."

Under his vehemence, I nodded tearily.

He kissed my hand. "I love you," he said as he left.

"I love you, too," I whispered, but he was gone.

I did as he asked.

Outside on the paved lot, a spot in the open let me view the house. Another quiet rumble emanated from the ground underfoot. The gray walls of the house swayed.

Or was the pavement moving beneath me? Unable to see, I wiped away tears.

Yes, the house shifted slightly and so did the pavement.

Three great dogs showed up from nowhere and seated themselves beside me. We watched the house in silence, their companionship comforting for me and I suspect for them. In a few moments that seemed a lifetime, Warwicks started streaming out, most coming from the side where porch steps led down from the first floor.

"Drat, I left my purse. Should I go back for it?"

"I hope nothing happens to my children's pictures. I always take them everywhere but I forgot to gather them up before—"

Deidre and her husband emerged in matching purple flannel pajamas while one of the musicians came out clutching his flute. An elderly man carrying an umbrella, marched out fully dressed in suit and tie. He had on pink bunny house shoes.

Over it all were the questions.

"Where's my husband? He was right behind me! Oh, Joe, there you are! Thank goodness!"

"Where's Serenity?" Or Matthias or Cindy or Narcissus or Hiram or Bill or Dorcas.

Everyone was looking for someone, but I looked only for Gareth.

He didn't appear.

Alonzo staggered out in a bright red robe, helped along by

Artemesia clad only in boxers and camisole. And Cavanagh, dressed in pajama bottoms and barefoot, looked frenzied as he scanned the crowd. When he saw me, he left the line of chattering Warwicks. "Your room was close to theirs. Have you seen my parents?"

"No."

At his naked fear, I pitied him, an emotion I never expected to feel for Cavanagh after what he had tried to do to Gareth. He turned back toward the front of the line, still searching.

As vigilant as any seaman's wife on her widow's walk, I resumed my watch. A tinkling came from the house as window glass shattered and fell, and then a crackling sound that was the frame itself breaking up.

The house was visibly falling apart. The ground beneath us continued to tremble. A plume of smoke appeared, frail at first but quickly growing larger and darker.

I caught my breath.

Others saw the smoke, too. Reassurances passed around me from one Warwick to another that help was on the way.

"I called on my cellphone so they—"

"I think that's a siren."

"Can you hear it, too?"

"The fire trucks have to come from town."

"Don't be ridiculous, everyone down there could be in the same situation we are up here. We need to find a water hose."

The smoke billowed and grew. Its black form floated overhead like an evil genie, overpowering the crumbling house and the people below.

I started walking toward the house.

Something was terribly wrong. My intuition teetered on the brink of telling me what but, as on the yacht when Gareth went overboard, wouldn't quite reach my brain.

Because I didn't need to be told.

Gareth was in there. He remained inside and the house was falling apart and something was wrong. My feet, leaden at first, began to run of their own accord.

"Gareth!" I screamed as I ran. "Gareth!"

Hands caught at me, pulled me back. Warwick hands, long and tapering and white. Like Gareth's hands.

"Gareth's all right." Warwick voices, accented and soft and calm, comforted me. "He's just checking to see that everyone got out safely. He'll be out shortly."

I fought them off, only to have others take their place.

He wasn't all right.

"Gareth's in there!" I sobbed as they held me. "He isn't all right! Don't you understand? He isn't all right! He may be trapped in there!"

They refused to listen.

"Gareth won't take chances. He'll be out soon," someone said.

"No!" Though I fought like a madwoman, I was defeated in the end. They dragged me a safe distance back where I gave vent to tears of frustration.

Someone was counting heads. Alonzo. How would he know who was missing and who wasn't? Who would go back for Gareth?

Gareth, who no one had welcomed when he came back.

"Who saw them last?" someone—Artemesia?—asked with a restrained urgency. Sirens threw out their mournful wail in the distance.

Another Warwick answered. "—and then Gareth helped me with Father. We had to get his wheelchair down the steps so Gareth and I grabbed—"

"We saw both of them through the smoke, after Gareth beat on our door to—"

"—isn't back either? We have to check out the garage, then. Alonzo, do we have time?" I recognized the down-to-earth Deidre in flannel pajamas and loafers.

Alonzo wrung his hands. "Eleanor knew to get out. I don't understand why they wouldn't have come when everyone else did. All of them can't be in there."

All of them.

I knew before I pushed my way to Deidre's side. "Who else?" I asked her. "Who else besides Gareth is missing? Who's he with?"

I think I screamed at her. I know my fingers seized her arm and I believe the bone would have snapped under my hand had she not answered.

She looked at me strangely. "Eleanor and Jeffrey. And Cavanagh. He went back to find them."

An image of Eleanor's face came to me, the look on it as Gareth and I had burst out into the hallway. "She was awake when Gareth and I came down. She looked out of her room when we went down. She would have known—Why didn't she get out?"

Had she deliberately lured Gareth back to his death? Could she hate him that much?

The house was now a flaming wall on one end.

In its reddish glow, I clenched and unclenched my hands. "I will kill her."

I didn't even feel the pain when my nails bit into the palms. My hair fluttered and fell in the wind from the heat of the blaze. The scent of roiling smoke filled my lungs. "If Gareth is harmed because of her, I will kill her myself."

My vehemence alarmed Deidre. "Come away," she said softly, for she was a kind woman. "Come away with me to where the rest of us are."

Like an automaton, I allowed her to lead me over to the parking area where Gareth had told me to wait. The Warwicks clustered in small groups, still whispering and watching for the most part although a few had managed to drag out a water hose and hook it up. A fire truck made its way up the mountain, sirens screaming and red lights flashing.

Still, Gareth did not appear.

A firefighter hopped out and directed the truck driver. Beyond them Warwicks met another uniformed man, pointing toward the house and telling him something. The man nodded, turned to shout orders to a fire crew scurrying behind him.

I knew what the Warwicks had told him. That there were other people in the house. That they had last been seen in the main part of the house.

The earth began to rumble again. The mountain opened up. The shock of tilting ground sent us to our knees.

Where there had once been solid rock was now a gaping cavern.

The house split in half. A great roar rose from people's throats. Timbers popped. The dogs bayed.

The remains of Paladins Rest began to slide down the chasm toward the lake below as plumes of smoke and dust obscured our view.

As it slid, a lone portion remained intact. Part of a room. The wall had been ripped away and the opening showed a gaunt, gray figure clinging to a shapeless bundle.

Eleanor turned her face toward us, but her eyes fastened on me. They no longer frightened me, for she was lost and she knew it. The mountain was about to claim her.

Still holding the bundle in both arms, she put back her head and howled like the dogs as the fragmented room went over the edge and carried her down to the lake below.

At the last moment, I saw that the form she held was that of a man. "No!"

Jeffrey, surely it was Jeffrey. Oh, please God, let it be Jeffrey.

The milling Warwicks had gasped along with me. Now they gave way to horror. "It was Eleanor! Eleanor!"

"Why didn't she leave?"

"Was that Jeffrey with her?"

"It must have been. Although it could have been Cavanagh or Gareth," one man said, giving voice to my fears.

Like the others, I strained to see into the rubble still falling below us. We looked to no avail.

There was no sign of Gareth's red shirt.

Maybe he wasn't in that part. Maybe . . .

The tremor ended. Where the house had once stood was a new hollow.

The garage doors in the rock were still closed. The newly created chasm was to the left of them, but above them lay empty air. The structure was gone. Not one stone, not one beam, not one wall was left standing.

Some of the firemen worked on the garage doors, trying to split them open with axes and force them apart. "They won't budge," they called. "We can't get in this way. We'll have to climb up to the top."

"No, it isn't safe." The chief waved them back. "We'll have to wait."

I rushed over to him. "Please, there may be people in there!"

"Sorry, ma'am. Those doors have been forced together tight. The mountain may have collapsed into the garage. And if we go up there"—he pointed to a pile of rubble, what was left of the house—"it could slide off at any moment. I can't put my personnel in that kind of danger. If your friends are in there, it may be hopeless anyway."

Not hopeless. I grabbed his sleeve. "There's another way into the garage."

The Warwicks took up my cry. "Yes, you can get in on the side!"

"The side!"

"Go around to the side door!"

Artemesia ran to lead the firemen to the door in the stone Gareth and I had used the day before.

Was it only yesterday we had gone through it in such happiness?

I went, too, crazed with fear.

This door was on the untouched side of the mountain but when it opened, smoke roiled out in black waves. A figure bulky with oxygen mask and flame retardant uniform entered cautiously.

Gareth, I thought in despair. *Gareth, I love you.*

If he was dead, I might as well be, too.

A shout arose from the Warwicks as the fireman almost immediately emerged, supporting one figure while behind them another staggered. A man covered with so much soot on his chest and face that he was unrecognizable.

Not to me. Despite the black grime, I knew him.

"Gareth!"

I cried and sobbed and laughed. I could not move quickly enough to get to him.

* * * *

LATER, AT THE hospital, Artemesia, Deidre, and I waited in the hospital emergency room with both men on gurneys. Deidre told Cavanagh that she had nearly given him and Gareth up.

"We nearly died." Cavanagh, oxygen tubes in his nose and lips cracked from the heat, could hardly rasp the words. "Father wouldn't come. He wanted to get his papers. All the deeds were . . . All the blueprints and drawings he'd worked on so long. He wouldn't leave them. He thought if he could get them out before . . . It would put us in a position to lead the corporation."

He stopped, exhausted.

"Was that what you wanted?" kind Deidre asked. "To save the papers?"

"They were important to Father." He lay still. "I just wanted to make it up to them."

"Make what up? To who?"

Gareth, with his own oxygen tubes, and black all over except for his red-rimmed eyes, listened intently.

I held his left hand, the undamaged one.

Cavanagh rasped, "Make it up to him and Mother. Her father left all his shares to Aunt Annora because he disapproved of their marriage. Mother wanted to prove Father was as good as everyone else. All my life, she's tried to make everyone see that."

"Oh, Cavanagh," Deidre said with real compassion. "Dear child. That's not why your mother was cut out of Falderby's will. She sto—"

"Not now, Cousin Deidre." Gareth roused himself. "Cavanagh's suffered enough."

I frowned. He shouldn't defend Cavanagh.

"Later." His hand holding mine tightened. "We'll talk later."

Cavanagh coughed. "Mother tried to get Father to leave but he wouldn't come. Even Gareth tried."

"You had to leave them. I understand," said Deidre, patting his hand. She was very maternal for a Warwick.

Cavanagh closed his eyes. "I made Mother go. Father told me to take her so I picked her up and carried her."

Conveniently leaving Gareth to reason with Jeffrey. I pressed my lips together.

"Mother was stronger than I thought. She got away and went back for the papers. By then, Gareth had persuaded Father to come out. She met them and saw he didn't have the papers. She went on. And then the second quake came. A beam fell on Father. She came back to him. I tried to reach them but . . . Gareth grabbed me when the house started to go."

A nurse in scrubs came and looked at Gareth's chart.

"You'll have to wait outside," she told me as she released the brake of his gurney. "We'll let you know as soon as they're through checking him."

Gareth gave me a weary smile and winked as she wheeled him away.

So Gareth and Cavanagh survived while Jeffrey and Eleanor didn't.

* * * *

"WE'LL NOT REBUILD," Gareth told me the next morning as he sat up on his hospital bed waiting for the doctor to come and sign his discharge papers. His right hand was bandaged but a cut on his face had scabbed over on its own. He had showered but still didn't look completely clean. "This area is getting too crowded. We'll move somewhere else. The Ozarks perhaps. Or Australia. We'll build a new Paladins Rest where there aren't so many people."

"Else where would the Warwicks congregate?" I murmured. "Yes, dear," I added as he looked at me suspiciously. "We'll rebuild it wherever you want."

"Wherever the family decides," he corrected me.

I had been waiting to ask. "Gareth, why did Eleanor's father disinherit her?"

"There's no reason to revive old scandals."

"You know all my family secrets."

"And you want to know mine." He took a deep breath. "Eleanor always had an emotional problem. When she was young, she took half her parents' assets without their knowledge and squandered them in different schemes. She justified her theft by saying it would eventually have come to her anyway. When her father died right after she married Jeffrey, he left everything to his wife but tied it up so that my grandmother, his other daughter, would eventually inherit. Which she did. I guess Eleanor convinced herself that he disowned her because of her marriage. She tended to warp things."

"How sad."

"Yes. Well. All families have black sheep. Everyone thought Eleanor had learned her lesson. She seemed not to care about her father's will. She kept on friendly terms with my grandmother and began to take an interest in the family business again. But after the fire, I began to wonder."

"So you blame her instead of Cavanagh for everything that happened? The fire? Your hit and run in New York?"

"I didn't at first, but after thinking about all their personalities, I think so. Jeffrey was weak. He did exactly what Eleanor said. Cavanagh wanted only to please his parents, but I don't think he could deliberately kill anyone. So yes, I blame Eleanor."

He saw my frown and hesitated before saying, "One thing I didn't tell you. Eleanor's mother died unexpectedly at their home in Switzerland not long after her husband. She fell from a balcony after a quarrel with Eleanor. At the time, everyone thought it an accident, but after the fire on the houseboat, Alonzo began to doubt it. He finally told me his concerns. I think he may be right."

I shuddered. "She was a monster. She . . ."

"Enough, Lindy. She's gone. Let it be." He sighed and then moved restlessly. "Right now all I can think about is getting out of here."

I tried to match his change of mood. "After what you went through, one night in the hospital shouldn't be getting you down."

"There's too much I need to be doing. Deidre's been great at arranging places where we all can stay. She's even found a motel that'll take Jacinth and the dogs. But the family needs to get together before everyone scatters. We have to discuss the future. I need to be there." He shook his head as if to clear it. "Where the hell is this doctor who's supposed to dismiss me?"

"He'll be here soon." Seeking to distract him, I added, "So is it decided yet? Are you going to make what's left of the mountain into a park?"

"We'll see. I haven't talked everyone around to that yet. Alonzo says the sentiment is to keep it undeveloped. I think the loss of the house and the northern peak of the mountain shocked everyone more than they care to admit."

"I thought your plan was to open it up to the public with walking trails. If you did that, you could charge a small fee, maybe enough to pay for an overseer. I guess if you wanted to rebuild and keep the house for your family, you could do that, too. Don't some of the great estates in England have public tours or something? How about something like that?"

"No. This will never be our home again." He put his hands around one knee and leaned back, wincing. "Ow. I remember now why I have to move slowly."

"The slower the better," I said wickedly.

He grinned at me. "Would you care to get me a drink since the damned doctor hasn't put in his appearance yet?"

I got up. "Sure. I'll get you whatever you want."

"An orange Fanta'll do for the moment," he said demurely. "After I get out of this place . . . Well, we'll see."

Down the hall, I met the doctor. "He can leave," he told me. "I can't for the life of me understand how he escaped with minor smoke inhalation. The other man's going to be recuperating for some time yet and may always have to deal with the residue. But your boyfriend is in great shape. Someone must have been watching over him."

I remembered my prayers. "Someone must have been."

The soda machine didn't offer orange Fantas. In fact, it seemed to be out of everything except diet drinks. Gareth would have to settle for water.

Annoyed, I turned back with change intact.

At the door of his room, Gareth stood, straight and tall, giving the doctor his funny twisted smile, holding a can of orange Fanta in his good hand. "So you think I'll live then?"

"This time. Don't try any more heroics though or I won't be responsible for the consequences." The doctor grinned, waved at me, and was gone.

I pointed to the orange Fanta. "Where did you get that?"

He looked at me and then the can. "Oh." He considered. "They must have put it out this morning. I found it on the table after you left."

I didn't remember seeing that can.

I hadn't seen that can.

I reached out to touch it. "It's still cold," I said accusingly.

He looked surprised and felt the metal. "Yeah, I guess it is. It wouldn't be good hot, would it? Want some?"

"No, thanks."

"Good. It's almost gone."

It hadn't been on his breakfast tray. I knew that for certain because I'd been there while he ate. The only other person in his room besides me and the doctor had been a nurse, but she'd carried a thermometer and a blood pressure gauge. Nothing else.

How the devil had he gotten that drink?

I stared at the Fanta and back at him.

Gareth didn't notice. He took one last drink before disposing of the can. Then he smiled his slow sweet smile. "Ready to go?"

"Yes." The Warwicks had always been different from other people. I'd known that all my life, but I'd learn to deal with it. "I'm ready to go."

His hand taking mine felt warm; the sterile hallway seemed the gateway to a wonderful future.

I didn't much care that the Warwicks were different from anyone else I knew. This one Warwick was all I wanted, all I'd ever wanted.

He wanted me, too, and I was glad.

He pressed the button by the elevator bank and chose an elevator on the left to stand in front of.

It opened immediately. Empty, naturally.

I lagged as he got on. He looked back questioningly, held the door open.

"How do you do that?"

He looked astonished that I should ask.

"Timing," he said. "Don't you remember me telling you that once before?"

I stepped in, took hold of his arm, and we entered the rest of our lives.

Other Fiction

by

Cheryl B. Dale

Romantic Suspense

Intimate Portraits
The Man in the Boat
Set Up

Paranormal/Gothic Romance

Treacherous Beauties

Light Mystery

Taxed to the Max
Overtaxed and Underappreciated

Vintage Mystery

Losing David

Thank you for reading this book. If you enjoyed it, please consider leaving a review to help others discover it. Among sites that offer places for reader reviews are:

http://www.amazon.com

and

http://www.goodreads.com

If you do have the time and take the effort to leave a review, please accept my sincere appreciation and thanks.

www.cherylbdale.com
cherylbdale.blogspot.com
cherylbdale@hotmail.com